THIS BOOK
IS IN THE CARE OF

D0964779

Katrina Martin

On the Edge of the Edge of the Dark Sea of Darkness

Adventure. Peril. Lost Jewels.
And the Fearsome Toothy Cows of Skree.

Andrew Peterson

The Wingfeather Saga Book One

WaterBrook
PRESS

THE EDGE OF THE DARK SEA OF DARKNESS

Paperback ISBN 978-1-4000-7384-9
ISBN 978-0-307-44665-7

right © 2008 by Andrew Peterson

-drawn maps and toothy cow illustration © 2008 by Andrew Peterson

ations © 2008 by Justin Gerard, Portland Studios

hed in association with the literary agency of Alive Communications, Colorado Springs,
0918.

ghts reserved. No part of this book may be reproduced or transmitted in any form or by any
, electronic or mechanical, including photocopying and recording, or by any information
e and retrieval system, without permission in writing from the publisher.

hed in the United States by WaterBrook, an imprint of the Crown Publishing Group,
ion of Penguin Random House LLC, New York.

BROOK® and its deer colophon are registered trademarks of Penguin Random House LLC.

ry of Congress Cataloging-in-Publication Data
on, Andrew.
n the edge of the Dark Sea of Darkness : adventure, peril, lost jewels, and the fearsome
y cows of Skree / Andrew Peterson.—1st ed.
   p. cm.—(The Wingfeather saga ; bk. 1)
ummary: Three siblings experience many fantastic adventures while looking for a lost
re.
BN 978-1-4000-7384-9
. Brothers and sisters—Fiction. 2. Fantasy.] I. Title.
P4431On 2008
—dc22
                                        2007047702

ed in the United States of America

2

2 9 18 17

For my brother

Contents

A Brief Introduction to the World of Aerwiar

The old stories tell that when the first person woke up on the first morning in the world where this tale takes place, he yawned, stretched, and said to the first thing he saw, "Well, here we are." The man's name was Dwayne, and the first thing he saw was a rock. Next to the rock, though, was a woman named Gladys, whom he would learn to get along with very well. In the many ages that followed, that first sentence was taught to children and their children's children and their children's parents' cousins and so on until, quite by accident, all speaking creatures referred to the world around them as Aerwiar.

On Aerwiar there were two main continents divided by one main ocean called the Dark Sea of Darkness. By the Fourth Epoch, the harsh land east of the sea had come to be known as Dang and has little to do with this tale (except for the Great Evil that came to exist there and waged a Great War on pretty much everybody).

That evil was a nameless evil, an evil whose name was Gnag the Nameless. He ruled from high atop the Killridge Mountains in the Castle Throg, and of all the things Gnag despised in Aerwiar, he most hated the High King Wingfeather of the Isle of Anniera. For some reason no one could guess, Gnag and his wretched hordes had marched westward and gobbled up the Shining Isle of Anniera, where fell the good king, his house, and his noble people.

Unsatisfied, the Nameless Evil (named Gnag) built a fleet that bore his monstrous army westward across the Dark Sea of Darkness to the continent of Skree. And he ravaged that wide land, nine long years before our adventure begins.

A Slightly Less Brief Introduction to the land of Skree

The whole land of Skree was green and flat. Except for the Stony Mountains in the north, which weren't flat at all. Nor were they green. They were rather white from all the snow, though if the snow melted, something green might eventually grow there.

Ah, but farther south, the Plains of Palen Jabh-J covered the rest of Skree with their rolling (and decidedly green) grasslands. Except, of course, for Glipwood Forest. Just south of the plains, the Linnard Woodlands rolled off the edges of all maps, except, one would suppose, those maps made by whatever people lived in those far lands.

But the people who made their homes on the plains, at the edges of the forest, high in the mountains, and along the great River Blapp, lived in a state of lasting, glorious peace. That is, except for the aforementioned Great War, which they lost quite pitifully and which destroyed life as they knew it.

In the nine years after Skree's king and all his lords—in fact, everyone with a claim to the throne—had been executed, the people of Skree had learned to survive under the occupation of the Fangs of Dang. The Fangs walked about like humans, and in fact they looked exactly like humans, except for the greenish scales that covered their bodies and the lizard-like snout and the two long, venomous fangs that jutted downward from their snarling mouths. Also, they had tails. Since Gnag the Nameless had conquered the free lands of Skree, the Fangs had occupied all the towns, exacting taxes and being nasty to the free Skreeans. Oh, yes, the people of Skree were quite free, as long as they were in their homes by midnight. And as long as they bore no weapons, and they didn't complain when their fellow Skreeans were occasionally taken away across the sea, never to be seen again. But other than the cruel Fangs and the constant threat of death and torture, there wasn't much to fear in Skree. Except in the Stony Mountains where hairy bomnubbles crept across the land with their long teeth and hungry bellies, and across the frozen wastes of the Ice Prairies where those few who made their home there battled snickbuzzards daily. Farther south, the Plains of Palen Jabh-J were as safe as they were beautiful, except for the ratbadgers that slithered through the tall grass (a farmer from South Torrboro claimed to have seen one as big as a young meep, which is about the size of a full-grown chorkney, an animal that stands about as high as a flabbit).

Before roaring over Fingap Falls, the River Blapp was wide and peaceful, clear as a spring, and the fish to be caught there were both delicious and docile, except for the many fish that were poisonous to the touch, and the daggerfish that were known to leap into boats and impale the stoutest fisherman.

An Introduction to the Igiby Cottage (Very Brief)

Just outside the town of Glipwood, perched near the edge of the cliffs above the Dark Sea, sat a little cottage where lived the Igiby family. The cottage was rather plain, except for how comfortable it was, and how nicely it had been built, and how neatly it was kept in spite of the three children who lived there, and except for the love that glowed from it like firelight from its windows at night.

As for the Igiby family?

Well, except for the way they always sat late into the night beside the hearth telling stories, and when they sang in the garden while they gathered the harvest, and when the grandfather, Podo Helmer, sat on the porch blowing smoke rings, and except for all the good, warm things that filled their days there like cider in a mug on a winter night, they were quite miserable. Quite miserable indeed, in that land where walked the Fangs of Dang.

1

The Carriage Comes, the Carriage Black

Janner Igiby lay trembling in his bed with his eyes shut tight, listening to the dreadful sound of the Black Carriage rattling along in the moonlight. His younger brother Tink was snoring in the bunk above him, and he could tell from his little sister Leeli's breathing that she was asleep too. Janner dared to open his eyes and saw the moon, as white as a skull, grinning down on him through the window. As hard as he tried not to think about it, the nursery rhyme that had terrified children in the land of Skree for years sang in his head, and he lay there in the pale moonlight, his lips barely moving.

Lo, beyond the River Blapp
The Carriage comes, the Carriage Black
By shadowed steed with shadowed tack
And shadowed driver driving

Child, pray the Maker let you sleep
When comes the Carriage down your street
Lest all your dreams be dreams of teeth
And Carriages arriving

To wrest you from your berth and bower
In deepest night and darkest hour

Across the sea to frozen tower
Where Gnag the Nameless pounds you

At Castle Throg across the span,
A world away from kith and clan
You'll weep at how your woes began
The night the shadows bound you

Away, beyond the River Blapp,
The Carriage came, the Carriage Black
By shadowed steed with shadowed tack
The night the Carriage found you

It's no wonder that Janner had a hard time sleeping once he heard the faint thud of hooves and the jangle of chains. He could see in his mind the forms of the crows circling the Carriage and perched atop it, hear the croaking beaks and the flapping of black wings. He told himself that the sounds were only his imagination. But he knew that somewhere in the countryside that very night, the Black Carriage would stop at some poor soul's house, and the children there would be taken away, never to be seen again.

Only last week he had overheard his mother crying about the taking of a girl from Torrboro. Sara Cobbler was the same age as Janner, and he remembered meeting her once when her family had passed through Glipwood. But now she was gone forever. One night she lay in bed just as he was now. She had probably kissed her parents good night and said a prayer. And the Black Carriage had come for her.

Had she been awake?

Did she hear the snort of the black horses outside her window or see the steam rising from their nostrils?

Did the Fangs of Dang tie her up?

Had she struggled when they put her into the Carriage, as if she were being fed into the mouth of a monster?

Whatever she had done, it was useless. She had been ripped away from her family, and that was the end of it. Sara's parents had held a funeral wake for her. Being carried off by the Black Carriage was like dying. It could happen to anyone, at any time, and there was nothing to be done about it but to hope the Carriage kept moving when it rattled down your lane.

The rattles and clinks and hoofbeats echoed through the night. Was the Black Carriage getting closer? Would it make the turn up the lane to the Igiby cottage? Janner prayed to the Maker that it would not.

Nugget, Leeli's dog, perked his head up at the foot of her bed and growled at the night beyond the window. Janner saw a crow alight on a bony branch outlined by the moon. Janner trembled, gripping his quilt and pulling it up to his chin. The crow turned its head and seemed to peer into Janner's window, sneering at the boy whose wide eyes reflected back the moonlight. Janner lay there in terror, wishing he could sink deeper into his bed where the crow's black eyes couldn't see him. But the bird flapped away. The moon clouded over, and the *thump-thump* of hoofbeats and the *creak-rattle* of the Carriage faded, faded, finally into silence.

Janner realized that he'd been holding his breath, and he let it out slowly. He heard Nugget's tail thump against the wall and felt much less alone knowing that the little dog was awake with him. Soon he was fast asleep, dreaming troubled dreams.

2

Nuggets, Hammers, and Totatoes

In the morning the dreams were gone.

The sun was shining, the cool of morning was losing ground to a hot summer sun, and Janner was imagining that he could fly. He was watching the dragonflies float across the pasture, putting his mind into a dragonfly's mind, to see what it saw and feel what it felt. He imagined the slight turn of a wing that sent it zipping across a meadow, whipping left and right, lifting on the wind up over the treetops, or scaling down the craggy drop to the Dark Sea. He imagined that if he were a dragonfly, he would smile while he flew (though he wasn't sure that dragonflies could smile), because he wouldn't have to worry about the ground tripping him up. It seemed to Janner that in the last few months he had lost control of his limbs; his fingers were longer, his feet were bigger, and his mother had recently said that he was all elbows and knees.

Janner reached into his pocket and, looking around to be sure no one was watching, pulled out a folded piece of old paper. His stomach fluttered as it had when he found the paper the week before while sweeping his mother's bedroom. He unfolded it now to brood upon a sketch of a boy standing at the prow of a small sailboat. The boy had dark hair and gangly limbs and looked undeniably like Janner. Big billowy clouds whitened the sky, and the spray of the waves burst up in splashes that looked so real and wet that it seemed to Janner that if he touched them, he would smear the picture. Beneath the drawing was written "My twelfth birthday. Two hours alone on the open sea, and the best day of my life so far."

There was no name on the picture, but Janner knew in his heart that the boy was his father.

No one ever talked of his father—not his mother, nor his grandfather; Janner knew little about him. But seeing this picture was like opening a window on a dark place deep inside. It confirmed his suspicion that there was more to life than living and dying in the Glipwood Township. Janner had never even seen a boat up close. He had watched them from the cliffs, specks cutting slow paths like ribbons through the distant waves, sailed by a crew on some adventurous errand or other. He imagined himself on his own ship, feeling the wind and the spray like the boy in the picture—

Janner snapped out of his daydream to find himself leaning on a pitchfork, up to his knees in itchy hay. Instead of feeling the ocean wind, he faced a cloud of chaff and dust shaken by Danny the carthorse, impatiently harnessed to a wagon half full of hay waiting to be carried across the field to the barn. Janner had been working since sunrise and had made three trips already, anxious to finish his chores.

Today was Dragon Day Festival and the only day of the year that Janner was glad to be in the quiet town of Glipwood.

The whole village waited all year for Dragon Day, when all of Skree seemed to descend on Glipwood. There would be games and food, strange-looking people from faraway cities, and the dragons themselves rising up out of the Dark Sea of Darkness.

As far as he knew, Janner had never left Glipwood in all his twelve years, so the festival was the closest he got to seeing the rest of the world—and a good reason to be quick about finishing up with the hay. He wiped sweat from his forehead and looked wistfully over his shoulder at a dragonfly zipping away. Then he dug into the straw with a grunt and pitched it into the wagon. As he did so, his foot caught on a stone hidden beneath the hay and he lurched forward, toppling face first into a neat, fresh pile of Danny the carthorse's nuggets.

Janner leapt to his feet, sputtering and wiping his face with fistfuls of hay. Danny the carthorse looked at him, snorted, and tore up a mouthful of grass while Janner ran, quick as the dragonfly, to the water trough to clean his face.

Across the field and past the fence, Janner's brother Tink (whose given name was Kalmar) straddled the cottage roof, two nails between his lips and a hammer in one hand. Tink was trying to repair a loose shingle but having a hard time of it, so violent was his trembling. When he was younger, just riding on his grandfather's shoulders made him nervous, and though he laughed, his eyes were always wide with fear until he was placed firmly on the ground again.

Podo, his grandfather, always assigned the reparation of the roof to Tink because he thought it would do him good to face his fear. But Tink, now eleven years old, was still as frightened as ever. Shaking like a leaf, he removed a nail from between his lips and hammered it into the roof as timidly as if he were hammering his own face. He looked out across the field to see Janner trip headlong into the water trough, and he wished he were finished with his chores so he could play a game of Zibzy[1] with his big brother at the Dragon Day games.

Tink was useless on the roof, but when his feet were on the solid ground he could run like a stag.

With the first tap of the hammer, the nail slipped from between Tink's

---

1. Zibzy gained wide popularity in Skree in the year 356. A lawn game played with giant darts (hurled high into the air by the offensive team), a whacker (a flat board with a handle), and three rocks. Injuries abounded, however, and because of the public outcry the game was banned. In 372, it was discovered that a passable version of the game could be played by replacing the giant darts with brooms. For complete rules, and a deeper look into Zibzy's fascinating and bloody history, see *We Played, We Bled, We Swept* by Vintch Trizbeck (Three Forks Publishing, Valberg, 3/423).

fingers. He tried to catch it, missed, and threw himself down, hugging both sides of the hot roof. Nail and hammer clattered down the roof in opposite directions and over the edge. Tink groaned because it meant having to inch his way over the edge and down the ladder again. It also meant that it would be that much longer before they were able to go into town for the festival.

"Lose something?"

Tink's fear turned to grumpiness. "Just throw it back up, will you?"

Tink heard laughter, then the hammer flew up, end over end, and landed a few feet from him. He gathered his courage to reach near the edge and grabbed the hammer with a trembling hand just before it slid back down.

"Thanks, Leeli," he called, trying to sound a lot nicer.

Leeli sat back down on the steps at the back of the cottage and continued peeling totatoes, humming to herself. Nugget was at her feet, tail wagging, panting in the welcome shade. Soon Leeli worked her way to her feet with a small wooden crutch and brushed the totato peelings from the front of her dress. Carrying the bucket, she limped into the house, Nugget close behind.

Her right leg twisted inward at an unnatural angle below the knee, and the toes of her bad leg trailed lightly along the wooden floor. When she was little more than a baby, she had learned to walk with a tiny crutch under her arm, and every year her grandfather made her a bigger one, each more ornate and sturdy than the last. This one was made of yew and had little purple flowers etched along its length.

Leeli plopped the bucket of peeled totatoes onto the table behind Nia, her mother, who was tossing ingredients into a large pot of stew.

"Ah, thank you, dear." Nia wiped her hands on her apron, then pushed a few stray hairs behind her ears. She was tall and graceful, and Leeli thought her mother was so beautiful that the plain dress she wore fit her like a royal gown. Nia's hands were strong and callused from years of hard work, but gentle enough to braid Leeli's hair or to stroke her boys' faces when she kissed them good night.

"Would you fetch your grandfather for me?" she asked. "He's been in the garden gathering herbs for at least an hour now, which can only mean one thing."

Leeli laughed. "The thwaps are back?"

"I'm afraid so." Nia turned back to her stew just as another clatter sounded above them. Her eyes followed the sound across the ceiling to the window, where she and Leeli saw Tink's hammer fall to the grass. A muffled moan came from the roof.

"I'll get it." Leeli limped out the back door and tossed the hammer back up to Tink.

Janner loped up to the cottage, sopping wet from the waist up, bringing with him a terrible smell and a swarm of fat green flies buzzing about his head.

As Leeli limped around to the front of the cottage to find her grandfather, she heard her mother shriek and shoo Janner out of the house, where he was promptly bonked on the head by a falling hammer.

3

Thwaps in a Sack

Leeli's one-legged grandfather was on his knees, growling at something in the garden. Fat red totatoes hung from the vines; round heads of lettuce burst quietly from the ground in long rows; sprouts of greenions, carrots, and sugarberries—her favorite—were yet bright and dewy.

Like Leeli, Podo got along fine with only one leg, though instead of using a crutch, he strapped on a wooden stump below the knee. He never talked about how he had lost his leg, but it was no secret that he had been a pirate in his wild youth, and he entertained his grandchildren nightly with tales of his adventures at sea.

Like the time all eighteen of his crew fell ill from eating a batch of bad ponkfin they had looted from a fishing boat near the Phoob Islands. Podo was the only one who hadn't eaten any and was left to sail the ship alone through a storm while his crew sloshed about, moaning in the hull.

"And that's not the worst of it," Podo would say. "I tell ye! That was with the Skreean Navy hot on me stern, cannons firin' and arrows whizzin' through me hair. That's how come it parts in three places, see? Still can't catch a whiff of ponkfin what I don't get the urge to trim a sail and run for cover…"

The Igiby children would squeal with delight, and old Podo often got so worked up that he'd need to dab the sweat from his forehead with a handkerchief.

He was wiping his brow with the handkerchief now as he squinted through the greenion sprouts.

"Grandpa?" Leeli said from behind him.

Podo whipped his head round, waving a knotty wooden club at her. His long white hair was frazzled, and he looked like a mad old hag. "Eh? Watch yerself, lass. I like to have banged you on the head with me whopper." His white, bushy eyebrows shot up and he held a gnarled finger to his lips. "Thwaps!" he hissed.

Suddenly, a small, hairy figure leapt out from beneath a totato plant and squealed.

Podo bounded after it.

Nugget, who had been whining happily, lost all restraint and pounced into the garden with a bark.

The common thwap was a little bigger than a skonk[1]—not much more than a ball of fur with skinny arms and legs standing as high as the middle of Podo's remaining shin. The old man's club found its target and sent the little critter flying through the air, but not before another one darted out of the garden and bit Podo fiercely on his stump, with its long, yellow teeth. The first thwap crashed into the trunk of a nearby tree and dropped to the ground, where it immediately stood up and hurled a pebble at the old man. It struck Podo squarely in the forehead, and he staggered for a moment, shaking his head while he beat at the thwap whose teeth were stuck in his wooden leg.

The thwaps squealed and darted back into the garden. A moment later they reappeared, one with a totato in its furry paws, the other with an armful of carrots. They dodged another swipe from Podo's club and shot into the garden again.

Podo roared and swung his club above his head. "Avast, foul rodents!"

A gust of wind moved the garden leaves in waves. Podo's white hair flew out behind him, and he leaned into the breeze with a fierce set of his jaw. A thwap appeared from behind a sugarberry plant and threw another rock. Podo swung his club and sent the stone zipping back into the garden as the thwaps dove for cover.

---

1. Bip Thwainbly, *The Chomping of the Skonk* (Publisher and date unknown).

"Aha!"

A few moments passed as the thwaps squeaked and twittered among themselves.

Podo's face wrinkled even tighter. He lowered his club and cupped a hand over his ear, as if he could have understood them.

Suddenly, a fat, red totato whizzed through the air and burst on Podo's face.

"Not the totatoes!" Podo blinked the juice from his eyes and batted another totato away with his club. "Not my totatoes!"

Just as Leeli turned away she saw him dive into the garden, headfirst, howling all the while. She smiled and limped back to the cottage, which was thick with the smell of breakfast.

Nia tromped past her to the garden without a word, snatched two leaves from a rosepepper plant, and returned to the kitchen, ignoring Nugget's barking, Podo's howls of rage, and the thwaps sailing through the air.

Janner, who had finally managed to clean the manure from his face and hair, walked back to the house, dripping wet.

Tink, skinny as a rake, sat at the table beside Leeli. His eyes were fixed on the large pile of sausage sizzling on the stove, and the sound of his growling stomach filled the room.

"Well! That's better." Nia folded her arms and tried not to smile at Janner. "I thought I'd see you with fresh grass growing on your face by now."

Janner blushed and shook his head as he took his seat.

Leeli and Tink tried to hide their giggles, as Nia pulled up a chair and sat with her elbows on the table and her chin in her hands, watching her children eat. Janner stared out the window, deep in his thoughts; Tink hunched over his plate like a buzzard, eating the hotcakes and sausage as if they might try to escape; Leeli watched her brothers and fidgeted with the hem of her gown, humming and bobbing her head back and forth while she chewed.

"Eat well, my dears. It's going to be a busy day," Nia said smiling.

The children's eyes widened. "The sea dragons!" they cried in unison.

Nia laughed and pushed herself up from the table. *"The summer dusk hath split in twain the gilded summer moon, and all who come shall hear again the dragons' golden tune,"* she sang.[2] "Coming just like they have for a thousand years. Finish up your breakfast and we'll go on to town. The chores will wait."

With a loud crash, the back door burst open and there stood Podo, drenched with sweat and out of breath. "THWAPS!" he bellowed, holding out a sack with something squirming and screeching inside. Podo smacked it with his club and the squealing promptly stopped.

Nugget yipped and danced at his feet, nipping at the sack.

"There are two more of the little stinkers out there, but these three"— he shook the sack—"won't be munching on any more of our vegetables, I can tell you that. Lousy, thievin' little thwaps…" He noticed his three grandchildren and his daughter watching him and cleared his throat. "Don't worry, now. I'll be tossin' 'em off the cliff straight into the Dark Sea after I eat a few of yer fine hotcakes, honey." He nodded to Nia, trying to sound less gruff.

Nia's mouth dropped open. "How could you throw them into the sea?"

Podo scratched his head. "Easy. See, I take this sack here, and I…dump it out. Over the cliff. Simple as that."

Leeli sat with her fork in her hand and a look of horror on her face. "Grandpa, you can't just kill them!" She pushed back from the table as the boys rolled their eyes. She hobbled on her crutch to her towering grandfather and looked up at him with a pitiful sweetness in her eyes.

Podo loved his little granddaughter like nothing else in Aerwiar, and she knew it.

"They're such *sweet* little things, Grandpa, and they never harm anyone."

---

2. From "The Legend of the Sunken Mountains," a traditional Skreean rhyme. A later version of the tale was printed in Eezak Fencher's *Comprehensive History of Sad, Sad Songs.* See page 283 in Appendices.

Podo sputtered and pointed to the scratches on his arms.

Leeli didn't seem to notice. "And all they take is a few of our vegetables each year to feed their baby thwaplings. I can't believe that you would do such a thing. Please, Grandpa, don't kill the little fuzzies." She grabbed his shirt, pulled his face to hers, and kissed him on a grizzled cheek. "Come on, Nugget," she said, and she left the kitchen.

The sack squealed and Podo smacked it again, but with less vigor. With a grunt, Podo plopped the sack on the floor beside the table and shoveled a hotcake into his mouth.

"Now Janner, lad," Podo said without looking up from his plate, "It can get rowdy out there with the festivities going on, and you know the Fangs get even meaner when it looks like we Skreeans are having a grand time of it."

"Yes sir." Janner looked down at his plate and clenched the sides of his chair, bracing himself for what he knew was coming.

"And you're the oldest, which bears a noble responsibility. It means—"

"It means that I have to keep an eye on Tink and Leeli and make sure they get home safely. I've heard the same thing every day of my life, and I'm not stupid." Janner surprised even himself. His cheeks reddened when he saw the look of shock on his mother's face. He knew he had gone too far, but it was too late to turn back. Years of frustration decided to explode over hotcakes that very morning. "What it means is that I'm a nanny, that I never get to do anything *I* want to do."

Tink snorted and tried to hide his laughter by shoving another large bite into his mouth. Janner kicked him under the table, which only made Tink snort again.

"I don't want to spend my life fretting over Tink and Leeli, following two little kids around, fussing over them like an old woman and wasting my life!"

"Son—" Podo started.

"I'm not your son! You're not my father, and if my father were alive, he'd understand." Janner already hated himself for what he had said. He was breathing hard, staring at the stove, afraid to look at his grandfather's face. His chest felt hot, and tears were coming. He put a hand in his pocket and squeezed the folded drawing of his father. Like never before, he wished he were on that boat, out on the Dark Sea of Darkness, far away from Glipwood and from the way he felt right now.

Podo chewed and swallowed his hotcakes slowly, considering his grandson in a heavy silence. "Tink, clear yer plate and go get dressed, laddie," he said without taking his eyes off of Janner.

Nia stood by the stove looking at the floor with her hands on her hips.

The grizzled old man wiped his mouth with a napkin and gripped the sides of the table with his big hands.

Janner was in trouble. He knew it.

4

A Stranger Named Esben

The door swung shut behind Tink as Nia pulled up a chair between Podo and Janner.

"Lad, do you know I love you?" said Podo.

Janner nodded, then added, "Yes sir."

"I know I'm not your father. He was a good man. A brave man. He fought well and died well in the Great War, and it's my duty to raise you children as near as I can to what your father would want."

Janner stole a glance at his mother. She fought back tears as she stood and busied herself with clearing the plates from the table.

"Now lad, you're getting long of leg and yer voice is getting thicker. I expect you figure you're nearing manhood, do ye?" Podo looked at Janner with one white bushy eyebrow cocked up and the other eye squinting at him. "Speak up, lad."

"Well, I'm twelve! I know that's not old, but…" He broke off, unable to think of what to say.

"Sometimes ye feel like yer brother and sister might weigh ye down like an anchor, is that it? Sometimes ye feel like this little town's too small for the notions in yer head?"

Janner stared at his hands. With a deep breath, he pulled the picture from his pocket. Nia stopped her cleaning as Janner unfolded the picture and spread it flat on the table. He could hold his tears back no longer; they dripped from the end of his nose onto the picture, mingling with the spray of the sea.

Nia hugged Janner's head to her chest and smoothed his hair for a long time. "I wondered where that picture had gotten to."

"It's him?"

Nia nodded slowly. "Yes."

"And he drew it?"

"Yes." Nia dabbed the tears from the picture with her apron. "That was a different time. A different world." She was quiet a long moment. "Before the Fangs. Your father would want nothing more than for you to sail your own seas, and one day you will. But if he were here he would tell you the same thing your grandfather is telling you. There's a time to sail and a time to stay put."

"Laddie, I understand more than ye might know." Podo's voice was softer. "But hear me: I was there when your pa died. I didn't see it, but I was there all the same."

Janner looked up sharply. "You were there? What happened?"

"Aye."

"Papa, no—" Nia said.

"It's time he knew something of where he's from, lass." Podo pointed at the drawing, then at Janner. "Look at 'im. He's the spitting image—"

"I don't see what that has to do with anything. Raising Esben's memory from the dead will do no good. *No* good." Nia's voice trembled.

Janner hated seeing his mother so upset but desperately wanted to hear more. "His name was Esben?" Janner hoped to keep Podo talking.

Podo and Nia looked at him with sad eyes.

Nia kissed Janner's hair. "No more. Please," she said to Podo and left the room.

Janner was silent.

Podo was silent.

The thwaps in the bag were silent.

Finally, Podo cleared his throat. "Well, you must trust me. I see your father in you. He was a great man. He fought for us. *Died* fighting for us. Your wee sister and brother are treasures, same as you, and we wouldn't have our treasures lost." The old man leaned forward and lowered his voice. "Blood was shed that you three might breathe the good air of life, and if that means you have to miss out on a Zibzy game, then so be it. Part of being a man is putting others' needs before your own."

Janner thought of Tink and Leeli. The idea of always having to look out for them still galled him, but he did love them. He wanted to be a good, brave man like his father—whose name he had just heard for the first time. "Yes sir. I'll try," he said, not quite able to meet Podo's eyes. Janner folded up the picture and looked at Podo questioningly. Podo gave his permission with a nod, and Janner placed the picture back in his pocket with care.

"So, lad, since you're so old now, why don't you and your brother and sister head over to the festival without yer mother and me for a while. We still have some chores to mind. You're in charge."

"But, mama said that Leeli couldn't—"

"Hee," Podo laughed. "I'll see to yer mother. Just keep yer sister close. Your mother and I'll be along directly. Can you handle that?"

"Yes sir," Janner said, suddenly unsure that he could.

Podo clapped his hand on the table. "Right, then. Now. There's something I need you to do for me before you three head out to the festival." He handed the sack of thwaps to Janner and lowered his voice. "Would you mind dumping these stinkers over the cliff for yer dear Podo?"

Janner's eyes widened. "What?"

"Aw, I'm foolin'," Podo said with disappointment. "I couldn't do that after Leeli's little performance." Podo reached into his pocket and handed Janner three grayish coins. He took another bite of hotcakes, swallowed and burped. "Buy yerselves some munches."

5

The Bookseller,
the Sock Man,
and the Glipwood Township

The Igiby children raced across the cottage lawn, though that was only as fast as Leeli could hobble. Janner resisted the urge to offer her his help. He had learned long ago that his little sister was capable of getting around on her own and that if she wanted help, she'd ask for it. He also knew that while she was fiercely independent, she fiercely wanted them to wait up for her.

Even with a crippled leg, Leeli was remarkably fast, and her brothers moved at a trot as they wound down the shady lane that led to the town of Glipwood. Nugget padded along beside Leeli, wagging his tail, and if the Igiby children had had tails they would have wagged too. They could already hear the uncommon sound of laughter from the direction of town, and wisps of happy music lifted over the tops of the oaks.

Janner suddenly felt pleased to be entrusted with the care of both of his younger siblings. He laughed at how quickly his feelings had changed. Only minutes ago he felt chained down by his responsibility—now he was proud of it. Going to town alone with Tink and Leeli was a far song from sailing alone in the open sea like his father had done, but it would have to do.

Janner wondered what his friend, old Oskar N. Reteep at the bookstore, would say when he saw the Igibys with no parents in sight. Would Oskar give him more work in the store or let him take home more books?

Maybe he'd finally allow Janner to read the books reserved only for older folks, the thick ones on the top shelves with the ancient binding. He smiled to himself. *Responsibility might not be so bad after all.*

"So what happened back there?" Tink asked as they jogged down the lane.

"Nothing."

"What do you mean, nothing?" Tink sounded disappointed. "No spanking?"

"No. No spanking."

"So when you're twelve you can be a stinker and not get whomped?"

"It's complicated," Janner said, thinking again of his father. He wondered when he'd show Tink and Leeli the picture.

"I can't wait to be twelve." Tink grinned deviously, and they rounded the corner onto Main Street.

Janner smiled back at his brother, but inside, he was troubled. *Esben. Esben Igiby,* he thought. Knowing his father's name made Janner think of him as a real person, not just a happy shadow from his dreams. Many days he didn't think much about him, but whenever the other children in Glipwood spoke of their fathers, or when they asked Janner why he lived with his old grandfather, he felt like an oddity. He knew that Leeli and Tink felt it too. Everyone else in Glipwood had grown up there, or somewhere nearby. But whenever Janner asked Podo or Nia where they had come from, the answer was always silence. All he knew was that Podo had grown up in the cottage, and that his great-great-great-great-grandparents (Janner's great-great-great-great-*great*-grandparents), Edd and Yamsa Helmer, had built the cottage two hundred years earlier, when Glipwood was little more than a cluster of buildings.[1]

---

1. Glipwood had prospered greatly over the years and was now a slightly larger cluster of buildings, thanks in part to the tourism generated by the Dragon Day Festival. Willibur Smalls, *It Happened in Skree* (Torrboro, Skree: Blapp River Press, 3/402).

Now Glipwood had one main street with several buildings on either side. Shaggy's Tavern stood on the left, its dark green shingle bearing a picture of a dog with a pipe hanging from its mouth. Beside it was the biggest building in town, Glipwood's only inn. Its sign read, THE ONLY INN at the top and below that, in smaller letters, "Glipwood's Only Inn." The Shoosters, a kindly old couple, kept the inn warm and clean, and the smells that floated out of the kitchen made the whole township hungry. Across the street was a barbershop called J. Bird's, where Mr. Bird usually could be seen sleeping in one of his chairs. Next to the barbershop squatted the town jail, where Fangs lounged on the stoop and hurled insults at passersby.

Wide, mossy oak trees stretched their boughs over the streets, offering welcome shade from the summer sun. Children with sticky faces straddled high limbs, munching on various desserts. Everywhere Janner looked were men and women of different shapes and sizes. The women wore long, flowing, brightly colored gowns, and the men who strolled beside them puffed pipes and sported silly round-topped hats. Occasionally a horse-drawn carriage would squeak by, its occupants peeking smugly out the window.

Janner, Tink, and Leeli, with Nugget by her side, made their way through town, past the inn (always full this time of year, being Glipwood's only inn), past Ferinia's Flower Shop and the old rickety building that housed Books and Crannies. A sign hung in the window:

OSKAR N. RETEEP
PROPRIETOR / BOOKSELLER / INTELLECTUAL / APPRECIATOR
OF THE NEAT, THE STRANGE, AND/OR THE YUMMY

Oskar N. Reteep, a round man with a short, white beard and very little hair on top of his head, waved at them from his front porch where he sat in a rocking chair puffing on a long pipe. He had combed long wisps of hair over his freckled brown egg of a head in a vain attempt to hide the fact that he was bald. The breeze was stirring a long tendril of hair about as if it were waving at the children too.

"Ho there, Janner!" he called, smiling and beckoning to the children.

"Hello, Mister Reteep," Janner hollered over the noise of the crowd.

From the window behind Oskar, a little man with pointed ears watched them. Zouzab Koit was a ridgerunner,[2] whom Oskar had adopted six years earlier upon opening a crate that was supposed to have been full of books from Torrboro. Instead, Oskar had been shocked to find a starving, frightened Zouzab cowering inside.

Ridgerunners were a little people, and little known in Skree, but Oskar, a self-proclaimed Appreciator of the Neat, the Strange, and/or the Yummy, decided that Zouzab most certainly qualified. Zouzab's descriptions of his homeland and harrowing life in the Killridge Mountains were very Neat, as were his stubbly hair and pointed features. His dress and behavior were quite Strange. He wore leather breeches and a patchwork shirt of many colors that billowed around him like a hundred tiny flags. Strangest of all, he couldn't help climbing on everything taller than himself, which was most things. As for his being Yummy, Oskar didn't care to speculate.

Janner thought how they looked rather silly together—Oskar round as a pumpkin and Zouzab short and thin as a shorn weed.

Leeli waved at Zouzab. His beady eyes widened and he ducked out of sight.

"Where's Podo?" Oskar asked wiping his glasses on his vest.

Janner tried to sound nonchalant. "Back at the cottage. Said we could come alone today."

"Ah-ho." Oskar eyed Janner through the spectacles perched back on the end of his nose. Janner beamed. "Come bright and early day after

---

2. Ridgerunners are a reclusive race that dwell primarily in the mountains of Dang. Their great weakness is fruit of any kind, in any form, whether plucked from the tree or baked in a crispy pie. Because of this, ridgerunners are the chief enemy of the people of the Green Hollows, who grow fruit of many kinds. Each year, swarms of ridgerunners descend the northern slopes of the Killridges and steal fruit from the Hollows. It's said that as long as you are not a fruit, a ridgerunner won't eat you. Since there was no fruit directly involved in the Great War, the ridgerunners of course remained neutral. Padovan A'Mally, *The Scourge of the Hollows* (Ban Rona, Green Hollows: The Iphreny Group, 3/111).

tomorrow, eh? I found an absolute trove of books on my last trip to Dug-town. I'll need help loading them in."

"Yes sir, I'll be there." Janner began to think of all the books he would read next.

Oskar squinted one eye at Tink and looked him up and down. "And bring that skin and bones brother of yours too. We could use the extra hand, and by the look of it, he could use the exercise."

Tink's eyes widened. "Really, Mister Reteep?"

"That's right, lad." Oskar smiled down at Leeli. "What do you think of all this fuss, lass? Glipwood is a different town for a day, isn't it?"

Leeli looked around at the folk milling past them, taking in the sights, sounds, and smells that were so foreign to the sleepy little township. She smiled. "I like it. But after a day of it, I'll be glad when things are back to normal."

Janner rolled his eyes. "Well, I wish Glipwood was like this every day. I wish The Only Inn was always full of travelers and merchants with news from Torrboro and Fort Lamendron or tales from explorers who've gone beyond the edges of the maps. Did you ever think about the fact that there might be whole continents that no one from Skree has ever seen? That no one *anywhere* has ever seen? We've never even been to Fort Lamendron, and Podo says it's only a day's ride from here. All these rich people from Dug-town and Torrboro get to really *see* Aerwiar, not just shovel hay all day…"

Oskar raised his eyebrows at Janner, whose speech trailed off at the quizzical reaction of his friend. Oskar then wiped his brow and pressed the single waving lock of Reteep hair back to his forehead. "So. Glipwood is too small for Janner. What say you, young Tink?"

Tink sniffed the air. "I want some sugarberry pie."

"Janner," Oskar said, "there's more to the world than just seeing it. If you can't find peace here in Glipwood, you won't find it anywhere." Oskar gestured at a carriage rolling by. "These folks may appear wealthy, but no one really is anymore. If you look close enough, you'll see the suits and dresses these so-called rich folk are wearing are tattered and patched.

No earrings or necklaces adorn the women. No rings sparkle on the men's fingers."

Janner saw that it was true. *Why hadn't he ever noticed that before?* Annoyed, he nodded to Oskar and toed at the dirt. *It was his day to be corrected by the grownups,* he thought.

"Lad, it's one thing to be poor in pocket—nothing wrong with that. But poor in heart—that's no good. Look at them. They're sad in the eyes, and it's a sadness no amount of money could repair. Why, they hardly remember what it's like to laugh from the belly anymore."

"But they seem to be happy, Mister Reteep, don't they? We could hear the laughter and music from up the lane," Leeli said.

"People come to Glipwood to see the dragons because it's one of the only freedoms they have left. Sure, they sleep under their own roofs with their own families, and broken though it is, this is still their own land. But this is a far fling from freedom, young Igibys. Some of us still remember what it was like to stroll through town after dark or to ride a horse through the forest without fear." Oskar's voice grew angry, and it seemed to Janner that he was no longer talking to them but to himself. "It's beginning to feel like the Fangs have always been here, that Gnag the Nameless has always ruled us, taxed us, and stolen our young."

Janner looked at the half smiles on the people's faces. He saw the way the people cowered away from the sneering Fangs on the jail stoop. There was sorrow underneath all the merriment, and for the first time Janner was old enough to feel it.

Oskar came back to himself and smiled at the children. "Ah. But it's a fine day, is it not, Igiby children? There's a time to think hard and there's a time to ease up. Now you run along. As the great Thumb of the Honkmeadow wisely wrote, 'The games are starting soon enough.'" Oskar waved them on with a wink while he puffed his pipe and palmed his hair back to his bald pate.

With somber hearts, the children made their way down the crowded street. Janner was deep in thought, staring hard at Commander Gnorm,

the fattest and meanest Fang in Glipwood. Gnorm's feet were propped on
an old stump, and he was gnawing the meat from a hen bone, his long purple tongue slurping noisily. Gnorm hurled the bone at an old man walking
by and the Fang soldiers hissed and laughed as the man bowed and wiped
the grease from his face. Janner found it hard to believe that there was a day
when no one in Skree had ever heard of the Fangs of Dang.

Past the jail, in front of the little building that housed the printing
press, a cluster of people stood in a circle laughing at something. Above the
heads of the onlookers, two ragged boots were kicking around in the air.

Janner and Tink grinned at one another.

"Peet the Sock Man!" Tink pointed and took off running. "Come on,
Leeli! Let's see what he's up to."

They pushed through the crowd and saw the strange fellow walking on
his hands in the middle of the circle. He was chanting the phrase "wings
and dings and purple things" over and over, kicking his feet to the rhythm.
His cheeks were sunken, his eyes were shadowed, and the creases around
them gave him the look of having just finished crying. He wore ragged
clothes and was filthy, as were the dingy knitted stockings he wore on his
arms up past his elbows.

Onlookers tossed coins, but to the residents of Glipwood, this was normal behavior for Peet. Earlier that summer, in fact, Peet crashed into the
street sign at the corner of Main and Vibbly Way (which was quite innocent, as it was standing still and in plain sight). After insulting the sign's
mother, Peet challenged it to a contest, though it quite stoically showed no
sign of retaliation. He took a hard swipe at it, missed, spun in a circle like
a circus dancer from Dugtown, and collapsed into the dirt where he snored
noisily all that night.

Janner applauded with the crowd as Peet flipped back onto his feet,
adjusted his hair with a flourish, and skipped away with one eye closed and
a socked hand in his mouth, leaving the coins in the dust. Janner grinned
after Peet, whose bushy head bounced up the dusty side street and around
the corner.

"And he's gone," Janner said.

"Do you think it's true that he lives up near the old forest?" Tink asked.

Janner shrugged. "He'd have to be crazy to live there." In the years before the war, rangers and trappers braved the forest and tamed the deadly beasts that prowled within it. But the Fangs had taken every weapon in the land. Every sword and shield, every bow and arrow, every dagger and spear, every farm tool that could be used as a weapon was locked away and guarded.[3]

"Well if anybody's crazy enough to go near the forest, it's Peet." Tink paused. "The Blaggus boys said they saw him riding a toothy cow like it was a horse up by the forest, whipping its rear with a switch and singing a ballad."

Janner snorted. "No way. Nobody could survive a toothy cow. Besides, the Blaggus boys are too jumpy to go anywhere near the forest. They're pulling your strings." Janner turned to go. "Come on."

But he stopped in his tracks and grabbed his brother's arm. He couldn't see Leeli. His head whipped to and fro, scanning the crowded street.

"Where's Leeli?" he cried. "Leeli!"

Tink tapped him on the shoulder. Janner whirled around to find his brother pointing to the ground at Janner's feet. Leeli was sitting there scratching Nugget's belly, looking up at him innocently. He sighed and felt his insides quiver with relief. In the space of a few seconds, he had envisioned Leeli lost or hurt, and he felt a tinge of the painful guilt he'd bear if something ever actually happened to her. *But nothing ever does,* he thought bitterly. *Here we are at the Dragon Day Festival, and I'm a nervous mess since the minute we arrived. Over nothing at all.*

What could possibly happen in just a few seconds?

---

3. In order for Podo to hoe the garden, he had to fill out the Permission to Hoe Garden Form, then the Permission to Use Hoe Form to borrow the hoe. If the tool wasn't returned by sundown, the penalty was much too severe to be mentioned in this happy part of the story. See pages 285–286 in Appendices.

6

A Bard at Dunn's Green

ome on," Janner grumbled, relieved but annoyed at himself for pan-
icking.

Tink reached down to help Leeli to her feet, but she ignored him and
got up with the help of her crutch.

Suddenly, the blast of a horn pealed through the summer air and the
crowd cheered. The games were beginning. All day long, games would be
played on Dunn's Green, the wide lawn on the east side of town. Participants and spectators would stay there for most of the afternoon watching
sack races, handyball,[1] Zibzy, and wiggle the chicken. Everyone lay on quilts
in the soft grass and watched the sports, nibbling treats purchased in town.

And that was exactly what Janner had in mind to do, if they could ever
get there.

Janner pulled Leeli along by her free hand and urged Tink to keep up.
"Could you two walk any slower?"

Tink was far more interested in the delicious smells wafting from the
kitchens and makeshift stands where merchants were selling baked butter-
dough pastries and fire-cooked swisher fins.

"Hang on, I want a berry bun." Tink dug into his pocket with the
hand Janner wasn't tugging.

---

1. A delightful sport in which each team tries to get the ball into a goal without using their feet
in any capacity, even to move. B'funerous Hwerq, *Ready, Set, Chube! A Life in Gamery* (Three
Forks, Skree: Vanntz-Delue Publishers, 3/400).

Janner was losing his patience. "I'll buy you a berry dumpling later if you want. Come on," he grumbled.

Tink relented, casting a long, regretful glance over his shoulder at a plump man in an apron basting a platter of buns with bright red jam.

When they finally arrived at Dunn's Green, the Igiby children sat on the lawn and watched the festivities all morning and into the hot afternoon. When the sun slipped westward and the shadows began to lengthen, the people chattered more and more. At dusk the sea dragons would come, and the people would perch on the cliffs to watch them dance by the light of the moon. Janner could feel the anticipation in the air.

To his delight, Tink had spotted a merchant selling blueberry gooey-balls just behind them. He had spent the few coins Nia had given him, so Janner had begrudgingly shared some of his own just to quiet Tink's stomach (and his mouth). Tink had no idea that his face was now smeared with dark purple. Leeli was content to passively watch the games while she tickled Nugget's belly or threw a stick for him to fetch. The onlookers had tolerated this until she'd accidentally thrown the stick onto the playing field. When Nugget chased it, one of the handyball players (who was rolling awkwardly across the field, careful not to let his feet touch the grass) missed a pass from another player because Nugget got in his way. All eyes had turned angrily toward Leeli, whose cheeks burned as red as Tink's were purple, but when the onlookers saw Leeli's crutch, they softened their glares and the game continued. Janner was glad that Leeli was too busy scolding Nugget to notice the crowd's pity, or she would have been even more upset.

Janner was as excited about all the unfamiliar faces around him as he was about the games. He wondered where all these people had come from, though the attire gave some folks away. The Torrboro citizens, for example, all dressed alike: The men wore little black hats, coats with long tails (in spite of the summer heat), and pants pulled up to a shocking height. The buckles of their belts sat just a little below their chins. The fashionable women wore frilly dresses with patterns that depicted the noses of various animals; their black shoes were pointy and oversized, as if their toes were as long as feet themselves, which made the women lurch forward when they walked. To Janner, it was like watching circus clowns (which he'd only read about) desperately trying not to be funny. Most of them wore white gloves, so when a handyball player scored a goal the sound of their applause was more like thopping than clapping, and they'd say things like "Good show!" or "Ho-lo, mommy-crack-a-whip!" or "Boozie!" or "Indibnibly fine shot!"

The long-haired folk from Dugtown weren't so odd in their dress, but their manner was shocking. Men and women alike were loud and their laughter sounded more like howling. Janner could tell that certain words they used were unacceptable to the Torrboro folk standing nearby, but the Dugtowners were oblivious. They growled and guzzled and made such a jolly racket that it was hard not to like them in spite of themselves.

Each stranger in Glipwood that day was a reminder to Janner that he had never, *never* left the town. They lit up his imagination and filled him with an ache to see the world. But then he would hear Leeli giggle or Tink burp and remember again that for now he would have to watch after his sister and brother in this dreadfully quiet little town—quiet, that is, except on the day the sea dragons came. He resolved to enjoy himself and pushed all unpleasant thoughts out of his mind.

Suddenly a commotion across the field interrupted Janner's thoughts—and the handyball game. Onlookers near the opposite goal had turned around, trying to make room for something or someone. Excited whispers circulated through the multitude, but Janner couldn't make out what anyone was saying. Voices rose up from the crowd, and even the players, sweating and covered with grass stains and dirt (though their feet were quite clean), stopped and focused on the fuss.

Janner and Tink stood up to try and see what was the matter, but there was nothing to see but agitated spectators shuffling out of the way while someone pushed in from behind them. The Fang sentries growled and hissed their irritation at the disturbance. They were charged with keeping the people under control, and something unusual was happening. As much as they hated the Skreeans, they weren't interested in doing any extra work on a hot day like this one.

Then the rumor finally reached Janner's ears. A portly woman to his far right gasped and said breathlessly to her portly husband that Armulyn the Bard had come unannounced and had been asked to sing by the honorable Mayor Blaggus of Glipwood.[2]

Tink and Janner looked at one another in disbelief. Armulyn the Bard was there, in Glipwood? Could it be that the very man who claimed to have visited the Shining Isle of Anniera,[3] the same Armulyn who wandered the captive lands and sang of the legends of Aerwiar,[4] of great deeds and great loves, was even now in Glipwood in his regal garb upon his majestic horse?

All thoughts of the handyball game vanished. The players were greatly relieved about this fact and stood up, moaning and stretching. Two burly men rolled an empty wagon to the center of the playing field. Mayor Blaggus mounted the makeshift platform with a grunt and it creaked

---

2. Blaggus's duties as mayor included running the town press, which now printed Commander Gnorm's various permission forms for tool usage. Being a person obsessed with paperwork and rules of order, this suited Blaggus well. He also organized which Glipfolk would prepare meals for the Fangs each week, who would clean the barracks, and made formal requests to Commander Gnorm on behalf of Glipfolk who wished to travel to Torrboro. Blaggus had lost his youngest daughter to the Black Carriage six years earlier, and Gnorm kept him in his employ under the threat of taking his two remaining sons as well. Understandably, because of this the people of Glipwood bore the mayor no ill will.

3. Many Skreeans doubted that the legendary Isle of Anniera existed at all. It is a sad truth that some people only believe something exists if they can see it with their own eyes. Bandy Impstead, for example, had argued for hours in Shaggy's Tavern one evening that there was no such thing as Wind for this very reason. His roof was torn off in a storm that very winter. Bandy's mind, however, remained unchanged.

4. The Legends of Aerwiar are a collection of stories about the Maker and the Beginnings of Things. The greeting of Dwayne and Gladys, the First Fellows, for example, is well known in all the lands of Aerwiar. The legends also include the tragedy of "Will and the Lost Recipe," "The Deep Holoré" (healing stones the Maker buried in the earth), and an early version of "The Fall of Yurgen." The legends were once contained in old books said to have been written by the Maker himself and given to Dwayne for safekeeping, but the old books—along with the Holoré, Will's famous cream of hen soup recipe, and Yurgen's mountains—are lost.

beneath his weight (he had eaten a few too many sugarbutter pastries in his day). He wore dark leggings and a bright red shirt. A gaudy yellow feather sprouted out of his hat, and he curled his moustache self-importantly. Blaggus held his hands out to silence the audience, then he turned to address the Fangs.

"With our all-wise and stunningly handsome and powerful and swift soldiers' permission," he said, bowing deeply so that his belly touched his knees, "we would like to hear a song or two from the bard Armulyn. We beseech your lordships this trite pleasure, for which we will give you our eternal thanks and servitude."

"Speak for yourself," Tink muttered with a sideways glance at the Fangs, whose scaly smirks showed how much they were enjoying the mayor's groveling. One of the Fangs nodded and let out a slithery growl that polluted the air like smoke.

"We thank you, kind masters." Mayor Blaggus cleared his throat. His tone changed abruptly to the regal, inflated voice he had used for many years before the Great War. "My dear friends and neighbors, an honor rarely bestowed has risen on us like a warm sun," he announced. "Armulyn the Bard, tale-spinner of the imaginary Shining Isle of Anniera, has chanced to join us in Glipwood on this fine day. He has accepted my invitation to perform for us. Please welcome this son of Skree to Glipwood by the Sea. Ladies and gentlemen, I give you Armulyn the Bard!"

A bedraggled man stepped up to the wagon with a worn whistleharp[5] under one arm. The smile on his leathery face reminded Janner of a mischief-minded little boy about to disobey. Armulyn winked at the crowd and bellowed, "Hello, dear Skreeans! Fangs are ugly!"

The applause ceased abruptly, and the four Fangs standing at the edge of the crowd roared a chilling roar and rushed, hissing, toward the bard.

---

5. It is unclear where the whistleharp originated. Each culture on Aerwiar claims to have invented the instrument, and each culture has good evidence to support its claims. Whistleharp tunes are referenced in the writings of Hzyknah, which date to the end of the First Epoch.

7

Barefoot and Beggarly

Janner felt a sheen of cold sweat break over him like a fever. It took him a moment to realize what he'd just heard. Had Armulyn just insulted the Fangs? Amidst the waters of his shock was a splash of surprise that the beggarly man on the platform was in fact the famous storyteller. Was there some mistake? Surely Armulyn the Bard would at least be wearing shoes, he thought. And by the filthy, callused look of the man's feet, Janner could see that he rode no horse but walked wherever he went. If not for the weatherworn whistleharp in his hands and the deep waters of his eyes, Janner would have believed the man was an impostor.

The Fangs pushed Glipfolk aside and bounded toward the wagon, drawing their swords as they ran. Janner's whole body tightened, and he tried to tear his eyes away from the moment when the Fangs reached Armulyn. Many in the crowd emerged from their shock in time to scream.

But the bard merely stood on the wagon and smiled. As the Fangs neared, Armulyn strummed his whistleharp and raised his voice in song. The Fangs faltered, jerked to a stop, and crouched before Armulyn, trying in vain to cover their ears and wave their swords at him at the same time.

"*Sssilence!*" one of them hissed.

Armulyn stopped singing and raised his eyebrows at them, as if annoyed at the interruption.

"Yes?"

"Careful, *bard*," the Fang spat. "It would be nothing for us to chop you into bits and gobble you in a broth."

Armulyn gazed at their sinister faces with that same reckless smile. "I doubt you'd like the taste of me. I'm wiry and ill fed." The only sound was the rattle of leaves in the wind. "Will that be all?" the Bard said after a moment, lifting the whistleharp to play again.

The Fangs stood frozen, but Janner thought he saw their black eyes shift sideways at the throng of people surrounding them on the green.

"Enjoy your petty songs," the lead Fang growled. He turned to the crowd. "And we will enjoy killing you all the moment Gnag the Namelesss decides he is finished with you. May that day come quickly." The Fang's tongue flitted out between his long narrow teeth, and his mouth curled upward in a grin. He clacked his teeth together and hissed at a little girl cowering at her parents' feet as those surrounding her on the field looked down at the ground or closed their eyes. The Fang who had spoken spat on the grass and moved away, his three companions following with hisses of their own.

The silence was broken by the strum of the whistleharp. The whiskery man raised his voice again in song, and there was no longer any doubt in Janner's mind that he was indeed Armulyn the Bard. The people sat enthralled as he sang the *Ballad of Lanric and Rube*,[1] and Janner and Tink found themselves pushing down tears as they listened to the tragic tale. After that he sang another for the rapt audience, then another, until the sun sank westward and the light grew golden, lengthening the shadows across the lawn.

As if the bard somehow knew, he ended his final song just moments before the sound of a low horn tore through the dusking air. Armulyn smiled widely and the many listeners gasped with excitement.

---

1. According to Eezak Fencher's *Comprehensive History of Sad, Sad Songs* (Torrboro, Skree: Blapp River Press, 3/113), Lanric and Rube grew up closer than brothers, but both fell in love with the same girl, a maiden named Illia. Armulyn sang of how they fought like bitter enemies for her hand in marriage before finally resolving to ride to her home in the green hills and ask her to choose which man she'd rather have. When they arrived they found her already wed to their cousin Doug, and the brothers went away weeping at their folly.

"The dragons," Janner said, grabbing Tink by his shoulders. Tink smiled back at him with his sticky, purple cheeks.

"Let's go," Tink said. "We have to find a good seat."

"Come on, Leeli!" Janner yelled, turning to go. People in the crowd were pulling one another to their feet and surging back toward the town. "Leeli?" Janner repeated, turning around when she didn't answer.

But Leeli was gone.

Janner told himself to calm down. The same thing had happened earlier. She couldn't have gone far. She had just been there on the lawn, rubbing Nugget's belly, hadn't she?

"Leeli Igiby!" he called, turning in every direction. People were everywhere, jostling the boys as they moved past.

"Out of the way, boy," said an old man with a cane, holding his pants up to his chin as he pushed by. The Torrboro women's wide dresses rustled past Janner and Tink, tugging them this way and that. Then a boisterous cluster of Dugtowners appeared like a wall before them. Janner found himself ducking under elbows and diving between legs, and twice he tripped over the Torrboro women's flopping, pointy shoes.

Tink was nowhere to be seen, but Janner knew he was near because of the shouts of surprise and the cursing coming from his left. Janner worried that the Fangs might be drawn to this new commotion, but to his relief the crowd finally thinned and he saw that the Fangs were gone.

"That was almost fun," Tink said, brushing himself off. Janner spun around and grabbed Tink by his collar.

"There's nothing fun about this, Tink. Do you realize that she could be hurt? She could have been snatched up by a Fang, or killed by one! *We have to find her.*" Janner glared at his brother. Was Tink really so foolish that he didn't realize how bad their situation was? As worried as he was for Leeli, Janner was also thinking of his own skin. What would Podo do when he found out that Janner had failed in his duty? How would he live with himself if something actually happened to his sister?

Tink flung Janner's hands from his shirt and backed away. He looked around Dunn's Green at the remaining people folding up their blankets and gathering their belongings for the walk to the cliffs. It finally sunk in for Tink that their situation was dire, and he put his hands to his mouth, turning in all directions, to yell over and again, "Leeli!"

Podo had taught them that if ever they were separated they were to meet at the last place they had all been together. Surely Leeli would be waiting for them innocently with Nugget in her lap once the rest of the throng had cleared.

"She must be right around here, Tink. I know she was here with Nugget just a few minutes ago." Janner scanned the lawn with a hand on his forehead.

Tink didn't answer. His eyebrows were scrunched together and he was wringing his hands, calling her name with a tremble in his voice.

"She'll be fine, you'll see," Janner said, trying to sound optimistic.

Tink and Janner called for her until the crowd was nearly dispersed, but still she was nowhere to be seen. Janner asked the stragglers if they'd seen a little girl, but they answered only with irritated looks; they were far more concerned with sea dragons than these pesky little kids. Finally, Janner and Tink stood alone on the lawn in the fading light.

Little Leeli Igiby was gone. The brothers looked at one another, unable to speak, unsure of what to do. Then a sound came faintly to their ears from the direction of the town—a sound that deepened their fear to terror and set them running as fast as they could run.

A dog was barking, and someone, a little girl—Leeli!—was screaming.

8

Two Thrown Stones

Faster, Janner!" Tink yelled over his shoulder as he sprinted toward town. Janner was huffing behind him, unable to keep up. As they passed the livery at the edge of town, Janner heard a deeper sound, below Leeli's screams and Nugget's growls: the dreadful, unmistakable hiss and snarl of a Fang.

Janner looked from one side of the street to the other, desperate for some clue as to where the screams were coming from, but they seemed to be everywhere. Tink bolted down the main street, which was mostly deserted. The few adults who remained were hustling toward the cliffs, thinking only of the annual dance of the sea dragons. If they heard the screams and the growling at all, they showed no sign of it. Out of the corner of Tink's eye, down a narrow alleyway between Ferinia's Flower Shop and J. Bird's Barbershop, he saw a Fang struggling with something. Tink skidded to a stop and Janner plowed into him, nearly knocking him down.

There in the alley, in a cloud of dust, Nugget was darting back and forth between the Fang's legs, evading the Fang's furious efforts to stab him with a spear. Leeli screamed again, and without a second thought her brothers ran down the alley to save her, though they both knew there was nothing two young boys could do, pitted against a Fang of Dang.

The narrow alley led around a corner to a small area between the back of Ferinia's and her stables. Leeli was curled into a ball while a second Fang held her in place with the butt of his spear. One Fang watched with grim delight as the other struggled with the little black dog.

Nugget was in a frenzy, pouncing in and out, snarling and snapping at the Fang.

The Fang standing over Leeli was chuckling in a thin, papery voice, "What's the matter, Slarb? Is the sssmelly little thing too much for you?"

Slarb growled as he jabbed again at Nugget. The spear nicked Nugget in the leg and he yelped.

Leeli screamed and the Fang jabbed at her with the butt of his spear just as her brothers burst around the corner, Tink in the lead. Leeli saw them and began kicking at the Fang with renewed vigor.

Janner found himself on Slarb's back, beating him with all his might around the neck and shoulders. It was the first time he had ever touched a Fang, and he was dimly surprised how cold the scaly skin was.

Tink dove past the second Fang, grabbed Leeli's arms, and tried to pull her away from it.

Slarb, with Janner on his back, hissed and thrashed, his long, sharp fangs dripping with venom that burned at the touch.

Nugget bit the lizard's leg and wouldn't let go.

The other Fang seized Tink by his shirt collar and yanked him backward and to the ground, where he lay choking and clutching his throat.

Leeli reached for her crutch, but the Fang snatched it away from her and crushed it into splinters. She saw bits of wood etched with purple flowers flying through the air.

The Fang then strode over to Slarb and kicked Nugget hard in the belly, sending him flying through the air with a yelp. The little dog crashed into the wooden wall and landed in a motionless heap.

Slarb hurled Janner over his shoulder and onto the ground. He bent over Janner's neck with his scaly jaw wide open, baring his dripping fangs to bite. The second Fang drew his sword and raised it to strike Tink. Leeli was helpless but to close her eyes and pray.

At that moment there was a dull *thunk*. Slarb's black eyes rolled back, and he fell unconscious on top of Janner. The second Fang had time to see that Slarb had been hit in the head with a fist-sized rock before he felt a stone smash into his own temple. He tottered for a moment then crumpled to the dirt.

Tink lay there stunned. "Where did those rocks come from?" he asked between gasps for air. Leeli's hands were folded tight and her eyes were still shut. She opened one of her eyes, amazed that the three of them were still alive.

They heard Janner's muffled voice from beneath the Fang, and Tink snapped out of his daze. After a few heaves, he pushed Slarb off and Janner scrambled away with a moan, wiping his neck where the Fang's burning venom had dripped on it.

Janner rushed over to Leeli and helped her up, inspecting her carefully. "Are you hurt?"

Leeli trembled but shook her head, pushing her hair from her face. She hugged her brothers and smiled through stubborn tears. "Nugget!" she cried, and hobbled over to the little black heap.

One of the Fangs groaned and stirred.

"We should get out of here," Janner said. "We don't want to be here when these things wake up."

Leeli was crying, stroking Nugget's face.

"Leeli, we have to go," Janner urged, pulling her away from the dog.

Suddenly, Nugget yelped and leapt to his feet. Hackles raised, he bared his teeth and circled menacingly. But his fierceness melted when he saw Leeli, and he set to licking her face and wagging his tail as if nothing had happened.

Leeli struggled to her feet and pointed at her ruined crutch. "I won't be going anywhere with that."

"Here," Janner said, sidling up beside her and pulling one of her arms around his neck. "It looks like you're going to have to let us help you for once. Let's go," he said, and they hurried out of the alleyway, leaving it completely empty.

Except, of course, for the two Fangs lying in the dirt, the two stones that knocked them unconscious, and the mysterious figure on the roof of J. Bird's Barbershop watching the three Igiby children flee.

9

The Glipper Trail

When they were back in the open street, two of the three children and Nugget felt a little better. Leeli was mostly happy that Nugget was fine, Tink was mostly glad that Leeli was fine, and Janner was mostly terrified because he was the oldest and had begun to think of the future. He knew Glipwood was a small town, and it would be only a matter of time—maybe hours, maybe just minutes—before the Fang called Slarb and his companion reported back to Commander Gnorm. Then terrible things would follow.

"We have to go home."

"Aw, Janner!" Tink wailed, already on to the next adventure. "Can't we see the dragons? Everyone's there, and as soon as the moon rises—"

"By the time the moon rises, you know what's going to happen?" Janner said hotly. Leeli and Tink were silent as they made their way through Glipwood's empty Main Street. Janner tried to calm himself down. "What's going to happen, *other* than the sea dragons dancing, is that those two Fangs will wake up. And once they do, every Fang in Glipwood will be looking for three kids and a little black dog. Oh, and the girl has a lame leg. Now tell me, do you think they'll have a hard time finding us?" Janner finished, more irritated than when he began.

"What do we do?" Leeli asked after a long pause.

"Mama will be at the cliffs watching the dragons, but that will probably be the first place the Fangs would look for us. Podo always stays home on Dragon Day. So that's where we're going. Podo will know what to do." Janner set his face for the lane that led to the cottage. "I hope he does."

"Here." Tink wrapped Leeli's other arm around his neck and picked up his pace.

Nugget trotted along beside them very seriously, as if he too had realized it was a bad situation indeed.

The light deepened as they hurried on, so when they were still an arrow's shot away from the cottage, they already knew that their grandfather wasn't home. No lantern burned in the window, no smoke lifted lazily out of the chimney. Janner stopped and Tink with him as they sat Leeli down on the grass, each bending over to catch their breath.

"Where...do you...suppose he is?" Tink said between gulps of air.

"Don't know," Janner said, pacing.

"Maybe he went to see the dragons this year." Tink was doubtful.

"But he never goes to the cliffs on Dragon Day," Leeli said, puzzled. "Why would he go this time?"

"Well, why wouldn't he be here at the cottage?" Tink asked. "I think we should look for him at the cliffs; then we might see the dragons after all—"

A glare from Janner cut him off. Janner looked east in the direction of the sea. Maybe Tink was right. Maybe for some reason Podo had decided to watch the dragons this year. "Fine," he said. "But we're taking the Glipper Trail. We can't risk the main road. There are probably Fangs everywhere. The Glipper Trail's faster anyway."

Tink moaned, but already Janner was helping Leeli toward the trail.[1]

---

1. The Glipper Trail had been there since long before Podo was born. Edd Helmer, Podo's great-great-great-great-grandfather had planned to take advantage of the cottage's nearness to the cliffs by doing his fishing from there. After carving out a path, he purchased a crate of fishing line from a merchant in Lamendron (later to become Fort Lamendron), tied a hook to the line, placed a horrified worm on the hook, and lowered the string down into the Dark Sea of Darkness. Just getting the hook down to the water took the better part of the morning, and, of course, Edd had no way of knowing from that great height whether or not the bait and hook were indeed submerged. Near dusk that evening, Edd felt a tug on his line and began hauling in his catch. Sometime after midnight Edd finally reeled in a small glipper fish. Yamsa wasn't happy about being awakened by Edd's cry of victory, or that in the dead of night he cleaned, cooked, and ate his little fish. Edd decided the next day that for all the trouble he had

An old walking path led through the trees behind the Igiby cottage and wound precariously near the edge of the cliffs. In the deepening shadows the children made their way through the trees.

When they emerged, the view was terrible and vast. Shale and tough grass littered the rocky verge of the land. The horizon was silent and wide, and a salty wind sighed upward, around their ankles and through their hair. The children stood without speaking, dizzy with the smallness they felt looking out over the Dark Sea of Darkness.

Janner looked to his right and could make out a precarious trail winding over stone and brush, leading away to where the people would be watching the dragons. The Glipper Trail stayed mostly level on a narrow shelf while the ground nearer the tree line rose steeply above them. Wiry shrubs and roots clutched the rock wall as if they too were afraid of falling.

"Janner, I can't do this," Tink said. He was standing with his back against the gray rock, eyes clenched shut.

"You have to," Janner said. "The Fangs that might find us on the road are more dangerous than this trail right now. You have to try, Tink."

Using the nearby boulders for support, Leeli hopped back to him and took his hand. "Come on," she said.

---

gone through for that one fish, he may as well have caught several. So he purchased a spool of rope from the same merchant in Lamendron, fastened it to a net, and once again spent all morning lowering the net into the sea. This time he fastened the line to a team of oxen and had them haul in the catch. By sundown the oxen were exhausted and the catch was only halfway up the face of the cliff. Edd tied off the rope and let it hang for the night. Early the next morning he set the oxen to work again. By noon, the net full of glippers, small sharks, pinchers, and squid was pulled over the edge and onto solid ground. Even Yamsa had to admit that it was a good catch, and they ate nothing but fish for the next three weeks. Fish and biscuits for breakfast, fish sandwiches for lunch, fried fish for dinner. They ate so many fish, in fact, that both Edd and Yamsa got sick, and they were never again able to eat fish without gagging. Edd never again fished from the cliffs, but the path by which his oxen pulled the heavy net remains.

Tink jerked his hand away and forced a smile.

"I'm not really worried about me, you know," he said with sudden bravado. "I just meant that, uh, I don't think Leeli should be out here."

"Oh, *thank* you," Leeli said wryly.

Tink sighed and peeled his fingers from the rock. He inched along behind Leeli and Janner, careful to stay as far as possible from the edge. As the light faded, the trail rose and narrowed. Leeli picked her way across, but Janner had to stop now and again for Tink to gather the courage to follow. Janner kept looking back to be sure that Leeli was able to navigate the trail without her crutch. With Nugget at her side and all manner of roots and rocks to hold, she seemed more like she was taking a stroll through a park than edging along a perch above the Dark Sea.

Finally, they topped the rise in the trail and it widened out to a grassy slope. Janner and Leeli tried not to laugh when Tink burst ahead of them and paced the safe ground. His shirt was drenched in sweat, and he was strutting like he had just won a race. Ahead and below them Janner saw the glow of torches where the people were gathered to watch the dragons.

"We made it," Janner said. "Tink, help me with Leeli."

As they scrambled down the slope toward the throng, the moon began its soft ascent. Then they heard the most achingly beautiful sound in all of Aerwiar.

10

Leeli and the Dragon Song

A long, warm note like the sound of a yawning mountain rose in the air and bounced off the belly of the sky. The deep echo was absorbed by the tall trees of Glipwood Forest and was answered a moment later by a higher sound that felt like a soft rain. Even Janner forgot to worry over the Fangs for a moment. His chest tightened and his eyes stung with tears.

"Quick!" Tink said. "It's starting!" Tink ran ahead, dangerously close to the cliff. His fear of heights was all but gone.

"Tink!" Janner called. But there was no stopping Tink—the sound of the dragons had changed him somehow. Janner even thought for a moment that he looked different, boldly making his way along the precipice.

Janner and Leeli moved as quickly as they dared till they could make out the dark cluster of people watching the ocean below them. The verge of the cliffs was cluttered with boulders between patches of tall grass, places where one could sit and comfortably watch the sea. The Dark Sea was so far below that it seemed if someone were to tumble over the cliff they would have time to stop screaming and take a final, breezy nap before crashing into it. Tiny, silent streaks of white on the surface were actually chaotic waves smashing into the jagged rocks below, and the mightiest spray was only faintly visible, like a poof of dust from a pebble dropped in the sand.

Janner and Leeli found Tink sitting on a flat outcropping of rock that depressed in the center. They were still an arrow's shot away from the crowd, enough to satisfy Janner that they were well hidden.

By the light of the big moon, Tink leaned out over the edge, straining to see something in the dark water below. *How could this be,* Janner thought, *when just that morning Tink had nearly wet himself on the roof of the house?*

From where they sat they could see the mighty Fingap Falls far to the north, roaring over the cliffs and pounding into the sea. To the south, the cliffs marched away into the distance, where they eventually curled backward and sloped downward to embrace Shard Harbor, home to Fort Lamendron, the largest Fang outpost in all of Skree. It was there the Black Carriage bore the children taken in the night.

Janner shuddered and tried not to think about Fort Lamendron or the Carriage. It wasn't hard, because the dragon song was rising in pitch and volume. Hidden in their cleft of rock, Janner forgot about the Fangs. He forgot about their desperate need to find their grandfather and mother. And, like Tink, he forgot the precariousness of the edges of the high cliffs as he leaned out over the empty air and felt his heart ache.

Tink was the first to see them. His breath caught in his throat and he found that he couldn't speak. He tapped Leeli on the knee with the back of his hand and pointed. She and Janner saw it as well.

In the churning white waters at the base of Fingap Falls, a long, graceful shape burst from the surface. Its skin caught and magnified the light of the moon. The sea dragon was easily twice the height of the tallest tree in Glipwood Forest. Its reddish body glimmered like a living fire. The head was crowned with two curved horns and its fins spread out behind it like wings. Indeed, it looked as if it might actually fly, but the dragon wheeled in the air and crashed into the sea with what must have been a sound like thunder but was inaudible over the constant roar of the waterfall.

At that moment, the dragon song rose into the air on a bright wind and filled the people gathered on the cliffs with a thousand feelings—some peaceful, some exhilarating, all more alive than usual.

A middle-aged man named Robesbus Nicefellow, who had spent his life balancing records for the famed button merchant Osbeck Osbeckson of Torrboro, decided he wouldn't spend one more day working behind a desk; he had always wanted to sail. Mr. Alep Brume, who was sitting beside Ferinia Swapleton (proprietor of Ferinia's Flower Shop), turned to her and whispered that he'd secretly loved her for years. Mayor Blaggus silently swore he'd never again pick his nose.[1] All of the passion and sadness and joy of those who listened wound into one common strand of feeling that was to Janner like homesickness, though he couldn't think why; he was just a short walk from the only home he'd ever known.

The few Fangs unlucky enough to stand watch at the cliffs, however, heard only screeching, a miserable wail that set their teeth on edge. Their green skin shivered and they snarled and hissed at the people closest to them.

Tink was leaning so far over the edge that it looked like he might fall to the sea. Eyes wide open, his jaw was clenched and his knuckles were white where they gripped the rock at his sides. Janner had the strange thought that he looked like a statue of a king, perched there so rigid and serene in the warm dusk.

The song continued, and more dragons exploded out of the water. They spun in the air and hung there for a moment before slamming back into the sea. Scores of horned bull dragons, amber and shimmering gold, swam circles around the thinner and more sleek mares that burst out of the water and over them in an intricate pattern. Now even the roar of Fingap Falls was not as loud as the crash of the many dragons into the Dark Sea. The strains of the song entwined and followed one another until a haunting melody emerged. Janner thought, as he thought every summer the dragons came, that there could be nothing more beautiful in all the world.

Leeli was still as a statue, her hands clasped at her chest. Janner heard a whisper of sound mingling with the dragon song as her lips moved like

---

1. Mayor Blaggus broke his vow on the walk back to town.

she was trying to remember the words to a song, or like she was praying. Her gaze was far away, resting somewhere beyond the dragons. A slight, sweet melody, the beauty of which Janner had never heard before, drifted from Leeli's mouth. Janner looked at her with wonder. He was so enthralled with her song he scarcely noticed that after a moment it was *all* he heard.

The dragons had fallen silent.

They had halted their dance and were gazing up at the cliffs. Though they were leagues away and the dusk made it difficult to see, Janner knew with a shudder that the sea dragons were watching them.

They were *listening.*

O holoré lay thee low
Holoél dark in the Deep
Down beneath the earth you go
Go holoré fast to sleep

Fast to sleep
Fast to sleep
Dark holoré in the Deep

Rise again holoré now
Spring abundant holoél
Render green the dying bough
Raise the rock where Yurgen fell

Raise the rock
Raise the rock
Spring abundant holoél[2]

---

2. Though it is impossible to be sure, most scholars agree that this is likely the song that Leeli Igiby sang at the cliffs that evening. *Holoré* is an ancient word with several meanings. Its most

A breezy sound of gasps and whispers rose from the crowd. In all the years the dragons had come, this was something new. Tink and Janner looked in awe at Leeli, who seemed unaware of the quiet commotion she was causing. The wind carried Leeli's voice along the cliffs so it seemed to the crowd that the song was coming from the air itself.

Finally her song ended. Leeli came to herself and focused on the shimmering beasts below her, silent and watching. For a moment the only sound was the wind and the sea and the distant waterfall. Then the dragons arched their great necks, spread wide their fins, and bellowed an answer that rattled Janner's teeth. It echoed Leeli's tune in a sad, hopeful reprise.

Then it stopped.

The dragons were gone as fast as they had come. The last fin disappeared in a swirl of water. Only the dull, even rush of Fingap Falls and the occasional cry of a gull interrupted the awed silence.

Mr. Alep Brume blew his nose. Whispers turned to hushed voices, which finally became the chattering of the multitude standing and stretching, then turning to walk back to town.

The moment was over. The dragons would make their way, so people said, back south to the Sunken Mountains to live out the winter.

Tink was still staring at the sea, at the place where the last dragon had sunk away. He blinked several times and came out of a trance of his own.

---

common definition is "the feeling of forgetting to do something without knowing what that thing is." For example: *Foom was overcome with holoré for the whole journey, but when he returned home to find his wife still waiting on the front steps, he realized what he had forgotten.* The word *holoré* is also used to describe the scent of burned cookies, and is often applied to any potentially good thing that has turned unexpectedly sour. For example: *When Foom realized he had forgotten to bring his wife on the three-day vacation, the holiday was holoré.* The ancient meaning of the word, which is how it is likely being used in the song, refers to the stones laid deep within the earth by the Maker at the creation of Aerwiar. The stones, according to *The Legends of Aerwiar*, are imbued with power to keep the world alive and growing, functioning much the same, it is assumed, as Water from the First Well. The meaning of *holoél* is uncertain, but very likely has to do with cookies as well.

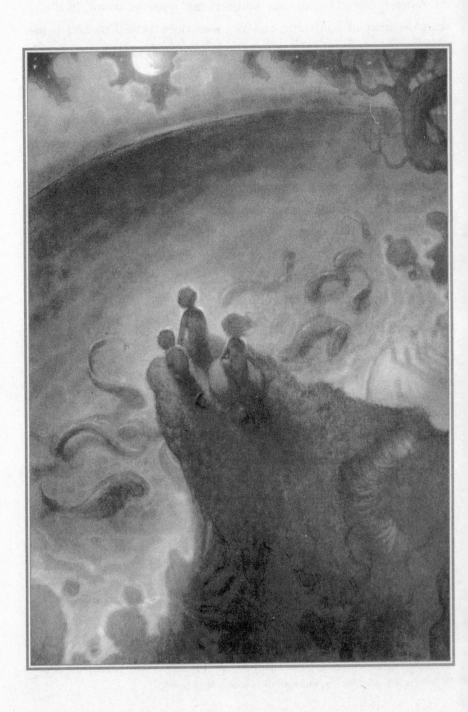

He looked down, his face turned pale and he squealed like a flabbit. He skittered back and lay panting on the ground five feet away, clutching the grass as if the world might lurch to its side and try to shake him over the edge.

Leeli giggled, her head full of music.

"What was that, Leeli?" Janner asked. "Who is Yurgen?"

She shrugged, blushing. "I don't know. I think it's a song mama used to sing me when I was little, or something like it anyway." She scrunched her face up, thinking hard. "It's odd," she said.

"What?"

"I can't remember it now," said Leeli, looking out at the Dark Sea.

"Well, it was...really pretty." Janner didn't know what else to say.

He was about to suggest that they find Podo and their mother when two cold hands grabbed him from behind. Janner was spun violently around to find himself face to face with Slarb the Fang, who had a swollen, bleeding wound on the side of his scaly face.

11

A Crow for the Carriage

The Igiby children stood frozen. Four more Fangs surrounded them with swords drawn. "Try to run if you like," Slarb said with a smile that exposed his long, sharp teeth. "It's a long way down to the sssea. I'm sure those ghasstly dragons would love a few plump vittles after their silly show, don't you think?" Two of the Fangs seized Tink and Leeli.

In a deep, gravelly voice, one of them said, "What d'you want we should do wif 'em, Slarb? Tosss 'em over or put 'em in the pen?"

Slarb considered the first option for a moment. His purplish forked tongue flicked over his fangs as his cold eyes went from the children to the cliffs a few feet away.

Janner looked over Slarb's shoulder at the dissipating crowd, praying that Podo and his mother would spot them, wherever they were. But not one of the people in the crowd was looking their way, and as far as he could tell, none of them was Podo or Nia. Janner was furious that he had allowed himself to be distracted from finding them. They probably would have been better hidden in the crowd anyway.

"Commander Gnorm told me to bring 'em in, but this cliff is *ssso* close and these humans are so very *sssmelly*, eh, Brak?" His tongue flitted a few inches from Janner's face.

There was no way out. One Fang would be hard to escape from. Five would be impossible. It was best to stay calm and hope Slarb followed orders. Being thrown in jail and sent to Dang in the Black Carriage was horrifying, but it was better than being tossed into the sea right there and then. Janner noticed that Nugget was long gone.

So much for the loyal dog, he thought, just as Slarb's fist slammed into the side of his head, knocking him to the ground. It was the first time he'd ever been hit so hard. He'd had his share of fights with Tink, but they were nothing to the explosion of pain he felt while he moaned and struggled to his feet.

Slarb snorted. "Let that be a lesson, boy. Touch me again and I'll eat you alive."

He stepped over to Leeli, grabbed a fistful of her wavy blond hair and jerked her head back. "And the same goes for you, ssstenchy little girl," he said, and he pushed her to the ground beside Janner.

Tink wrenched free from the Fang who was holding him and swung a fist at Slarb, but Slarb brushed the punch aside and rammed his knee into Tink's stomach. Tink doubled over and collapsed, gasping for air. Slarb bent over him and drew his knife. With one greenish-scaled hand, he held Tink's head flat against the ground while he ran the point of the blade softly down Tink's cheek. "And you, you ssscrawny little thing," he growled. "Remember Slarb with *thisss.*" He flipped the dagger in the air, caught it by the blade, and cracked Tink in the head with the pommel. Janner and Leeli cringed at the sound it made as Tink cried out, then clenched his teeth and fought back the tears as a little patch of blood emerged from his hairline. At the sight of the blood, the Fangs became agitated, hissing and snorting like dinner had just been served.

"Bring them with me," Slarb said, turning away.

The brothers were yanked to their feet and shoved forward. Leeli tried to stand, but her poor twisted leg buckled beneath her, and she crumpled to the ground. Janner bent to help her up, but the Fang named Brak stepped between them with a growl.

"I'd let the little ssstinker alone if I was you," he said.

"She can't walk without help!" Janner said hotly, and Brak bared his fangs at him.

"Let the boy help his little crippled sister, you fool. Unless *you* want to carry the sssmelly thing all the way back to the jail," Slarb hissed.

Brak's nose twitched and his scaly lips curled with disgust while he regarded Leeli. He relented, and Janner helped her up again.

The side of Janner's face was pounding from the blow, and above Tink's ear an egg-sized knot was growing. Leeli cried as she limped along, looking around for Nugget.

By now most of the tourists had made their way to either The Only Inn for dinner or to their camp at the opposite edge of town to cook something they'd bought at the market that day. A few people were milling around the lamp-lit streets, but when they saw the procession of five armored Fangs carrying torches and prodding the three frightened children along, they averted their eyes and shuffled out of the way.

Commander Gnorm was a fat, scaly thing with sagging eyes and yellow crooked fangs. He lazed on the front porch of the jail almost all the time, sharpening a dagger and eating whatever happened to be on hand.

Janner's mind was racing. They had gotten themselves into a hayload of a mess. Commander Gnorm's decisions were as swift as they were ruthless, and for all he knew they would find themselves in the Black Carriage on their way to Fort Lamendron before the sun rose.[1] They were shoved up the few steps onto the jailhouse stoop where Commander Gnorm was leaning back in a chair, sharpening his dagger in the shadows.

"Well, get 'em inside," he said without looking up.

They were marched into a lamp-lit room and past a desk littered with fish bones. On the wall facing the desk, a crude circular target had been painted and a score of daggers were jutting out of the wall. Whoever had

---

1. When townspeople broke the law or were singled out for no reason by the Fangs, they were sometimes brought to jail where they were beaten by Gnorm and his soldiers. If this happened, it was considered by the Glipfolk to be a wonderful fortune, and upon a prisoner's release (if he was conscious), his family and friends congratulated him and carried on as if he'd just won a major award. If one wasn't lucky enough to receive jail and torture, Gnorm sent a messenger crow to summon the Black Carriage.

thrown them was disturbingly accurate. Slarb pushed the children into another room that was as dark as a grave. The light of Slarb's torch revealed three barred cells, the floors strewn with hay and filth. He lifted a ring of keys from the wall, opened the barred door, and shoved the children into a cell. With a look of great satisfaction he locked the door, replaced the keys, and left.

Tink and Leeli curled up next to Janner on the floor as if it were cold, though it was quite stuffy.

"Let me see, Tink," Janner said, taking his brother's head in his hands. He parted Tink's hair and squinted in the darkness at the lump, though he had no idea what he was looking for. "It doesn't seem too bad," he said, trying to sound much older than he was.

"How's that face of yours?" Tink said.

"It'll be fine," Janner said, wincing as he touched the bruise forming on his cheek.

The brothers turned to Leeli.

"You going to be okay?" Janner asked.

"This was all my fault," she said, wiping her nose with her forearm. "I'm so sorry I got us into this mess."

"What happened back there, anyway?" Janner asked.

"While you were watching the handyball game, I was throwing a stick to Nugget near the lawn, behind the crowd. A thwap plopped out of a tree, right in front of him, and Nugget ran after it. I followed them and before I knew it I was all the way back here on Main Street. I saw Nugget chase the thwap into the alley, and when he turned the corner, he tripped that Fang."

"Slarb?" Tink asked.

"Yes. I think so. And that thing—Slarb—picked up Nugget and was about to bite him, so, I kicked it in the shin." Leeli said this as if it were the most natural thing in the world.

"You *kicked* a Fang?" both boys repeated.

"Well, what was I supposed to do?"

"I don't know, but that's about the dumbest thing I've ever heard," Janner said.

"And the bravest," Tink said.

Leeli sat with her head down, her long hair almost touching the dirty floor.

"And the bravest," Janner agreed after a moment.

Leeli sniffed and wiped her nose.

"Hush," Tink said with a hand on her back. "It wasn't your fault, anyway. It was that dog of yours," he said, trying to be funny. Tink regretted it as soon as it came out of his mouth. Leeli sobbed.

"It's not like him to run away like that," she said, and buried her face in Tink's chest. "What if one of those awful things kicked him over the cliff?"

"Listen," Janner said. "Be *glad* that Nugget isn't in here with us. We're the ones who are in trouble. Either we're about to have the snot beat out of us, or we're going to be shipped away to Dang. I'd rather not see Dang or the Castle Throg or Gnag the Nameless this week, so let's hope for torture."

When the door to their cell opened, in wobbled Commander Gnorm with Slarb at his side.

Janner, Tink, and Leeli stood and stiffened as Gnorm regarded them with his greenish scaly arms folded and resting on his large gut like they were resting on a table. He looked them over with black, droopy eyes.

"Yesss, Commander," Slarb said, "These are the ones."

"And these children somehow left you unconscious in an alley." Gnorm turned to Slarb with a sneer. "They must be valiant warriors indeed to best *two* armed Fangs of Dang," he said, his voice deep and wet-sounding.

Like bubbling mud, Janner thought.

"Well, sir—"

"It would ssseem that you are curiously incompetent if it takes five of you to bring in three children. I sssit on my green rump all day long, growing fatter with every rat I gobble, and I believe I could whip this rabble with my eyes closed. You do have fangs, don't you, Slarb, you tadpole? And you say these stones came from nowhere, do you? A little rock hits your ssskull and you sleep like babies in the dirt? Did some old mammy come tuck you in?"

Slarb tried again and again to interject, but Gnorm gained momentum as he spoke until Slarb stood silent, his pale green cheeks puffing. Gnorm had his hand on the hilt of his dagger, itching for an excuse to draw it and bury it in Slarb's soft belly.

Slarb gave him no opportunity, however.

"I beg pardon, Commander. My incompetence is inexcusssable," Slarb said with his head bowed low. Gnorm grunted, satisfied with groveling. He turned to go with a snort, unaware that Slarb bared his fangs at his back. "What about the children, sssir?"

The fat Fang stopped in the doorway and looked over his shoulder at the Igiby children on the floor of the cell. He considered them for a moment with his droopy black eyes. "What would you like to do with them?"

Slarb grinned maliciously. "Commander, if it would please you, I'd like to torture them. The whips, perhaps?"

Janner's heart pounded. Tink squeezed Leeli tighter.

"Would you, now?" Gnorm said coldly. "In that case, don't touch them. If you tried to whip them, they'd probably bessst you anyway. We'll have them sent to Dang tonight." He laughed as he turned away. "Send a crow for the Carriage."

12

Not the Same
as Ships and Sharks

The door closed with a thud, and Janner felt his heart drop like a stone over the cliffs and into the sea. Suddenly a growl filled the air. Slarb arched his back and opened his jaws impossibly wide, baring his fangs and clenching his fists. Janner could see the pinkish muscles in Slarb's mouth, the black, moist tongue wriggling about like a worm, and worst of all, those yellowed, dripping fangs. He shuddered at the thought of those poisonous teeth biting into his skin, of those clawed hands tearing into his flesh. It was easy to see why it was said that no Fang had ever been killed by a human. Black Carriage or not, any fate seemed better to Janner than dying at the hands of Slarb.

The Fang strode over to the ring of keys, panting, a bit of poisonous drool dripping from the corner of his mouth. He ripped the ring from the wall, strode to the cell door and jammed a key into the lock, infuriated when the first key didn't work. Tink and Janner slid Leeli into the back corner of the cell, then stood in front of her, wondering what they could possibly do other than grit their teeth and fight with all that was in them when this maddened Fang burst through the cell door.

But Slarb never opened the cell. The door behind him opened, and the burly Fang called Brak lumbered in.

"Hullo, Slarby."

Slarb straightened quickly and turned around, hiding the ring of keys behind his back. "Brak," he said, "I told you not to call me that."

"So we get to deport 'em, eh?" Brak said with a hint of glee. "I love watchin' 'em wriggle when we put 'em in the Carriage, don't you, SSSlarby?"

Slarb was straining to speak in a level voice. "Yesss. Deporting them all." He wiped the poisonous drool from his mouth with his forearm and casually hung the keys back on the wall. "It's probably worssse for them in the long run anyway," he said with a wicked grin, turning his black eyes on the children. "*Much* worse in the long run."

The two Fangs left the room. Janner and Tink collapsed to the floor beside Leeli.

"We have to figure a way out of this," Janner said, trying again to sound older than he was. "If there's anything Podo taught me, it's that there's always a way out."

"But that's grandpa, a one-legged man playing Ships and Sharks[1] with little kids," Tink said. "*This* isn't a game."

"I know it's no game, Tink. But it won't do any good to argue with someone bigger than you." Janner punched Tink's shoulder playfully.

Deep down Janner didn't have the slightest idea how they would get out of this mess—and he feared that they wouldn't. But as the oldest, he felt the need to keep up their spirits. From what he'd heard, much bigger and braver people had been forced into the Black Carriage, so why shouldn't they? Those bigger and braver people were never seen again, so why should they? All he knew was that it was better to be in a Fang jail cell with a little bit of hope than without it.

Leeli fell asleep with her head on Tink's lap, and before long Tink drifted off too. Janner paced the cell for hours, wondering what Podo and

---

1. Ships and Sharks is a yard game introduced to Skreeans by merchants from the Green Hollows. Typically, the children play the role of Ships, and the adults are the Sharks. The game begins when the Shark says to the Ships, "Gwaaaaah!" which is generally agreed to be the sound a shark would make if it weren't a Sea Creature. The Ships then run like mad to escape the Shark. If a Ship is overcome by a Shark, the Ship is rolled in the dirt and tickled severely. This brutal simplicity is typical of games invented by the Hollowsfolk. Another popular game from the Green Hollows is called simply Trounce.

Nia were doing. By now they had to know the children were missing, and they likely knew from the townspeople that the children were in the jail. He pulled himself up by the bars in the high window, but it faced the shadowy rear of the jail. There was nothing to see. The cell door was locked fast and the keys were unreachable. There was nothing to do but wait. Tink was right; this wasn't Ships and Sharks, and maybe there wouldn't be a way out.

Janner wished he could sleep like Tink and Leeli, but his anxious thoughts kept him from it. He tried to think about anything but the dreaded Black Carriage that was making its way over dark hill and starlit vale to Glipwood. He thought about how fine his breakfast had been that very morning, and how warm the hearth was in the Igiby cottage, nestled beneath the boughs of Glipwood trees. His heart was sad for Podo, his dear scruffy grandfather, who had lost his wife in the Great War. He was sad for his mother, whom the Great War had widowed. Now they would again be bereaved, all because he had failed to keep a close eye on Leeli.

Janner sighed and leaned against the wall with his head hung low, thinking of his father. He wished more than ever that he was sailing on a boat in the open sea, and he thought to take his father's drawing out again before he realized that there would be no way to see it in the dark. Surely his father would know how to escape from this dreary cell and their terrible ride in the Black Carriage. Or, if he were still alive, surely he would come to their rescue. But young Janner Igiby had no father and very little hope, there with his brother and sister in that bare, awful cell.

Leeli lifted her head and looked up at the window.

"Did you hear that?" she said.

Tink woke up with a start and said, "Pass the gravy."

"I think it's Nugget," she said. "Nugget! Is that you, boy?"

Three pairs of eyes turned up to the window. The children listened. They heard a whine and a worried sound somewhere between a bark and a howl. Janner felt happy, though he didn't know why. There wasn't much a dog could do for them in their predicament, but knowing that Nugget had come back made hoping easier. Then they heard Fang voices arguing in the outer room of the jail. One of the voices—maybe Slarb—was cut short by a thud and a crash.

Commander Gnorm growled something about obeying orders, then footsteps clunked toward the door.

The door creaked open to reveal Gnorm's chubby silhouette. Janner could see Slarb sprawled on the floor behind him. For the second time that day, because of the Igiby children, Slarb's head had found itself in the path of a blunt object. Gnorm took the keys off the wall and unlocked the cell door.

"You're most fortunate, children," he gurgled. "Someone thinks you're worth a few shinies."

He wiggled his pudgy fingers at them. They were studded with four golden and bejeweled rings that hadn't been there before. Glittering bracelets covered his forearm and a golden medallion on a silver chain hung around his neck. The jewelry looked out of place on such an ugly creature. Gnorm swung open the door and waved out the children.

"So…we can go?" Janner asked timidly.

"Yes. Out of my sight," he said impatiently. Gnorm admired his new jewelry while the children eased by. But as Janner passed him, the Fang snatched him by the face and jerked him close. The Fang's baggy face filled Janner's vision. He saw his terrified reflection in the black bottomless pools of the Fang's hateful eyes, felt his claws digging into his cheeks.

"Touch one of my soldiers again and a *thousand* chests of gold won't ssssave you or your family," Gnorm said in a low, menacing voice. He thrust Janner away so violently that he fell to the floor. Tink helped him up, not daring to look at the Fang or to breathe a word. The boys helped Leeli past the soldiers, past Slarb, who by now had picked himself up off the floor and was seething with anger as he watched the children leave unscathed.

In the faint lamplight in the middle of the street stood their mother, Nia, whose face was as pale as the moon.

13

A Song for the Shining Isle

Janner, Tink, and Leeli stepped down the wooden steps to the dusty road, looking carefully sideways at the Fangs who lurked on the porch. Janner could hardly believe they were free. Was this a trick of some kind?

Commander Gnorm waddled out and plopped down in the chair on the porch, still admiring the jewels shining on his hand. Leeli between them, the boys walked slowly to their mother, whose eyes were brimming with tears.

"Let's go home," she said with a strong voice as she put her arms around her children and turned carefully away from the Fangs. They moved down the street in silence, as if they had stumbled upon a sleeping dragon and were loathe to disturb it. Janner wanted to run, to get as far away from the Fangs and the jail as fast as he could. All the children felt that way, but Nia sensed it and held them back.

She walked her children through the empty thoroughfare of Glipwood with her back straight and her chin thrust out. Quiet laughter drifted from The Only Inn, the lampposts flickered yellow, and the wind whipped up swirls of dustlike ghosts in the moonlight.

When they were well up the road and out of sight of the jail, Nia spoke first.

"I don't know what I would have done without you."

At the sound of her voice, Janner, Tink, and Leeli felt a rush of relief, as if they'd been holding their breath underwater and their mother had just pulled them to the surface. "I just don't know what I would have done," she repeated. She knelt down, gathering them to her and hugging them tightly. Leeli looked up to see Nugget racing toward her. He was on her in a flash, whining and ferociously wagging his tail, licking not just Leeli but each of them wherever he could find exposed skin. Leeli laughed and tumbled backward as she squeezed Nugget's neck.

"Where were you, boy?" she said, rubbing his neck and the sides of his face. Why did you leave us like that?"

"We looked for you at the cliffs," Nia said. "Your grandfather and I were worried. But there were so many people there. We waited until after the dragon song and the crowd had mostly gone, but we still couldn't find you. We rushed back home, thinking that maybe we'd just missed you..." Nia bent down to the little black dog in Leeli's arms. "That's when little Nugget here found us. He led me to the jail." She scratched behind Nugget's ears. "I made your grandfather stay home. He would have torn the jail to pieces and fought an army of Fangs to bring you home, but it would have just gotten us all killed. So I came alone."

"Where did those jewels come from?" Janner asked. "The ones on Gnorm's hand?"

Nia looked back toward the jail. "They were stored away in case of an emergency," she said simply. She looked Janner in the eye. "This was an emergency."

"But where did you get them?" Tink asked. "That was a lot of gold."

Nia sighed. "From your father." Nia turned to Janner, clearly wanting to change the subject. "Your cheek." She touched the bruised and bloodied spot. "Did they hit you?"

Janner nodded.

Nia tilted Janner's head toward the light for a better look, then kissed his cheek.

Janner grimaced and wriggled away, though secretly he enjoyed the warm feeling it gave him. He wanted to ask more questions about the jewels that came from his father, but his mother had already turned away.

"And you, sweetie?" Nia asked Leeli.

"I'm okay, Mama."

Nugget was lying on his back in the dust with his tongue lolling out while Leeli rubbed his belly.

Tink showed his mother the lump on his head, and she winced for him and kissed it.

"Did you see the dragons? Did you see how they stopped and listened when Leeli started singing?" Janner said.

Nia looked startled, but she collected herself quickly.

"That was you, dear?"

"Yes ma'am."

Nia smiled down at Leeli and put a hand on her hair. "It was beautiful."

"But why would the dragons do that?" Janner said. Nia's answer was a shrug. "And why wouldn't Gnorm have just taken the jewels and killed us anyway?" He felt like every question led to another, and his head was swimming.

Nia took Janner's shoulders in her hands and looked him square in the face. "Because I told him I could cook the finest maggotloaf in the four seas and that if he let you go, I'd cook it for him every third day of the week, once the meat had plenty of time to fester. I told him I had a secret recipe that involved hogpig sweat. The gold was just to get his attention, you see. Fangs have a weakness for jewelry."[1]

"You know how to cook maggotloaf?" Tink said.

"I have no idea. I suppose I'd better learn," she smiled. "Now, enough questions from you three. Janner, what happened to your neck?" She turned him again into the lamplight to see the bright red splotch on his neck, where Slarb's venom had dripped on him.

"Fang venom. From the one called Slarb," he said, touching his neck with the tips of his fingers. "The one that attacked Leeli."

"So that's what happened," Nia said. "Why did he attack you?"

Nia put an arm around her crippled daughter, who recounted the

---

1. The women of Skree had a similar weakness for jewelry, but they were less inclined to kill one another for it.

events with Janner and Tink adding bits as the Igibys continued up the lane. Nia listened until Janner told about the two rocks that struck the Fangs in the alley. She stopped walking.

"And you saw no one? No sign of who might have thrown the rocks?"

"No one." Janner looked puzzled. He saw his mother's brow crease as they continued walking. His head buzzed with questions. *Where had she hidden all those jewels—enough to buy half the town of Glipwood? And why did she keep the secret from the family all these years? Couldn't they have used just a bit of it to make their lives a little easier?* Janner had never seen so much gold in one place, and the thought that they had been in his family all these years made him—what? Angry? Thankful? Janner didn't know what to feel, as if his insides were as clumsy as his outsides. *All that gold, all those precious stones, gone. No, not gone. Adorning Commander Gnorm's fingers and wrists.* Janner wondered what their family needed and didn't have and was humbled to realize that there was nothing. He had to admit to himself that his mother and Podo had provided all that they needed. The jewels wouldn't have changed a thing, except that without them Janner would still be sitting in that jail cell with his siblings. *Still,* he thought with a sideways glance at his mother, *what else was she hiding?*

But his tumble of thoughts was interrupted by the sound of someone singing.

On the lawn in front of old Charney Baimington's[2] cottage a small fire was burning. Several people lounged around it, listening to Armulyn the Bard sing. The orange glow of the fire lit his face and cast a large shadow on the house behind him. Armulyn was singing a song of Anniera, and his eyes seemed to glow with their own light as he looked out past the dark around him. It was as though he could see before him the fair island itself with its kingdom of sailors and poets, its high green mountains and shaded

---

2. Of the Torrboro Baimingtons, who prided themselves on having an ancestor who coined the phrase "Jouncey as a two-ton bog pie." The Baimingtons were careful to insert the phrase into every conversation of which they were a part.

vales, the bright city where a good king once reigned and the people sang in the fields while they gathered the harvest. Somehow, Janner felt that it was more than just a song. Armulyn had put his secret dreams to music. Janner felt pulled to those mountains, and he saw it in the faces around the campfire too.

The song ended and for a moment before the applause, the small gathering of listeners was silent. Janner looked up to see that his mother's face was wet with tears and that she, like the bard, was staring into the distance.

"Why are you crying?" he asked, squeezing her hand.

Nia jumped a little, like he'd just woken her from a nap. She smiled down at him. "It's nothing, child. And why are *you* crying?"

Janner hadn't realized it, but his cheeks were wet as well. "There's just something about the way he sings. It makes me think of when it snows outside, and the fire is warm, and Podo is telling us a story while you're cooking, and there's no place I'd rather be—but for some reason I still feel... homesick." Janner looked down, embarrassed.

Tink and Leeli were silent, for Janner had spoken their thoughts as well.

Armulyn, still barefoot, was shaking hands and shyly nodding his head in reply to people's compliments. He picked up his whistleharp and bid them farewell, walking toward Janner and his family. Nia sucked in a breath of air and quickly bustled the children on down the shadowy lane.

"Mama, can't we meet him?" Tink asked, looking over his shoulder at Armulyn, who was making his way directly toward them.

"No, it's time we got home. Papa will be worried sick."

"Mama, please?" Leeli said.

"I said *no.*" Nia picked up the pace. Leeli, even with Nia's hand on her arm, lost her footing and fell to the ground. Nia stopped to help her up, apologizing while she brushed the dirt from Leeli's dress.

"I like your dog," a kind, raspy voice said from behind them.

The children froze. Nia stopped brushing Leeli's dress and straightened. She worked her way around to face the silhouette of Armulyn the

Bard. He was bent over, patting Nugget on the head. Janner and Tink were speechless.

"Thank you. His name is Nugget," Leeli said, and she scooted over to where Nugget sat wagging his tail. She peered up at the dim silhouette of the bard. "I like your singing."

"Why thank you, little princess," Armulyn said, squatting down in front of her.

Nia was still strangely silent, standing a little ways back from them. Armulyn held out his hand to Leeli. "My name is Armulyn. I don't like it here," he said with a smile that Janner could barely see in the dark.

Leeli smiled back at him, unfazed by the strange remark. "My name is Leeli. I can't walk very well."

At her name, Armulyn's smile faded and he leaned a little closer to better see her face. He looked up at Nia and the boys, who still hadn't moved. "And who might you kind people be?"

"Our name is Igiby," Nia said stiffly. She stepped quickly to Leeli and pulled her away from the bard. "We wish you a good evening," she said. She led the children once again toward home, leaving Armulyn standing in the middle of the road staring after them.

When they approached the warm cottage nestled among the trees, they could see lamps burning in the windows. Fireflies flickered in the night air, and Danny the carthorse snorted in the pasture. Janner felt another rush of gladness that he wasn't dead, or worse, trapped in the Black Carriage.

Before they reached the door it flew open wide. Podo's tall, one-legged form filled the doorway. He had a stout club in one hand and brandished a wooden spoon in the other. "WHERE IN ALL THE GREAT GOOD GOAT GOB-BLIN' WORLD HAVE YOU BEEN, OUT TRAIPSING THE FROLLOCKY HILLSIDES WHILE I'VE BEEN HERE GNAWIN' ON MY GUMS! YOU JUST MARCH YER SOGGY FEET OVER HERE BEFORE I YANK OUT YOUR INNARDS AND STEW 'EM IN A..."

Their grandfather's torrent lasted at least two minutes, and would have gone on much longer, but the children broke free from Nia and tackled the big man with hugs. His club and deadly spoon dropped to the floor, and he nearly toppled over, but years of practice with one leg had made Podo Helmer quite agile.

In a moment he had Tink in a headlock and was poking his ribs with one of his gnarled, callused fingers while Janner and Leeli tried to wrestle him to the ground. Finally, he gave in and toppled backward dramatically, howling all the while about rotten children and their disrespect of their elders. They tumbled about on the floor by the light of the crackling fire in the hearth until the match ended and the old man stood up with a groan. Out of breath and sweating, he beamed down at them and pushed a wild lock of long white hair out of his eyes.

"You'll be wantin' some of my cheesy chowder and butterbread, won't you, my little warriors?" he said, panting. "It's been simmering all evening, along with a thousand prayers that ye'd make it back to yer Podo safe and uneaten."

At the mention of food, Tink moaned with pleasure and disappeared into the kitchen, rubbing his stomach.

Podo hoisted Leeli onto his back and carried her. "Lost yer wee crutch, eh? We'll make you up another in the bright morning," he said as the kitchen door swung shut behind him.

Janner watched Nia wearily close and bar the front door. She bowed her head and whispered a prayer of thanksgiving.

"I love you, Ma," Janner said, pushing down the lump in his throat. "I'm sorry I lost her."

"Shh. It's all right," Nia said. "You did well, son." And with a weary smile she ushered him into the kitchen.

14

Secrets and
Cheesy Chowder

Janner joined Leeli and Tink at the table to gobble down the cheesy chowder. After the day he'd had, this seemed the finest meal he had ever eaten. A vat of steaming soup filled the kitchen with a rich, buttery smell, and a fresh loaf of butterbread had been sliced and set on the table. Janner got up to refill his bowl (Tink had already eaten three) and heard a snippet of conversation between Nia and Podo in the next room.

"What in the name of smelly seaweed and sour salad happened to the bitties?" Podo demanded, pounding his club on the plank floor.

"Well, Papa, that granddaughter of yours wandered off. I told you I didn't feel good about letting them go into town alone. Janner and Tink didn't notice she was gone—"

"What? If I've told that boy once I've told him a jabillion times! He's to watch over them—"

"Hush, now, Papa. They're safe. That's what matters now."

A long pause. Janner's cheeks burned with shame. "Aye, aye. He's just a lad yet. I shouldn'ta let 'em into town alone, not on a day like this. Then what happened?"

"Leeli tried to protect Nugget from a Fang. She kicked it."

"The dog?"

"The Fang."

"She did? My little warrior lass had the sweet pluck to round on a Fang?"

Janner couldn't see Podo, but knew he was smiling proudly with his bushy eyebrows raised. He also knew his mother's expression would be disapproving.

Within seconds, Podo cleared his throat and said gravely, "She did, eh? Reckless child. Oughter've known better."

"And the boys tried to save her," Nia said.

"Aha!" Podo thundered, and Janner grinned. Podo cleared his throat again and said in a loud whisper, "I knew those lads had a fire in their bellies! Two wee fighters against the Fangs of Dang! I tell ye they've got their ol' Podo's growl and girth in 'em! If their father could see them now—"

Janner stopped smiling, as Podo stopped short.

A heavy silence divided them all. "Sorry, lass," Podo said after a moment. He was suddenly tender in a way that surprised Janner. "Go on," Podo urged Nia. "What happened then?"

Nia took a deep breath. "I'm not sure, but I think I have a guess. The kids said that someone threw two rocks that knocked the Fangs flat. They didn't see where the rocks came from. Then they ran to find us. It wasn't until after the dragons sang that they were caught and taken to the jail."

Again, neither spoke for a moment. Podo broke the silence. "Well grab my gizzard, honey, do you think it was…him?"

Podo's voice had suddenly lowered and Janner heard his own heart quicken. *Does she think it was who?* he wondered as he eased away from the stove and pressed his ear to the door.

"I don't know," Nia said, "but it certainly sounds like something *he'd* do." There was another long pause. "Whoever it was, I'm thankful. The children are alive."

Janner could tell by his mother's tone that the discussion was over.

"Jnnnr, gimmph s'more chrrdrrbrph," Tink mouthed from the table.

"Huh?" Janner said, turning around a little too quickly.

Tink swallowed his mouthful of food and belched loudly. "Get me some more chowder, eh? Since you're up."

Deep in thought, Janner filled Tink's bowl and sat back down at the table. Leeli was feeding Nugget bits of food, and Tink was oblivious to anything but the steaming bowl of soup in front of him. Janner thought back over every detail of that afternoon, and he couldn't think of one clue as to who could have thrown the rocks. The alley was deep enough that whoever threw them had to be an excellent shot. Only two rocks thrown, and they hit their marks perfectly—and they came at the very last second. How could that be? And how was it that Podo and his mother had a guess as to who the mysterious rock thrower was?

Suddenly, with a crash and a pirate growl, Podo burst into the room. "WHAT'S THIS I HEAR ABOUT BRAVE LITTLE RENEGADES TERRORIZING THE TAR OUT OF THE LOCAL LIZARDS?" he roared. Hobbling over to Leeli, Podo swept her up over his shoulder with one of his giant tattooed arms as she squealed and pounded playfully on his back.

"Now get in here, lads and lasses and tell me a tale that'll make me quiver in me boots." Podo kicked open the door with his wooden stump and carried Leeli out of the kitchen like a kidnapped maiden.

Janner and Tink smiled at one another and pushed away from the table, Tink with a mouthful of butterbread and Janner with a head full of questions.

15

Two Dreams
and a Nightmare

That night, after telling the story to Podo four times, the children slept. Tink dreamed of sea dragons and pie. Leeli dreamed of sea dragons and dogs. Janner dreamed of sea dragons and his father.

Janner had one of the nightmares he often had about his father, and all he could ever remember in the morning was a boat and fire. There was another dream, one in which he could almost make out his father's face, a dream full of golden light and green fields. That bright dream filled him with the same feelings as Armulyn's song had the night before, feelings that somehow hurt and felt good all at the same time.

But this night he had tossed in his bed with the heat of the dream fire surrounding him, roaring in his ears.

When Janner woke he was sweating, but birds were chirping and the golden light of dawn eased through the windows. It felt as though the previous day's events were part of his nightmare, and the world of his warm bed and the sturdy old cottage so full of life was the only real one. The Fangs seemed about as dangerous as weed snakes.

Janner stretched and sat on the edge of his bed. Happy beams of sunlight landed on the floor and scattered the shadows. Leaning against Leeli's bed was a freshly made little crutch that Podo must have spent most of the night making. Carved into the crosspiece in small, neat letters was the inscription LEELI IGIBY: LIZARDKICKER

Janner could hear the clatter of Nia preparing breakfast in the kitchen, humming in muffled tones. He smiled to himself, stretched, and ambled into the main room where he lay down on the cushioned couch, yawning while he scratched his head. He was staring up at the timbers in the ceiling, letting the fresh fire in the hearth warm him when he heard the familiar *tap-clunk, tap-clunk, tap-clunk* of Podo approaching the front of the cottage. Janner heard him grumbling to himself even before the door opened.

"Rotten stinking rodents…teach *you* to touch my totaters…lucky I've only got one leg, you, you, worm-eating, ankle-biting…"

Janner peeked over the back of the couch to see Podo hobbling through the door with a sack full of vegetables over his shoulder, his boot and the bottom of his peg leg wet with dew. The grumbling resumed as Podo made his way through the kitchen door. Janner was barely able to keep from snorting with laughter. When the door swung shut, the smell of cooked eggs and bacon drifted into the room, and Janner's stomach rumbled. Just as he got up from the couch, he heard the thump of Tink dropping down from his bunk, right on cue with the arrival of breakfast.

When Janner entered the kitchen, his mouth was watering. On the table sat three plates of hot food. His mother smiled at him from the stove where she was frying more eggs and bacon.

"Good morning, jailbird," she said. The back door was ajar and Podo was already bounding through the field toward the garden, bellowing something indecipherable. Janner sat down at the table and dug into his food just as Tink bumbled through the kitchen door and headed straight for his chair. Nia pecked them both on the cheek.

"Leeli coming?" she asked. Tink nodded with a mouthful of bacon.

Leeli came through the door and stretched so taut that her nightgown came up to her shins. Nugget trotted past her to nose his way out the back door, eager to assist Podo in wrathful pursuit of the thwaps.

Leeli greeted her brothers with a light backhand on each of their shoulders as she scooted past with the LIZARDKICKER crutch from Podo. Tink and Janner grunted, their mouths full of bacon.

"I see you have a new crutch, dear," Nia said.

Janner and Tink took sudden interest in their sister and complimented her between gulps of milk.

"The three of you slept late, so eat quickly and get dressed. The Dragon Day festival is over and life goes back to normal today," Nia said, placing a plate of food in front of Leeli. "Your chores and studies are waiting."

Janner thought that his mother looked tired, which was odd since he always had the feeling that she'd been awake for hours before he stumbled in for breakfast. There was something in her eyes—*was it worry?*—and she seemed to move a little slower. But when she put two more slices of hot bacon on his plate and tousled his hair, he decided it was probably his imagination.

For as long as they could remember, Nia had taught the children what she called T.H.A.G.S.[1] Janner studied writing and poetry. Tink spent his time painting and drawing. Leeli learned to sing and to play the whistle-harp. Tink had asked his mother once what was so traditional about learning the T.H.A.G.S. when not one other child in Glipwood was forced to spend hours upon hours drawing the same tree over and over from different angles.

"You're an Igiby," she said, as if that answered the question.

No other boy in Glipwood had to read as many old books or write as many pages as Janner, and no other girl in town knew how to play an instrument. All three of the children had some proficiency in each of the T.H.A.G.S. but spent the vast majority of their time perfecting only one.

Janner remembered with a stab of panic that later that day he and Tink were supposed to help Oskar N. Reteep in the bookstore, which was right across the street from the jail. What if Commander Gnorm saw him and changed his mind? He might send for the Black Carriage after all. What if

---

1. Three Honored and Great Subjects: Word, Form, and Song. Some silly people believe that there's a fourth Honored and Great Subject, but those mathematicians are woefully mistaken.

Slarb attacked again? Then he thought about Books and Crannies, about all the stories on all the shelves in the store, and the warm thrill of being there overshadowed his fear. Janner swallowed the last of his breakfast. "Mister Reteep asked me and Tink to help him with a big shipment today. Is it all right to go into town?"

Nia took her time flipping the eggs and bacon in the frying pan while they waited for an answer. "Not really, no. It's not all right. It's never safe for you to go into town, especially after what happened yesterday." Janner's shoulders slumped. "But we can't live in fear," Nia said. "We *won't* live in fear." She turned and looked hard at her boys, wiping her hands on her apron. "Just be careful, and stay clear of that awful Slurp."

"Slarb," Tink said.

"And don't forget to return the books you borrowed, Janner. You've finished them, haven't you?" Nia asked.

"Yes ma'am."

"What did you think?"

"I read *In the Age of the Kindly Flabbits*.[2] It was okay. The other one was better," Janner said, clearing his dishes from the table. He had devoured a second book, one about dragons that actually flew and battles and a band of companions. It was full of high adventure, and Janner was sad when it ended, mainly because his life in Glipwood was so uneventful by comparison.

Nia turned back to the stove. "Your father loved that story."

---

2. By Jonathid Choonch Brownman, the explorer known to have been the first to find passage through the Jungles of Plontst. Though no one contested that the expedition itself was successful, people questioned the truth of many of Brownman's claims about his discoveries. When his memoir of the journey was published in 421, most of it was believed to be a fabrication. This was due in part to Brownman's insistence that while in the jungle he had lived for a time among a community of flabbits. Brownman insisted that they were docile, unlike flesh-eating flabbits in Skree. Scandalized, his readers challenged him to go and fetch one of the so-called tame flabbits back from Plontst, and Brownman agreed. It was the last anyone ever saw of Jonathid Choonch Brownman, though people still enjoy saying his middle name.

Janner smiled at the thought of his father, whoever he was, enjoying the same book. With a great commotion, Podo *tap-clunked* up to the back door and kicked it open. He was out of breath, holding two furry thwaps in an outstretched fist for the world to see.

"Two!" he roared, and thrust the thwaps into the same sack he had used the previous morning. The old man bent over Nugget and rubbed his head fiercely, then stepped inside. "No fear, no fear, ladies. I'll not toss 'em over the cliffs," he said with a wink at Janner.

When Podo saw Leeli his face lit up as it always did. "There's my little lizardkicker, Leeli the Brave!" He squeezed the back of Tink's neck. "And you! Tink the Quick, who dove into the fray—weaponless—and wrested the lady from the snake man! Now where…" He searched the room for Janner, who was standing by the kitchen door, unaware of the grin on his own face. "Ah! Janner the Strong! Backbreaker, who leapt onto the Fang like a toothy cow and lived to tell the tale!"

"Oh Papa, stop it," Nia said, filling Podo's plate. "Now children, go on and get dressed," Nia said, waving them off and setting Podo's hot breakfast on the table. While the smiling children filed out of the kitchen, he growled with a twinkle in his eye and swept Nia into the air and over his shoulder. The last thing Janner saw as he exited the room was his mother demanding to be "placed back down this instant."

After feeding Danny the carthorse and the hogpig, the boys had to help Podo collect fertilizer (compliments of the hogpig) and spread it over the summer garden (for food that would eventually be eaten by them all, including the hogpig). This set Janner thinking all kinds of thoughts about life, death, and fertilizer.

Leeli stayed inside with Nia, preparing food, stitching a tear in a pair of Podo's breeches, and cleaning the ashes out of the fireplace. When she was finished, she sat in the front room practicing a new song on her whistleharp and memorizing the words to the holiday classic, "Round the Gumpkin Danced the Meep."

They each went about their chores with gladness, even Tink and Janner when they shoveled the hogpig droppings into the wheelbarrow.[3] It was hard to complain when the sun was warm and their bellies were full, not to mention the fact that they had escaped death and torture three times the day before. But if Janner had been watching closely that morning, he would have seen how often his mother peeked out the window toward the town, and he might have noticed the troubled look in her eyes. If Janner had thought about it, he might have wondered why Podo had stayed so close to both boys all morning, and why his trusty club remained at his side.

---

3. This was done with a shovel Podo had checked out from Mayor Blaggus early that morning by filling out the Permission to Shovel Hogpig Droppings Form. See page 287 in Appendices.

16

In Books and Crannies

Janner, Tink, and Podo walked to town after their lunch of apples and butterbread. Podo had insisted on accompanying them, which made Janner and Tink feel safer. The closer they got to Main Street, the more anxious they were about being seen by Slarb or Gnorm or any of the Fangs they'd been so unfortunate to meet the night before.

Glipwood was eerily quiet now that the many visitors had packed up their belongings and left town for another long, sad year in Fang-infested Skree. J. Bird's lanky form could be seen inside his barbershop, sweeping. Ferinia's Flower Shop had a CLOSED sign in the window. The Only Inn's windows and doors were wide open, and Podo waved at Mr. and Mrs. Shooster, the proprietors, busy changing the bedding and shaking out the rugs. Shaggy sat snoring on a bench outside his tavern.

Without turning his head, Janner stole a glance at the jail. Commander Gnorm, to his relief, was dozing in his rocking chair on the jail stoop with his pudgy greenish hands folded across his chest. The rings on his fingers glimmered, even in the shade. Janner pulled his eyes away and moved a step closer to Podo.

"You lads run along to Oskar's," said Podo. "I'll be watching over ye from the tavern. I feel the need to wake up old Shaggy and wet my whistle."

Janner started to protest but caught himself. While he didn't want to spend even a minute alone so close to the jail, he also wanted Podo to know that he could be brave and responsible. "Yes sir," he said, straightening his back to his full height. "Come on, Tink."

The brothers moved carefully past the jail to Books and Crannies, where Zouzab was perched like a vulture at the apex of the roof, his patch-work shirt waving like a flag in the breeze.

Janner waved to the ridgerunner.

"And hello to the Igiby men," said Zouzab. His voice was soft and deli-cate. "I trust your time at the festival was pleasurable?"

Janner was surprised that Zouzab didn't seem to know about their near-death experience the night before. "Yes," he replied. "It was an eventful day."

"Is Mister Reteep inside?" Tink asked.

"Inside, yes. Many are the boxes that arrived by wagon not an hour ago. Many new books for you to read, Janner Igiby." Zouzab was courte-ous, but Janner always felt like there was far more going on behind his lit-tle eyes than his mouth ever spoke.

Zouzab said no more and watched them enter the bookstore.

Books and Crannies was a place of wonder. Rows upon rows of books, many of them tattered, charred, and ancient looking, filled every shelf and corner nearly all the way to the high ceiling. Tall books, skinny books, books about daggerfish, books about the lineage of the kings of Skree, books about the rise and fall of the use of sugarberries in cake, books of leg-end about Anniera, books about books about other books, all organized according to subject in a maze of shelves.

But it wasn't just books. Rolls of maps and odds and ends and surpris-ing surprises were lying here and there among the many volumes, in plain sight but easy to miss in all the clutter. No matter how many times Janner had been inside Oskar's store, he still managed to get lost at least once before he made it to the office at the back of the building.

When the door clicked shut behind them, Janner smiled and took in a deep breath. He loved the musty smell of the place. Tink had only visited a few brief times, so his eyes shot back and forth, trying to take in all there was to see. As they made their way toward the back of the store, they saw a wooden bowl full of dusty old spectacles. Beside the spectacles was a tiny, beaked skull with three eye sockets.

"Look!" Tink whispered.

Janner smiled, enjoying Tink's excitement. On another shelf was a jar of dead, bright orange insects, and on yet another was a miniature wooden castle with a mouse watching them from the spire window. Janner came to a dead end and stopped in front of a shelf labeled BOOKS ABOUT BLACKSMITHING AND/OR PIE, and Tink, so focused on trying to read the spine of every book he passed, collided with him. Janner's feet got tangled in themselves and he pitched forward. He tumbled to the floor, knocking over a fat, round candle from the shelf. Glaring at Tink, Janner picked up the oily greenish candle and set it back in place. A handwritten label on the candle said SNOT WAX. Janner retched, wiping his hands on the front of his tunic.[1]

"Eh? Who's there?" came a muffled voice from somewhere nearby. Suddenly several books on the shelf to their right slid backward and vanished—replaced by Oskar's spectacled face peering at them from the other side. "Ah! Janner, Tink, I didn't hear you come in," he said with a smile. "There's a lot of work to be done, so no dillydallying. Time for browsing later. Follow me."

The books slid back into place and Oskar's footsteps thumped toward the back of the store. After three more dead ends, Janner and Tink found the owner of Books and Crannies pacing the floor of his storeroom with a pipe in his mouth.

"Now lads, I'd have thought your Podo would have taught you better than to laze about while an old man like me needs your help. What in Aerwiar have you two been doing out there?" he said.

"We took a wrong turn at SKREEAN HISTORY," Janner said, "and then another at POINTLESS POEMS and—"

"No matter," he said with a wave of his hand. "I believe it was the great Chorton who wrote, 'To worry over dallying brothers is not worth the trouble when a large shipment has just arrived.' Or something to that effect."

---

1. Snot wax is too repulsive a thing about which to write a proper footnote.

Oskar's wide desk was cluttered with stacks of parchment, various kinds of pipes, feather quills, and bottles of ink. A nearly spent candle sputtered on a brass candlestick and lit up an ancient-looking map that was unrolled on the center of the desk. Tink moved closer to examine it.

"Easy, young Igiby," Oskar said, scooting behind the desk and turning over the map. "Surely your big brother's told you that not everything here is permissible for young eyes. There are mysteries in the world that should remain mysteries for the young."

Tink flushed, embarrassed that he was already in trouble. Janner caught his eye and gave him an encouraging wink.

"Where did all these books come from, sir?" Tink asked.

Oskar's eyes twinkled as they took in his shop with pride. It was easy to get Oskar to talk about his books. "The real question, young Tink, is where *didn't* these books come from. I traveled all over Skree after the Great War, salvaging what could be salvaged. You wouldn't believe the rubble. Those rotten Fangs burned our homes and cities to the ground. But as it always does, the dust settled. As the Skreeans began to unearth a life again, they also unearthed these treasures. Books. Only they weren't treasures anymore. Not to everyone. I knew that I had to gather them up, preserve them."

At the mention of the Great War, Janner's thoughts once again returned to his father. He had never asked Oskar if he had known his father, or if he knew any details about his death. Until recently, the subject was studiously avoided in the Igiby cottage. When he had found the picture in his mother's room, it was as if a crack formed in the dam that held back his father's memory; Esben Igiby was seeping into Janner's thoughts, and there was no way to seal the leak.

Janner wanted to ask Oskar what he might know, but Oskar was busy dusting off piles of books and rambling. "Most people were working so hard at rebuilding and adjusting to life with evil snake men breathing down their necks that they didn't have time for books," he muttered. "They were given to me or sold for pennies. As the infamous Bweesley the Leaf Thief said in his memoir, 'Cheap is almost free.' Look around you, lads. This is the best of the old Skree. Or at least, it's what's left of it."

Janner and Tink stood in the silence of the study. Suddenly the piles of books and cluttered shelves were somehow more than that. What Oskar had preserved was the memory of a world that had passed away—as surely as Esben Igiby had passed away. Oskar too seemed lost in thoughts about the past. He tenderly cradled a stack of books in his hands. "On Dragon Day," he said, "the people who visit me come to remember who they were. They always leave sad."

Janner pictured in his mind the faces of the people in town with their weak smiles and hollow laughter.

"Now then," Oskar said, interrupting Janner's thoughts. "Here's what I need from you two. I'll sit here at the desk and keep record of the books and their categories—very taxing on the mind, I assure you—and you two unload the crates and stack them where old Oskar Noss Reteep tells you. Just holler out the title and author. Can you handle that?"

Janner's and Tink's nods halted as Oskar swung open the large double-door to reveal a stack of eighteen wooden crates of various sizes sitting on the lawn, piled precariously high. On top of the highest crate perched Zouzab, who smiled at the shock on the boys' faces.

"Well! We have much to do, I'd say!" Oskar chuckled as he sat at his desk and lit his pipe. "What was it the great poet Shank Po wrote?"

"Huh?" Tink asked.

"Ah yes," Oskar said with a puff of smoke. "'Get thee busy.'"

17

The Journal
of Bonifer Squoon

Janner and Tink worked for hours while Zouzab skittered here and there, giving unwanted advice on how they should proceed and occasionally serenading them with sad, haunting songs on his odd little flute.

Oskar N. Reteep sat at his desk with glee, his spectacles on the end of his nose, recording the titles and authors in a large leather-bound tome while he directed the boys where to stack each book according to its subject.

"*The Sound of Sidgebaw* by…Riva Twotoe," Tink read.

"Ah, a fine work. Very rare. File under SITTING UTENSILS, there in the corner, see?" Oskar pointed above Tink's head.

"*I Came and I Wept Like the Sissy I Am* by Lothar Sweeb," Janner read from another spine.

"Sweeb? Ah, yes, a mediocre talent, but very prolific. File under BACON SONGS, just behind the lampstand there."

"*Bonked* by Phinksam Ponkbelly."

"GARDENING. Excellent book."

Hours of this later, the boys were sweaty and exhausted. Tink's stomach growled constantly. Twice, Oskar bade Zouzab to fetch water for them, which he did without complaint before scampering back up the pile of crates and leaping across to the roof of the building like a squirrel.

Podo appeared from the front of the building, announcing his arrival with a bone-rattling belch. "Not bad manners, just good ale," he said with a wink. "I see old Oskar's puttin' ye both to good use."

Janner and Tink were grateful for an excuse to rest a moment. "Yes sir," Janner said. "We're almost finished, then Mister Reteep's going to let us bring a few books home."

"Aye, that's kind of him," Podo said with a nod. "If you lads are fine and well, I'm off to the cottage to fetch the shovel. Need to turn it in to the blasted Fangs before sundown. Will you two be okay to walk home without me?"

Janner and Tink looked at one another. Janner was still anxious about being so close to the Fangs, but he was determined to show his grandfather that he could be trusted. "Yes sir, we'll be fine."

"If anything happens," Tink said, "we'll call for Leeli and she'll come kicking."

This brought a hearty laugh out of the old pirate. "Ho! Let the lizards beware of Leeli Igiby and her deadly dog!" Podo looked them both in the eye. "You lads just keep to yourselves and come straightaway home, eh?" And with a clap to Janner's shoulder that nearly knocked him over, Podo was gone.

The last crate was smaller than the others. It appeared to be much older too. On the lid was one horrifying word: DANG.

Janner and Tink gasped. Even Zouzab, who had been watching so quietly all day, gasped.

"Aha! I've been waiting all day to look through this one, my boys," Oskar said, appearing behind them. He looked to his right and left and whispered, *"It's from Dang."*

"But—how? Who—who do you know in Dang?" Tink asked.

"Shh!" Oskar put a finger to his lips and looked around again. "There are Fangs afoot in Skree if you haven't noticed. Do you want to be thrown in jail again?"

It was the first time he'd shown any sign of knowing about the Igibys' troubles the night before, and Janner noticed it.

Tink lowered his voice, "Sorry, Mister Reteep. Who do you know in—"

"I don't know anyone in Dang. I found this old box along with the others, but I didn't want to draw any attention to it, so I piled it at the bottom of the wagon. I opened it long enough to see that it's full of books. That's all I know." He rubbed his hands together like a happy child about to eat a piece of cake, then lifted the lid. The brothers took a step closer to the crate and looked inside. They looked like ordinary books, but knowing that they were from a faraway land of danger and mystery made them fascinating to behold.

"Just bring these to me one at a time so I'll be able to record them properly." Oskar smiled and stared at the books longingly, "I mean to read them all tonight." He came to himself, cleared his throat and raised his eyebrows. "The afternoon is nearly spent, boys. These may be from *you know where*, but they're still just books after all. As the great explorer Jinto Qweb said, 'Hurry! Reading is fun!'" Oskar lit his pipe and shuffled back to his desk, humming as he went.

Janner pulled the first book out of the crate. It was worn and heavy, the cover decorated with intricate loops and knots. In the center, flowing letters said *Ridgerunner Rhyme: Poetry of the Mountains.*[1]

Zouzab squealed with delight and leapt to the ground. He was back on the roof of the building in the blink of an eye and left Janner standing there, empty-handed. Already the book was open and the little ridgerunner's lips were moving while he read.

"You asleep out there?" Oskar called from his desk.

As Janner and Tink scampered to bring Oskar book after book, he sat at his desk with pipe smoke drifting about his head, scribbling notes in his ledger, and mumbling.

---

1. According to Padovan A'Mally's *The Scourge of the Hollows* (Ban Rona, Green Hollows: The Iphreny Group, 3/111), "Ridgerunners are particularly fond of artful verse, though their subject matter is almost exclusively fruit. A free-thinking ridgerunner named Tizrak Rzt scandalized the ridgerunner culture when he composed a poem entitled 'Love, Love, Love Hath No Endingness' and famously made no mention of fruit."

"Mmm. Fascinating! *Nasal Dysfunction in the Woes of Shreve...*"

Janner tried his best to inspect each of the books as he carried them, and he only accidentally dropped four. Some of them were written in strange runes. Others contained maps of lands of which he had never heard. One book was titled *Mostly True Tales of the Pirates of Symia.* Janner thought of his grandfather and cracked it open. On the first page was a picture of a sleek ship lifting over a giant wave. The deck of the ship was full of pirates in flamboyant clothing clutching swords and daggers. He could barely contain the delight he felt holding that book in his hands, imagining salty seas and reckless sailors. He handed it to Oskar reluctantly.

"All in good time, lad," Oskar said, taking the book with one hand and pressing one long lock of his white hair across his forehead with the other.

Tink found a book with drawings of creatures that he could never have imagined; small dragonlike creatures with saddles and men astride them, horses with wings and clawed feet, great hairy beasts that walked upright and had teeth as long as a man's arm. Beside each picture were notes and specifics on the creature's weaknesses and strengths. Tink walked slowly to Mr. Reteep's desk, enthralled by the pictures. Oskar smiled and held out his hand.

"Pembrick's *Creaturepedia,*[2] son. Don't worry, that's one I'll let you look at. There'll be time enough to peruse all you like."

With that, Tink quickened his pace, and before long Janner was reaching into the crate for the last book of the bunch. Smaller than the rest, its worn leather cover was decorated with the image of a dragon, wings outstretched.

Janner flipped open the book the same way he had all the others, but

---

2. See Appendices for a sampling of Pembrick's seminal work. Bahbert Pembrick, *Pembrick's Creaturepedia* (Ban Rona, Green Hollows: Graff Publishing, 3/221).

the inside was different. He was surprised to see handwriting, not printed type:

This is the journal of Bonifer Squoon
Chief Advisor to the High King of Anniera
Keeper of the Isle of Light.
Read this without my permission
and I will pound your nose.

Janner's breath caught in his throat. *High King of Anniera? Could this be real?* Everyone had dreamed of Anniera's fair shores at least once, even those who denied it existed. Yet here he was, holding the king's advisor's own thoughts in his hands. Of course, the journal could be a hoax, but like everyone else in Skree, Janner wanted to believe that such a place existed— or had before Gnag the Nameless destroyed it. Janner showed the opened book to Tink, whose eyes grew wide. But just as Janner started to turn the page, the book was snatched from his hands.

"Zouzab!" Janner hissed, and he turned to face not Zouzab, but Mr. Reteep, whose face was stern.

"That'll be all then, Igiby boys." Oskar put the book under one arm and gestured at the crates with his pipe. "Stack those by the woodpile, and you can come in and browse the rest of my books all you like. Each of you can take home three volumes, but I must approve of them before you go."

Janner and Tink stood still, feeling the weight of Oskar's gaze. Janner wanted desperately to know what was in the journal, and he wondered why Mr. Reteep would be so secretive with it.

"Tink," Oskar said. "You like to draw, don't you? Come with me. As I recall I have an extensive collection of art books that you might find helpful." And he wandered into the maze of bookshelves.

By the time they caught up with Oskar, the light was fading and he was fumbling with lanterns for each of them to carry through the store.

The book spines looked richer somehow in the lantern's glow, and Janner thought of Oskar's words at the start of the day: *"Look around you, lads. This is the best of the old Skree. Or at least, it's what's left of it."* He was eager to roam the store, agonizing over which three books to borrow.

"This way, young Tink," said Oskar. "I'll show you where to start, then you're on your own." With a helpless look at Janner, Tink lifted his lantern and followed Oskar down the corridor out of sight.

Twice, Janner and Tink rounded a corner and nearly crashed into one another, but eventually they took their own ways deep into the labyrinth of shelves.

Tink found two art books, one of fantastic landscapes the likes of which he'd never dreamed, and the other an anatomy book that taught how to draw a chorkney in any number of positions.[3] He was still seeking book number three when his foot bumped something. He saw the snot-wax candle on the shelf and realized he was standing right where Janner had tripped earlier. He lowered his lantern to the floor for a closer look.

A narrow panel had come loose on the bottom of the shelf where it met the floor. *Janner's foot must have bumped it.* Tink bent to shift the panel into place, but his eye caught something in the shadows of the cavity below. He reached in and slipped it out just enough to see it was a rolled-up parchment, yellow with age and dusty.

Tink's heart quickened. He looked back down the aisle, wishing Janner was nearby. Nothing. Then he scanned the aisles in the other direction, but all he saw were rows of books fading into shadows.

"Janner!" he whispered.

---

3. Chorkneys are large flightless birds that live mainly in cold climates. The settlement of Kimera in the Ice Prairies boasts a chorkney ranch where the large birds are saddled, bridled, and trained to function much the way of horses in southern Skree. The webbed feet of a chorkney bear a cluster of retractable barbs which allow the bird to keep its footing in ice and deep snow. On rare occasions, male chorkneys are born with wings large enough to sustain short flights, though it isn't considered prudent to be riding one when this happens.

Silence. *There's no telling where he is,* Tink thought. He scanned the aisles again. It was his first day helping at Books and Crannies, and he already felt like he'd tried Mr. Reteep's patience. Tink didn't want to upset the proprietor any further, but his curiosity was maddening.

He took one last look in each direction, set the lantern on top of his art books, and carefully pulled the parchment the rest of the way out.

Fingers trembling, Tink unrolled it.

18

Stumbling onto a Secret

The map was drawn with a careful hand and remarkably detailed, though riddled with tiny holes. Tink recognized the Dark Sea of Darkness, complete with little drawn sailing vessels. He saw a road that led from some cliffs to a little cluster of buildings, all neatly rendered and labeled. He bent closer to read by the yellow glow of the lantern: FERINIA'S FLOWER SHOP, JAIL, and MY BOOKSTORE.

He realized with surprise that he was looking at a map of Glipwood, drawn by Oskar N. Reteep himself.[1] With his finger he traced the main road toward the cliffs to the lane that led to the Igiby cottage, and sure enough, there it was. It was even labeled IGIBY.

Across the top of the map was scrawled, "In the immortal words of Loshain P'stane, 'If anyone reads this without permission, he will be most certainly and brutally slain. Or at the very least I'll chop off a finger or two. Or three.'"

Tink wrung his hands as his heart shriveled with fear and the parchment started to roll shut. With trembling fingers, he smoothed it out again.

Near the top of the map, at the edge of the forest, was a house labeled ANKLEJELLY MANOR. Over the house was a large X, and beside it, this was written:

Be you friend or be you foe
Beware to all who follow

---

1. See Oskar's map, page xiii.

For in the catacombs below
Is hidden in the hollow
A way that leads to pain and woe
Sadness, grief, and sorrow
The hungry ghost of Brimney Stupe
Awaits your bones to swallow
So think you long before you go
Exploring here tomorrow

Tink jolted as the dreadful sound of Oskar N. Reteep's heavy footsteps came thudding toward him. Panicked, he rolled up the map, slipped it up his shirtsleeve, grabbed the lantern and his art books, and reached for a random book from the shelf in front of him.

Mr. Reteep's round figure turned the corner and floated into the lantern light just as Tink pulled the book from its place on the shelf.

"Ah, young Tink! I see you've found your books. What have you got there?" He squinted at the two art books, and then at the third. Tink stood still as a stone, praying that Oskar wouldn't notice the funny way his shirtsleeve was bulging.

"*The Art of Itching,*" Oskar read. He looked over the top of his spectacles at Tink and raised an eyebrow.

Tink knew that he was caught. He wondered whether or not Mr. Reteep would actually slay him or if he'd show mercy and merely cut off a finger. *But which finger?* he wondered. *And what kind of instrument would the old man use?*

"Is something wrong?" Oskar asked, narrowing his eyes at Tink. "You're hiding something."

Tink's face went pale and he felt as though he might faint.

"I understand, boy," Oskar said. "It's a very private thing. And as a matter of fact, it's none of my business is it?" Oskar lowered his voice and leaned toward Tink with a hand at the side of his mouth. "But if you've got an itchy rash of some sort, there are much more extensive books on the subject than *The Art of Itching*. Believe me, I've read them *all*." Oskar cleared his throat. "If you know what I mean."

Tink was so overcome with relief, he could barely speak. He forced a laugh, set down the book he'd just grabbed from the shelf, and with the free hand scratched at his belly and armpits. "Oh, I do know what you mean, sir. Ha. Ha-ha-ha."

Janner walked around the corner with three large books under his arm, frowning at Tink's odd behavior.

Tink stopped scratching as Oskar turned and approved Janner's selections, and before Tink knew it, he found himself walking out of the store with his brother, map up his sleeve, thankful that he still had all ten fingers.

It was nearly dark when Janner and Tink began their short walk home, and Tink could barely contain himself. He waited just till they were an earshot away from Books and Crannies and blurted, "I stole a map!"

Janner stopped in the middle of the street. "You *what?*"

"I didn't mean to. It's in my sleeve right now, so I stole it, but I didn't mean to, I promise," Tink stammered, looking around.

Janner stared at his brother in shock. "Keep walking, make sure you don't let that thing show, and tell me what happened."

They walked fast down Main Street, past the jail where a dozen Fangs lurked, yet felt no fear. Tink was too excited to tell what he'd found, and Janner too absorbed by the story to notice Slarb the Fang watching them closely from the jail's porch with hatred in his eyes.

Commander Gnorm stood behind Slarb, but he stared down the street as though waiting for something.

"And I'd just read that whoever looks at the map without permission would get their fingers cut off, when I heard Oskar coming," Tink panted.

"There must be some kind of mistake," Janner said. "Can you imagine old Mister Reteep cutting off someone's fingers?"

It was Tink's turn to stop in the middle of the street. "Yes," he said, eyes wide, head nodding.

"Well, I can't," Janner said. "He's a kind old man."

"*You* haven't seen the map," Tink said, shaking his head. "When we get home, you'll see for yourself."

A sudden, steady *clop-clop-clop* of hoofbeats and rattle of rein and bridle stopped the Igibys—a sound that curdled their blood. A whip cracked in the dusky air, and the brothers turned to see a shadowy carriage round the bend at Dunn's Green, driven by a figure in a black robe.

Janner grabbed Tink's arm, and they ran around the side of The Only Inn and flattened themselves against the wall. Janner closed his eyes to shut out the evil, but his head echoed with the sound of the approaching carriage. In his mind, he could see the iron bars and the pale arm of the black-robed driver swooping down to snatch him and Tink and lock them in the cage.

He opened one eye to see Tink peeking around the corner.

"*What are you doing?*" Janner hissed.

"Look! It stopped in front of the jail," Tink whispered over his shoulder.

Janner stayed put. "What's happening? Is it the Black Carriage?"

"I can't tell...wait... Commander Gnorm's talking to the driver..."

Janner could stand it no longer. He peeked around the corner and saw the two horses stamping the ground and snorting. The hooded driver addressed Gnorm, then slithered down from the seat and opened the carriage door.

Janner sighed. The door wasn't made of iron, but of dark, polished wood. No crows perched on the carriage roof or circled above. *It wasn't the Black Carriage at all.*

Gnorm heaved himself into the coach and made himself comfortable. The door clicked shut and, with another crack of the whip, the steeds heaved. The carriage lurched forward, turned, and departed just as it had come, while the rest of the Fangs watched from the street.

But not every Fang.

"And how isss your lame little sister and that mutt of hers?" a familiar voice hissed into Tink's and Janner's ears.

19

Pain and Woe and Sorrow

Tink and Janner spun around to see Slarb in the shadows, his black eyes like two empty wells. They cried out and backed away into the street as he emerged from the darkness, teeth bared.

"It's time to finish what I started yesterday, boysss." Slarb clacked his teeth together hungrily. He cocked his head sideways and considered Janner and Tink for a long moment.

Janner thought he looked just like the snout-snake he'd once seen in the pasture. It had reared its neck back and cocked its head sideways just before striking dead an unfortunate field mouse. *So this is the end,* Janner thought.

Commander Gnorm or no, Slarb was going to kill them right then and there.

"Slarb! Are those the Igiby woman's boys?" called another Fang from the jail porch. "Gnorm will stew you alive, if you come between him and his maggotloaf!"

Slarb sneered at the Fang on the porch and hesitated. Then he spat at Janner's feet. Little tendrils of smoke rose from the toe of one boot where the venom landed.

Janner resisted the urge to scream and rip off his boot.

Slarb snarled and seemed about to spring but, with a sullen look at the other Fangs, instead slunk back into the shadows behind The Only Inn.

Janner and Tink turned and raced home.

Oskar's mysterious map seemed of little importance. Living in a land crawling with Fangs was bad enough; now they had an enemy of one—and the only thing keeping Slarb from killing them now was the hope that Gnorm would find their mother's maggotloaf agreeable.

Janner and Tink each felt their spirits lift when they arrived at the cottage, however. The fire was burning, the lanterns were lit and the smell of a pot roast filled the air. Podo was napping on the couch beside the hearth, snoring so loud the windows rattled.

Tink slipped quietly to his room and hid the map under his pillow just as Nia called for supper.

When Janner and Tink sat down at the food-laden table they realized how tired they were. They told about their day, the crate from Dang, and the Annieran journal. Janner thought it odd that Nia and Podo were very interested in everything the boys had to say until they mentioned the journal. Janner saw them exchange glances, then his mother abruptly changed the subject.

What could that mean? Janner wondered whether his mother and grandfather were suddenly keeping secrets from them, or if he was just now beginning to notice something that had always happened.

Leeli interrupted his thoughts. "Have you seen any music books hidden away at Books and Crannies? I'd very much like to see one."

Janner laughed. "If Oskar doesn't have a hundred music books, I'll eat a worm."

When they talked about their encounter with Slarb, Podo made several promises to kill the Fang in several different ways.

Nia reminded them that every few months the Fang regiments were replaced. "It won't be this way forever. We just need to lie low and hope that my maggotloaf is truly horrendous."

"Maybe you should let grandpa cook it then," Tink said, spooning more roast onto his plate. "His totato porridge turns my insides to woodchips."

Everyone but Podo burst into laughter.

"What's the matter with my totato porridge? Scrumptious!" His eyebrows were raised so high they blended in with the rest of his hair. "A pinch of wortroot, a dash of cornpepper—WOODCHIPS, you say!" The more Podo protested, the harder the rest of his family laughed.

"Scrumptious!" Podo said again with indignation. He folded his arms across his barrel chest and thrust out his chin. But even Podo couldn't keep from laughing. His lips quivered like jelly, then a grin spread across his face, and soon he was slapping his knee and roaring with the rest of them.

Janner couldn't remember the last time they had laughed so hard, and he knew, as they all did, that they weren't laughing at Tink's comment so much as they were laughing because their fear-weary spirits needed it like medicine.

Finally, like a fit of rain that comes and goes and leaves everything damp and shining, the laughter stopped.

"Did you bring home anything interesting from Books and Crannies?" Nia asked, wiping the corners of her eyes.

Tink's smile vanished. He gave Janner a hard, pleading look that begged him not to tell about the stolen map.

"Tink," Janner said, looking innocently at his brother. "Is there something you want to say?" Tink glared at Janner, shaking his head as subtly as he could manage. When he didn't answer, everyone looked up from their plates. All eyes were on him.

"Tink, what is it?" Nia said. Tink's cheeks flushed and he glowered at Janner.

"Speak up, lad! Your meat's gettin' cold," Podo said.

"Well, see, I found…I found…" he stammered and hung his head so low that his hair nearly dipped into his plate of roast.

"He found an itchy rash," Janner said, grinning as he filled his cup from the water pitcher. "Has it spread to your armpits yet?"

Tink's head whipped up. "What? No. Not yet."

Janner winked at him, but Tink wasn't laughing.

Podo demanded to have a look at Tink's rash right there at the dinner table, and to Janner's enjoyment, the interrogation regarding the rash lasted the rest of their meal.

Convinced that Tink was fine, that the rash was probably just his imagination—something brought on by stress, Podo allowed Tink to go to his room.

"It's just a little stressful to know your fingers might be cut off," Tink muttered to himself once safe on his bunk.

"Maybe one of those could go in the maggotloaf," Janner said, laughing. "You know, your grubby fingers might make an excellent addition to the recipe."

"That's *not* funny," Tink said.

A melody from Leeli's whistleharp came from the main room, where she was playing a rousing sailors' tune at Podo's request.

Janner and Tink climbed up to the top bunk and spread out the map. They read and reread the inscription beside the building labeled ANKLE-JELLY MANOR, trying to imagine what might be hidden there that would make Oskar keep a secret map.

Tink shuddered at the line in the poem about the ghost of Brimney Stupe. "I don't like ghosts," he said.

"Come on, Tink. Ghosts aren't real."

"That's what you say. Podo says he's seen ghosts."

"Well, he told us he saw an abandoned ship on the Dark Sea of Darkness with a crew of ghost pirates," Janner said, "and he also said that he'd been awake for three days straight. You see strange things when you don't sleep." He shook his head. "Ghosts aren't real."

"What do you think all these little pinholes are all over the map?" Tink asked.

"I dunno." Janner shrugged. "Probably from mice. Or bugs. Look!" Janner pointed at an image of a dragon in the bottom, right corner of the map. "Does that look familiar to you?"

Tink shook his head.

"Remember the Annieran journal in the crate from Dang? That looks like the same dragon."

Tink pointed to an inscription above the dragon. "The Jewels of Anniera," he read, his face puzzled. "What are the Jewels of Anniera?"

Janner shrugged.

"I don't know, but I'm sure Mister Reteep has a good reason for keeping the map hidden. And for hiding the Jewels of Anniera or whatever's in Anklejelly Manor. One thing is for certain. I don't mean to find out. It's too close to the forest, and even *before* the war that place was creepy. It's been abandoned for years."

"Why?"

"I don't know. I read about it in a book on the history of Glipwood,[1] and Podo said the place was haunted, that people heard noises coming from inside. It's been avoided for so long that no one remembers who built it, or even who Anklejelly was. I've never even seen the place. According to the map it's a ways north of town, right at the edge of the forest."

Tink stared out the window into the night. "If we left right after lunch tomorrow, we'd have time to—"

"Are you *crazy?*" Janner interrupted.

Tink stared blankly at his brother, who looked at the door and lowered his voice.

"No way." Janner shook his head.

Tink's eyes twinkled. "You're the crazy one. How can you find a treasure map and not want to find the treasure?"

"It doesn't say 'treasure' anywhere on this map! In two days we've been in fights with two Fangs, thrown in jail, and almost taken for a ride in the

---

1. Janner is probably referring to *Between the Blapp and the Bay: A Town Called Glipwood*, by Randolt Mynerqua (Dugtown, Skree: BrookWater Press, 16/404). It was a popular read for the Glipwood Township, partly because it boasted only seventeen pages.

Black Carriage. You've stolen a map, and Slarb's informed us that he means to kill us all! And now you want to follow a map to a haunted house near the forest because of a riddle that says that it leads to pain, woe, and sorrow?"

Tink grinned. "Yes."

Janner let out a wail.

"Shh!" Tink grimaced. "I'm just saying there's a lot more to this little town than we thought. Our mother has a hidden stash of jewels that we didn't know about. Mister Reteep gets an Annieran journal in a crate from Dang. He has a hidden map. And some mysterious person with perfect aim saved our lives yesterday."

Janner cocked his head. "You're right," he admitted. "I heard Podo and Ma say they think they know who saved our lives too."

Tink's brow creased.

Janner looked hard into Tink's eyes. "And there's something else. Something about our father."

Tink was silent.

"His name was Esben."

"Who told you that?" Tink asked softly.

"I heard Mama say it yesterday. I don't think she meant to."

"Esben," Tink said to himself.

The brothers sat on the bed with the weight of their father's absence heavy on them until Leeli opened the door. "What are you both doing on the top bunk?" she asked, smiling and climbing into her own bed, Nugget right beside her.

"Nothing," Janner and Tink said in unison—and a little too quickly.

But Leeli didn't take notice, and soon she and Nugget were asleep.

Janner climbed down to his bunk where he lay awake long into the night, his head swirling with questions and his heart full of worry. The look of hatred in Slarb's eyes had burned itself into his mind. He could hear the Fang's hissing voice, smell the rotten breath, and feel all over again the sting of the venom dripping onto his neck; he was all too aware of the responsibility he had to keep watch over his brother and sister.

Tink's head appeared, dangling down from the top bunk.

"You awake?" Tink whispered.

"Yeah."

"We leave right after lunch," Tink said, and disappeared again.

"No!" Janner whispered, but Tink was snoring loudly, pretending to be asleep.

20

Into the Manor

Even as they treaded north toward the Blaggus Estate for a brief game of Zibzy, Janner knew they would be visiting Anklejelly Manor that afternoon. He had argued with his stubborn brother in heated whispers during their chores that morning, but it soon became clear that for Tink, fear and common sense were no match for his curiosity.

They were no match for Janner's either. He had been unable to stop thinking about that mysterious warning on the map, right next to the alluring X. Besides, he told himself, Tink was going with or without him. Who else would protect his little brother?

So in the hot early afternoon, the Blaggus boys won the game as usual, and Janner and Tink bade them farewell. When they were sure they weren't being watched, they struck out running through the high weeds of the old lane, around a bend, and up a hill until they were well out of sight of the estate.

The lane north of the Blaggus Estate was overgrown. Few had traveled it since the homesteads beyond the Blaggus family's estate had been burned and abandoned in the war. It wasn't long before Janner doubled over with his hands on his knees, gasping for air. Tink had outrun him and was waiting several yards ahead, looking at the countryside, trying not to look winded himself. The oaks that shaded the road had grown scarce, and the grassy land sloped upward, away from the town and the cliffs, and toward the dark edge of Glipwood Forest.

Janner stood up with great effort and wiped his forehead with the front of his shirt. Tink pointed down the slopes at the roof of the Blaggus home peeking from the trees below them. Beyond was the Glipwood Township, a tiny strand of buildings in the distance. The Only Inn could be made out easily since it stood a story higher than the other buildings, but eastward the land dropped away into gray expanse. The Dark Sea of Darkness.

Somewhere, each brother thought to himself, at the edge of the sea, beneath the shade of those glipwood trees, sat the Igiby cottage.

For an hour Janner and Tink followed the ancient lane as best they could. Each time the road began to blend into tall stretches of heather and disappear, they would search anew for the faint depression of the path in the swaying grass. The line of the forest loomed ever closer, and soon Janner was pointing to the shape of what must be the ruined structure of Anklejelly Manor.

Tink picked up his pace and soon they stood before the manor, its craggy back to the forest. The two gaping second-floor windows made Janner think of the eye sockets of a skull watching their approach. He stopped in front of a rusty iron gate that hung sad and crooked on ancient hinges. Neither brother spoke, unwilling to admit they were afraid and wondering what foolishness had made coming here seem sensible.

It was clear that the manor had once been a beautiful place. Several tall and mildewed statues of people in various poses dotted the courtyard. One was of a fat man eating a lamb chop (the sight of which caused Tink's stomach to growl loudly, the sound of which made Janner jump an inch off the ground). Another statue nearer the house depicted a laughing woman swinging a terrified cat by its hind leg. Another statue, covered in vines, was of a weeping man scratching his large belly with a rake. Dangling from the rake handle was a cluster of stone grapes.

The roof of the mansion had long ago collapsed, and everywhere weeds and vines had begun the slow work of pulling the stones and aged timbers back to the earth.

Janner turned and looked back down the long slope at the distant town.

"We came this far, didn't we?" he said uncertainly. He took a deep breath and passed through the gate.

The air was quiet as a grave. No bird sang. No wind blew.

Janner shuddered at the thought of the many beasts that roamed the forest. He wondered how often those beasts ventured beyond the trees and into places like Anklejelly Manor. Or were the animals afraid of ghosts too?

Tink followed his older brother past an old stone bench in what appeared to have been a flower garden lined with stones, now overgrown in a tangle of budding weeds. The front of the bench bore an inscription.

Janner pulled the vines away and read: BRIMNEY STUPE ENJOYS HIS SOUP.

Tink's stomach roared. "Did we bring anything to eat?" he asked, knowing they hadn't.

Janner ignored him. "Let's have another look at the map," he said.

They sat on the bench and Janner examined it, trying hard to ignore the dire warning about entering the place they were about to enter.

The edge of the forest behind the house was a tangled green wall, silent and grim, and as Tink stared into it, he couldn't shake the feeling that it was staring back.

"Is there anything on here that tells us exactly where to go?" Janner said. "It says, 'In the catacombs below is hidden in the hollow.' I guess that means we need to find a way down." He pointed to the foundation of the manor. "Under there."

Tink looked long at the skull-like stare of the manor and shivered. "Why are we here again?"

"Because you talked me into it, that's why."

"You know, a snack would be good about now," Tink said. "Maybe we should head back and—"

"Nope," Janner said firmly. "We came this far, and you're not backing out."

"It was just a suggestion," Tink said, forcing a chuckle. The sound of his laugh was unnatural there in the ruins.

Janner told himself there were no ghosts in the manor, and the warnings on the map were only there in case it fell into the wrong hands. Never

mind that it had, he argued with himself. But if that were really the case, Oskar hadn't bargained on two young boys finding it. He must have forgotten that in the mind of a boy, a warning isn't much different from an invitation.

"Come on," Janner said with resolve, and Tink followed.

They crunched through the thick brambles that surrounded the stone manor, looking for any sign of a cellar entrance. Janner smelled the musty scent of old things, and inside every window passed, he saw tumbled stones and fallen rafters in the dim light. From the rear of the manor, he and Tink peered through a back door that led to what must have been the kitchen. Vines covered a long, cracked counter with stone-cut wash basins. The ceiling of the first floor had caved in above the kitchen, allowing shafts of sunlight to cross a tangle of old wood, pots, and fallen stones on the floor.

They moved on through the brush around the mansion and passed a dry fountain that housed a prickly rosebush on the rear lawn. Beyond the fountain, the forest glared at them.

Janner's skin crawled. "Let's go back around to the front," he whispered.

Tink nodded gravely and followed his brother back around the house. Neither brother would admit it, but they each felt better with something between them and the trees.

That is, until they rounded the corner. The two brothers stood at the main entrance to the house, peering into shadows. The air was still and heavy with the afternoon heat.

"A lantern would be nice," Janner said, eyeing the dark entrance.

Then they each took a deep breath and walked side by side over the threshold, into the ruins of Anklejelly Manor.

21

The Horned Hounds

At first, Janner and Tink could see nothing but darkness. Then they realized they were in a wide, empty room with stone walls. A once-elegant staircase led upward, into the light of the roofless upper level. Rubble, old wooden beams, and scraggly weeds covered the floor. Everything of value had long since been plundered, but the faded glory of the manor was apparent. It wasn't hard to imagine dinner parties long ago with well-dressed men and women ascending and descending the wide staircase, or eerie laughter echoing in the huge, empty rooms—or Brimney Stupe, whoever he was, strolling through the corridors of the mansion at night with a candle held above his head.

It was not hard to imagine, in other words, that there were ghosts.

"Did you say something?" Janner asked, his nervous voice echoing in the room.

"No, did you hear something?" Tink whispered.

"No, did you?"

"Only you, asking if I said something."

"Then why did you ask?"

"Because you did."

Janner stepped carefully through the debris of the main room and peeked through the doorways that led deeper into the house. He led the way back to the kitchen area, where the ceiling was gone and the sunlight made them feel much more comfortable. Tink poked around in the empty cupboards while Janner peeked under fallen beams, hoping to find some hint of the treasure Oskar had mapped.

Just as Janner began to relax, and Tink began to think he might like to visit more often, a crackling noise sounded from just outside the kitchen window.

The Igiby brothers froze.

It was the same sound they had made when they walked through the brambles around the house. Something was outside, and it was getting nearer.

Janner held his breath and put a finger to his lips. He motioned for Tink to follow. Quiet as mice, they tiptoed back to the front entrance of the manor and peeked out the door.

Across the yard, a gray creature was sniffing the bench where they had sat. It looked exactly like a dog—except for two tusks jutting upward from its snout and a dangerous-looking horn that crowned its head, and the fact that it stood at least as tall as Janner.

A horned hound, Janner realized. "Don't move," he whispered.

Tink stood perfectly still. But it had been hours since he'd eaten. *We really should have brought something to eat,* he thought. The sight of the stone bench reminded Tink of the inscription on it, which reminded him of Brimney Stupe enjoying his soup, which reminded Tink that he hadn't eaten a thing since they'd left the cottage that day. His stomach rumbled. Loudly.

Janner froze in horror as the hound looked directly at the boys standing just inside the house. It raised its horned head and howled a piercing, hungry howl. Then it whirled and bore straight toward them.

"Quick!" Janner said, bolting through a doorway on their left. In the distance, an awful chorus of other howls answered the first. Janner could think of nothing to do but move further into the manor and hope to find some place to hide from the hounds.

The doorway led to a long hallway, where occasional holes in the ceiling allowed for thin shafts of sunlight. The hall was lined with doors on either side, so Janner picked one at random and pulled Tink after him. Outside, the howls grew in volume and number.

"Psst! There's another door!" Tink said. In the rear of the room was a doorway, smaller than the first, leading to an even deeper darkness.

"Come on! It's dark, so stay close," Janner said, running to the doorway. He stepped through—into empty air. Tink caught Janner by the shirt and pulled him back. Janner gasped and steadied himself on the door frame. Tink dropped to his knees and reached down into the opening, hoping for steps or a ladder.

There were none.

"This is a dead end," Janner said. "Come on!"

But their way was barred. Standing in the doorway from which they had come was the dim shape of a horned hound. The only sound in the room was the creature's panting. Its hungry eyes glistened in the dark, and a low growl filled the room. The hound stepped forward and two more of the horned beasts appeared in the doorway behind it.

"So this is what the map meant about pain and woe, huh?" Tink said, his voice shaking like a leaf in a storm.

Janner thought about his duty as the eldest. Only days ago, Leeli nearly died at the hands of a Fang because he hadn't paid attention. Now this. *Why can't I be like our father,* he wondered. *He died in the Great War, trying to protect those he loved.* For one shameful moment Janner felt a flash of anger at Tink for talking him into coming to Anklejelly Manor in the first place. *Why should I be the one to risk my life for my little brother when it's his fault we're here in the first place?* Janner was tired of bearing the responsibility for his brother's folly, and he wanted to forget Tink and run for his life. Maybe he could push his way past the hounds and find a better place to hide in the mansion. Maybe—

The idea to flee was only a brief thought. Janner knew he wouldn't—couldn't—leave his little brother behind. He could hear Podo's raspy voice in his mind. *"Part of being a man is taking much care of those you love."*

The first hound in the doorway twitched.

Janner felt it more than he saw it, and he knew that it was about to spring. Without another thought, he stepped between Tink and the beasts, spun his little brother around, and shoved him through the doorway.

Tink screamed as he fell, and Janner heard the beasts lunging, their hot breath on his neck as he too leapt into blackness.

22

The Catacombs Below

Janner's head throbbed. The world spun, and he felt like he had been asleep for days. When he managed to open his eyes, he saw a rectangle of dim light above him, and the shapes of the frenzied beasts filled the doorway, snarling and barking. One of them yelped and backed away. Janner looked to his right and could just make out Tink hurling a stone up at the horned hounds.

The stone missed its mark and popped through the rotten wood ceiling as if it were nothing more than paper. A shaft of sunlight stabbed into the room. Janner shook away the dizziness and wobbled to his feet to help his brother.

Rock after rock flew at the horned hounds, and when struck the hounds yelped like puppies and backed away. The brothers began to enjoy themselves as only boys can do when they're throwing rocks, and a contest ensued as to who would hit the last hound.

The largest of all the hounds, as tall as Janner, snarled and bared its tusks, prancing in the doorway. Tink hefted the rock in his hand, reared back, and with a mighty roar let the stone fly. The rock struck the last beast squarely in the eye and the hound crumpled to the floor, its head lolling over the edge.

The brothers doubled over with hands on their knees, panting.

Janner grinned at his brother. "Nice shot."

Tink smiled back. "You all right?"

Janner put a hand to the side of his head. "I…think so. The fall didn't hurt you?"

"No, but if you ever plan to push me over the edge of something again, let me know first. I almost wet my pants."

Janner looked around the room but could see very little in the dim light. He picked up another rock.

"What are you doing?" Tink asked.

Janner pitched the stone through the brittle ceiling, letting in another beam of sunlight, then threw several more stones until they could see their surroundings clearly.

The side of the cellar opposite the high door was cluttered with a pile of old crates and dry timber, but the room was otherwise bare. The only way out was the way they had come in; the doorway was twice as tall as Janner, and the walls too smooth to climb. Janner poked through the stack of timber, hoping to find something he could lean against the wall and climb. But all the planks that would have been long enough were too brittle to hold him. Most of the old wood was rotten and eaten through.

"Tink, get on my shoulders. Maybe you can reach the door."

"Oh, I don't know," Tink said, eyeing the doorway above them. "That's a long way up."

"I'm taller than you, and you can't hold me up. Besides, you just fell from up there and you're fine. Now come on."

Janner bent over and with much grunting managed to stand up with Tink's feet on his shoulders. Tink trembled and strained but still couldn't reach the doorway. *Even if he could,* Janner thought, *the horned hound whose head is dangling over the edge might still be alive. It probably was good that Tink couldn't reach.* Janner paced the cellar floor trying to think of what to do, and the more he thought, the more frustrated he became at himself for being there at all. This treasure-hunting business was foolishness, and Janner needed to get his little brother home. If they didn't get back soon, Podo and Nia would be at least as terrifying as the horned hounds.

Tink was at the other end of the chamber, toeing at the pile of wood.

"Janner!" he called. "A stairway!"

Thank the Maker, Janner thought. *We can get out of here.* He crossed the room and looked, and his shoulders slumped.

Tink was grinning, pointing to a narrow passageway that led *down* into shadows.

"No, Tink," Janner said.

"What do you mean?"

"What do you mean, 'what do you mean'?"

"We're so *close,* that's what I mean. We can't just go home!"

Janner was speechless. *How can I be expected to watch over my brother when he has no appreciation of the danger we're in?* Only moments ago they'd been nearly eaten by a pack of horned hounds, and now Tink was more concerned about poking around in a cellar than his own life.

Tink took the first few steps down into the passage for a better look. "Aha!" he said, sounding a lot like his grandfather. He reemerged with an oil lantern and a box of matches covered with cobwebs. Blowing dust from the lantern, Tink lit it, and started down the stairway without another word.

Janner looked around the room again, wishing desperately for another doorway to appear, but there was none. He had no choice. With a sigh, he followed his little brother deeper into the bowels of Anklejelly Manor, trying not to think about the warning on the map: *For in the catacombs below is hidden in the hollow, a way that leads to pain and woe, sadness, grief, and sorrow.*

The deeper their descent, the more the air grew cool and heavy. Cobwebs dangled from the passageway's low ceiling, and Janner's ears were full of the sound of his own breathing and the echo of footsteps on stone.

After several cracked and broken steps down, Tink and Janner came to the bottom of the stairs. The passageway was more of a cave than a tunnel; the walls rough and moist. The floor was damp enough that neither Janner nor Tink wanted to crawl, but the ceiling was too low to allow them to walk without stooping.

They inched along in an uncomfortable hunch, Tink holding the lantern and peering ahead into the blackness beyond the lamplight; Janner could scarcely see anything but Tink's rear end.

Neither of the boys had thought about the possibility of ghosts since their narrow escape from the flesh-and-blood horned hounds, and Janner was smiling in spite of himself. He couldn't deny the thrill of creeping through a secret passageway in the cellar of an ancient house, and he knew that Tink was smiling too. Janner broke the silence with a whisper.

"How does it look up there?"

"Nothing to see yet—wait, the passage is turning a little..."

The passageway veered right and the ceiling rose enough that the boys could stand up straight. They groaned with relief and stretched their backs. Their tension, fear, and excitement bubbled to the surface as nervous laughter. They walked a few more feet, slowly, and the passageway widened enough that the two of them were able to walk side by side. Neither of them spoke as they inched their way deeper into the corridor.

At last they came to the end of the passage, where a rusty iron door barred their way. Its hinges were embedded in the tunnel rock, and it was set as square and solid as if it had always been there. Whoever had put the door there had meant to keep out intruders. In the center of the door was a metal plate with several neat rows of round metal buttons the size of knuckles. There was no keyhole.

Tink tried the handle and found it locked.

"Of course," Janner said with disappointment.

A moment passed, both boys studying the door.

"Hang on," Tink said. He pressed one of the rusty buttons. With a loud click, it sunk into the door. "Janner, look. I think this is a lock. We just have to figure out the right combination of buttons to push, and the door will open. See?" He pressed another button. "There are…ten rows of…eight buttons each. That's only eighty buttons."

"That's ridiculous." Janner shook his head. "We have no idea how many buttons need to be pressed, or in what order. We'd be here for the rest of our lives, which I don't plan to spend here." He paused. "Besides, it could be a trap."

Tink took a deep breath and placed a hand on the handle.

Janner felt a moment of panic. "Don't."

Tink winked at Janner and tried the door handle again. The door didn't budge, but the buttons Tink had pressed clicked back out, flush with the rest.

Janner braced himself for something awful. But nothing happened. He tried once more to convince Tink to give up, but his little brother continued to ignore him as Janner sank to the floor and waited. Surely Tink would grow bored soon and give up on his own.

But he didn't.

Instead, Tink unrolled the map and examined it by the lantern light. "There must be something here…"

"Tink." Janner sighed, exasperated. "If there's a lock on the door, maybe it should stay locked."

Tink ignored his brother, intent on the map. He mumbled, "Some kind of a code…" He held out the map with one hand and raised the lamp with the other, casting the map's shadow on the tunnel wall.

Just before Tink gave up and began to roll up the parchment, Janner saw it—points of light in an uneven pattern cast by the tiny holes in the map. Janner's frustration vanished. "Tink, unroll the map."

Tink stared in confusion as Janner shone the lamp on the map and carefully guided Tink's hands to position the map in front of the buttons on the door. The points of light were too closely clustered at first, so Janner took a few steps back. Then Tink saw it too, plain as daylight: four of the points of light lined up with the four corners of the button rows, and the rest lit up seven more, roughly in the shape of the letter W.

Janner held the map and lamp steady while Tink pressed each of the corresponding buttons. Tink reached for the handle again.

"Wait—" Janner said, putting a hand on Tink's forearm.

Tink looked at Janner like he was out of his mind.

"Are you sure about this?" Janner asked.

Tink rolled his eyes.

"Well at least open the door slowly," Janner said.

With a deep breath, Tink turned the handle and with a click, it unlocked. Then he pulled open the door with a loud creak.

23

The Groaning Ghost of Brimney Stupe

Janner and Tink found themselves in a large room about the size of their whole cottage. All around were piles of odd-shaped objects covered in a thick layer of dust. At first, neither of them could tell what the piles consisted of, so Janner walked to the nearest one, a few feet to the right of the doorway, to get a better look. He leaned close to one of the dusty shapes and without warning, sneezed violently.

The eruption scattered the dust in a cloud, and the lamplight was reflected back by a flat piece of polished metal.

Janner had never seen a battle axe. Podo had often returned from town with a borrowed woodcutting axe, but this was nothing like it. The weapon was double edged, and the two blades combined were as wide as Janner's chest.

Tink stood beside him with his mouth hanging open. "What is it?" Tink asked in a quiet voice.

Janner didn't answer but ran his finger along the shining edge of the blade.

Tink blew the dust from another shape beside it, revealing a sword. Rubies and gems glimmered in the hilt, and an inscription in a language neither of them recognized ran the length of the blade.

Janner found another sword, stouter and less ornate, but polished and fine. Slowly they turned, their eyes wide with wonder. All around them were piles upon piles of swords, axes, shields, and daggers. Suits of armor stood like sentries along the wall. There were enough weapons for a small army, hidden in the cellar of Anklejelly Manor for who knew how many years.

After the initial shock, they hurried about the room, blowing and brushing dust from the weapons. Tink found a short sword and donned a small wooden shield. Janner tried to pull the axe from the pile but it was so heavy that as soon as the head was free it clanged to the floor. He wondered that any man could pick it up, let alone swing it in a fight. He found a dagger that suited him. He tied the scabbard to his belt and snatched the blade out several times, stabbing at the air. Tink put on a spiked helmet that was far too big for his head, and when Janner saw him he roared with laughter.

"Look at this!" Tink called, tossing the helmet aside. He had found hundreds of steel-tipped arrows, and beside them a pile of unstrung bows leaning in the corner.

Janner uncovered a coil of rope, which reminded him that they were trapped. They had been so enthralled by the weapons that he had forgotten the horned hounds and the unreachable cellar door. Janner took a good look around him at the trove of weapons. *Are these the Jewels of Anniera?* he wondered. What did dear old Oskar N. Reteep have to do with these weapons, anyway? He shuddered to think what the Fangs would do to them if they ever discovered this secret. Oskar had traveled all over Skree collecting books and curiosities. He must have gotten the weapons at the same time and hid them here. *But why?* Janner's mind whirled with all the answerless questions that had recently found a home there. But he would have time to think about all this later—right now he knew that he and Tink had to get home safely.

"Tink, we have to go."

Tink looked up from the oversized breastplate he was trying to buckle, and after a moment's thought, nodded. Even Tink realized they couldn't stay in the chamber forever.

Janner held up the rope. "Maybe this will help."

"Good. I'm starving. Maybe Grandpa will make some more of that cheesy chowder."

Janner was relieved that for once, Tink didn't argue. "Leave everything here. The last thing we need is to be caught by a Fang—"

"Or Ma," Tink said.

"—with a weapon."

They laughed together, took one last look at the shimmering room, and shut the door with a clank. The depressed buttons all clicked back out again, sealing the chamber from anyone without the map. They hustled back through the low tunnel, Janner with the rope slung over his shoulder, wondering how he would use it to escape.

Suddenly from the darkness behind them came a sound that turned their blood cold.

Drifting up from the weapons chamber was a wordless, menacing groan.

They had awakened the ghost of Brimney Stupe.

24

The Road Home

Janner and Tink stopped in their tracks and looked behind them, but beyond the lamplight—nothing. The moan floated to them again, and Tink's hands shook so violently that he dropped the lamp to the damp floor, where it snuffed out.

That was all Tink could take. Squealing like a meep, he scrambled through the tunnel.

Janner hurried after him, cold fear shivering through his veins. He imagined a thousand bony fingers clawing at his back and flew up the stairs in two bounds.

Tink was already at the top, wielding one of the old boards dangerously.

Janner wondered what Tink thought he would do with the plank, if the ghost of Brimney Stupe actually did come whooshing at him, but he admired his brother's intentions—and snatched his own short, sturdy-looking plank from the woodpile.

The long moan rose up out of the mouth of the passageway again as Janner frantically tied the rope to the center of the board. *Please, please work,* he thought. He took aim and hurled the board through the doorway, noticing dimly that the horned hound was no longer there. He tugged on the rope, but the board clattered back to the floor. On the second try, Janner jerked the rope so that the board was pulled flat against the door frame. Praying that the beasts were long gone and that the plank would hold, he clambered up the wall and through the door.

Janner reached down from the opening. "Tink, come on!" he cried over the moaning that echoed in the black room.

Tink tore his eyes from the tunnel opening to see that he was alone in the cellar. "Awk!" he cried as he tossed his board aside and scurried up the rope like a mad squirrel. He bypassed Janner's hand and zipped up and through the door where they both collapsed onto the floor, panting.

Janner kicked the plank and rope back into the cellar, thinking that it would be best to remove as many traces of their presence as they could. Just being out of the dark cellar made Brimney Stupe seem less frightening, but now they had to contend with the horned hounds.

The brothers crept back through the house and peeked out the front door, squinting in the brightness. The late afternoon sun was as warm and welcome as life itself.

Janner scanned the edge of the forest for any sign of movement. "I don't see them," he whispered.

Tink's face was pale.

Another chilling moan drifted up to them from the bowels of Anklejelly Manor.

"You ready?"

"I've never been so ready," Tink breathed.

"Run!"

The Igiby brothers ran past the stone bench, through the iron gate, down the long lane that sloped away from Anklejelly Manor and the border of the forest, and they didn't stop until they reached the field just behind the Blaggus Estate.

Unable to move another step, they lay sweating in the tall grass until they could breathe again. Then they rose to walk home, unable to believe that they were still alive and making solemn oaths to never again set foot in that horrid, wondrous place.

Janner and Tink approached the cottage in the late afternoon just as Podo was walking down the lane with a wriggling sack over his shoulder.

"Lads! It looks like the ol' Blaggus boys beat ye pretty smart again, did they?" Podo eyed their filthy, sweaty clothes.

Janner and Tink each forced a laugh.

"Where are you off to?" Janner asked, changing the subject.

Podo bent closer and put a hand to the side of his mouth.

"Don't tell yer ma—unless she asks, of course—but all these thwaps I've been snagging? See, I take 'em and I dump 'em into old Buzzard Willie's yard across town. Tee hee!" Podo laughed, slapping his knee. "That rascal never gave me a moment's peace when we were wee lads here in Glipwood, not to mention how he wooed sweet Merna Bidgeholler right out from under me nose. And besides," Podo's white eyebrows bunched together, "his totaters and sugarberries are always plumper than mine." He scratched his wild head of hair and muttered, "I don't know how he does it." He held out the sack and whacked it happily, bringing forth a chorus of chatter from inside. "So I'll see you lads a' supper!"

Podo limped away toward Buzzard Willie's, whistling and twirling the sack as he went.

Janner and Tink stood side by side a moment to watch Podo until he was out of sight. Then they made their own way back to the cottage, grateful to be home again.

But they were not the only ones watching. From behind a glipwood tree on the back lawn, Slarb the Fang squinted at Janner and Tink entering their cottage. Slarb had been slinking around the Igiby place all day, careful not to be seen. He had watched in agony, holding his hands to the sides of his head while Leeli practiced her whistleharp on the front porch. He had watched with loathing as Nia washed the clothes just outside the back door. And several times, when Leeli had played fetch with Nugget, it took all of Slarb's willpower to keep from snatching up the dog for once and for good.

Even now, clacking his teeth in the shadow of a glipwood tree, he yearned to sink his teeth into anything Igiby unfortunate enough to come near.

25

In the Hall of General Khrak

Meanwhile, in the city of Torrboro, Commander Gnorm was just arriving at the Palace Torr after traveling through the night and most of the day. By the reckoning of the old maps, Torrboro was a two-day journey from Glipwood by the main road, but the Fangs stopped for neither rest nor food as they drove their horses mercilessly across the barren prairies to the city.

The city of Torrboro sprawled on the south bank of the River Blapp and bustled with activity. No one who lived there seemed to know where anyone else was going or why, and many had very little notion as to where they themselves were going at any given moment. People were walking, pushing carts, driving carriages, leading sheep, carrying sacks of totatoes, loading wagons with fish; selling, buying, yelling, talking—all without smiling or thinking about much at all.

Lurking among the people were armored Fangs of varying sizes and shapes.

Lurking among the Fangs were trolls, and a single troll stunk worse than a hundred Fangs. If a troll brushed against some unfortunate passerby, the poor fellow would stink up his home for weeks; so wherever the trolls went, the people scattered like windblown leaves.

The citizens of Torrboro could scarcely remember the days before the war when Fangs and trolls were only rumors from across the Dark Sea of

Darkness. Now the sight of monsters walking among them seemed as normal as the seagulls that swooped and chattered in the air above the city.

Commander Gnorm started to open the carriage door but stopped when he saw the jewels glittering on his fat arms and fingers. He hastily removed the bracelets and rings and placed them in his pouch, relieved that he had remembered to conceal them. He didn't want any fights over his newly acquired shinies.

Gnorm squeezed himself out of the carriage with a long grunt and picked at the pieces of flabbit stuck between his teeth. He had been snacking on the drive. The exhausted horses wheezed and staggered while the plump commander climbed the long stairway to the mouthlike entrance of the Palace Torr.[1] The once-beautiful castle stood tall and sharp against the gray sky, the windows of its spires black, its banners tattered and swaying limply in the thick air as if in mourning for their former glory. Two troll guards stood watch at the main door, looking down at Gnorm and the driver.

"What businesss have you wi' the general," one of them said in a booming voice that rattled Gnorm's armor.

"The same business I had last time, and the time before that, and the time before that, horse maggot," Gnorm scowled. The troll burped and moved aside, motioning for the other troll to open the great wooden door.

"Oafs," Gnorm hissed as he passed over the threshold and into the palace.

The main hall was littered with bones and garbage. The stench would

---

1. Thorn the Torr, the warrior king who built the palace at the beginning of the Third Epoch, was fond of kittens. On every spire of the Palace Torr were statues of kittens in varied posture. From a bluff on the north bank of the Blapp it was plain that the palace itself was built to resemble a happy, crouching kitty. The uppermost spire was the tail, the portcullis resembled teeth, and the drawbridge was undeniably tonguelike. For ages the Torr Dynasty nursed a disturbing fondness of all things kitten. Then came the Great War, when Fangs captured King Oliman the Torr and forced him to watch as the kitten statues were pulled down and shattered, one by one. When all the kitties in the kingdom were placed on a raft and set adrift on the River Blapp, Oliman the Torr dropped dead with grief. To the citizens of Torrboro, however, it was the one good thing the Fangs ever did.

have made a human sick, but to Gnorm it smelled like dinner. Fangs lounged here and there, sleeping on the floor or leaning against the walls. Trolls huddled over a dice game in the corner; some of them looked up when Gnorm entered, then turned back to their business.

Gnorm looked around for a moment, smiling. *Always good to be back in the thick of it,* he thought. He lumbered down the center of the hall to the Fang sentries posted outside the throne room.

"Greetingsss, Commander Gnorm," one of the Fangs said, lifting his spear so that he could pass.

"Bleah," replied Gnorm, and he entered the throne room of the most powerful Fang in all of Skree.

Unlike the main hall, the throne room was empty but for General Khrak and a Fang servant who was filling his goblet with black sludge. Gnorm bowed so low his scaly gut almost touched the floor, and for a long time, he waited. He knew that many commanders had lost their heads by rising without permission. Finally, he heard the general grunt and Gnorm rose from his bow with a great deal of difficulty.

"Gnorm," Khrak said, his voice echoing in the empty hall. He sipped from his goblet. The ceiling was high and a pale light streamed in through narrow windows. The room was bare of furniture but for the gilded throne, now covered with filth. The general was one of Gnag the Nameless's oldest servants. It was Khrak who led the army that destroyed Anniera, and Khrak who had sailed the Fang horde across the Dark Sea to Skree. It was Khrak whose orders sent the Black Carriage roving across the land to kidnap Skreean children, and he whom even the Fangs feared.

His torso and abdomen were long and lithe, and though his arms and legs were shorter and thinner than those of most Fangs, no other was a match for Khrak's prowess. His teeth were longer and sharper than Gnorm's, and it was said that his venom could kill a sea dragon.

"What newsss do you bring from Glipwood?" the general asked.

"No news, lord. A scuffle on the day the sea dragonsss came, but it was quickly resolved." Gnorm absently scratched his belly. Usually the meetings with General Khrak were short, and he was hungry for some of Dugtown's famous fish entrails at a tavern called The Gargle and Slurp. The city of Dugtown crouched on the north bank of the River Blapp and was Torrboro's grubby neighbor, a maze of decrepit buildings crawling with thieves and beggars. Gnorm hated having to travel so far for such a short conversation, but at least he was able to slink over to Dugtown for a few days.

"Come nearer, Commander Gnorm. I have newsss from the Castle Throg."

Gnorm moved closer, hoping the general wouldn't take too much time. He pictured in his mind the gloriously filthy lower streets of Dugtown, where he would soon be gobbling little squirmies over a game of dice.

"The Namelesss has sent word," said Khrak, savoring the news, "that he is musssstering another army. He says it will be a greater army than any Aerwiar has ever known." Khrak paused and let the announcement hang in the air.

"And what does our lord plan to do with this great army, sir?"

"The Namelesss One has kept his purposes hidden from me, but I believe he plans to march west into the unknown lands. As you know, he still seeks the Jewels of Anniera. He no longer believes them to be in Skree, but beyond it, beyond the edges of all the mapsss."

"Sir, why does the Nameless One seek these jewels?" Gnorm bowed slightly. "If I am permitted to ask, sir."

The general's tail curled up and around the armrest of the throne. He toyed with the end of it while he spoke. A fat yellow centipede squirmed from the sludge in a desperate attempt to escape the goblet, but Khrak's tongue whipped out and snapped the creature into his mouth. The Fang closed his eyes and swallowed carefully.

"When we sacked...*Anniera*"—he said the word as if it tasted vile in his mouth—"many writings of King Wingfeather were found. In them, he spoke of the Jewels of Anniera and the ancient power they hold, a power that could destroy the Namelesss One and restore Anniera to its glory."

Gnorm had figured as much. For years Gnag had been consumed with finding the jewels, though Gnorm had often wondered how they would ever locate something that could be hidden so easily. Besides, what power could possibly overcome the mighty Gnag and his army?

"He believes the jewelsss are hidden...beyond the maps?" Gnorm asked, though he was quickly losing interest. Every moment he spent there was a moment he wasn't spending in the Gargle and Slurp, dining on chorkney brains.

"He has sssought them in Skree all these years," said Khrak, "and he grows impatient. The Skreeans have no knowledge of what lies west of the plains, but if there are peoples there to conquer, I'm sure he means to do it. It is not our job to know what our master's great mind intends," he said with a wave of his hand. Khrak leaned forward. "But he does require something of you, Commander Gnorm."

"Anything, my lord," replied Gnorm with a slight bow. He could taste the rat tails, feel them slipping deliciously down his throat.

"The Nameless One needs more prisoners sent to Dang. I'm ordering the commanders of all the sectors of Skree to double their arrests. Not just the children anymore, but whole families. We will fill the Black Carriage with Skreeans and send them by the shipload to our lord Gnag Who Has No Name." Khrak took another long sip of sludge and smiled. "I trust you will find this enjoyable?"

"Oh, yes, lord. Very enjoyable." Gnorm smirked, thinking of which Glipfolk he would seize first. Then he thought again of the taverns of Dugtown, and asked, "Will that be all, General?"

Khrak caressed his tail and glared at Gnorm.

"Yesss, commander. Go."

Gnorm again bowed low, and as he did, a gold medallion on a silver chain slipped from where he had tucked it into his breastplate. The necklace glinted in the light and dangled from his neck alluringly.

"Wait," the general said, slithering out of the throne and down the steps.

The click of his claws on the marble floor echoed throughout the chamber. "And where did you acquire this trinket?"

Gnorm felt clammy sweat seep from between his scales. He dared not move.

"From one of the townspeople, lord. A woman. It is yoursss, if you please," he stammered.

The general snatched the medallion from Gnorm's neck with a hiss and snaked his way back onto the throne with a grunt of dismissal. He eyed the medallion with satisfaction.

"I like the way it sparklesss," the general said to himself as he slipped it on. "Now go." Gnorm rose and exited the throne room. He stormed back through the hall where trolls and Fangs continued to lounge and heaved himself back into his carriage.

"Take me to Dugtown," he growled. "Now!"

The driver scurried onto the carriage and drove the disgruntled commander down the cobbled streets to the ferry to Dugtown, where he would feast on guts and drown his anger at losing his favorite bit of loot.

Trouble at the Bookstore

The next morning, Podo was pleased to find more thwaps in the garden. He took such pleasure in overhearing Buzzard Willie complain about them at the tavern that Podo had begun looking forward to waking up every morning at sunrise to catch the little thieves at their business; part of his daily routine was sneaking into Buzzard Willie's backyard, dumping sacks full of thwaps, and watching them scatter. To be fair, after setting the thwaps loose, Podo would sneak around to the front door and hand Willie a basket of vegetables, compliments of the flourishing Igiby garden.

Janner, Tink, and Leeli did their morning chores and studied their T.H.A.G.S. Tink was excited that the two art books he'd borrowed from Oskar were helpful and overflowing with beautiful pictures. Leeli spent her time memorizing the words and melodies to several old tunes that Nia knew from childhood. But Janner sat on the front steps with his journal in his lap, staring out past the trees. Nia had asked him to write a book report on *In the Age of the Kindly Flabbits,* but try as he might, Janner couldn't make it past the first few words without thinking about Oskar's map.

Oskar N. Reteep was quite a different man than Janner had thought, hiding secret maps and hoarding weapons in a haunted manor. Janner shook his head and smiled wryly, thinking about all the jewels his mother had kept secret. She wasn't exactly who he thought she was, either. *Do all grownups have something to hide?*

"Janner, are you almost finished?" Nia's voice startled him. She stood behind him, frowning at the mostly blank page on his lap.

Janner's cheeks reddened. He'd been sitting there for most of the morning and had nothing to show for it. "I just have…too much crammed in my head to write about flabbits and the Jungles of Plontst," he stammered. He stared at the ground, wondering why he suddenly felt the need to cry. He waited for a rebuke of some kind, but instead felt his mother squeeze his shoulder.

"Then write about that. It'll do you some good," she said, turning to go. "And I promise not to read it."

He looked down at the quill in his hand and remembered the feel of the sword he had swung in the weapons chamber. It had felt good, like he was no longer a powerless boy in a boring town but someone whose life could mean something, like his father's had. All the tears that had gathered in him just moments ago changed into words, and he began to scratch them into his journal.

Janner filled pages in his journal for hours. By the time he finished relating the details of the last two days' adventures—the head full of questions they had raised, and the heart full of emotions they had awoken—his hand ached and the ink bottle was almost dry.

Nia called for a lunch of henmeat salad and roundbread, and Janner closed his journal with a feeling of lightness in his chest, as if he had been carrying a feed sack on his shoulders for two days and had just heaved it to the barn floor. But his mind still swirled.

Tink appeared and tried to push toward the kitchen door, but Janner grabbed his elbow.

"Henmeat and roundbread," Tink said, patting his stomach. "What is it?"

Janner lowered his voice. "We have to return that map."

Tink's face grew serious and he hid his hands behind his back, thinking about how much he wanted to keep the fingers attached to them. "Do we have to? What if Mister Reteep finds out?"

"He'll find out soon enough, if he notices it missing, and I'm sure he'll suspect we took it. I think our safest option is to try to slip it back when he's not looking. Trust me. We'll do it today when we go to the bookstore."

They gobbled down lunch and headed out, Leeli and Nugget in tow. Once again, Podo escorted them into town as far as Shaggy's Tavern.

"After I chew the bone with Shaggy for a spell, I'm heading home to tend to the garden. I'll be back to get ye at sundown." With a warning to be wary and to stick together, he sent them on, complaining loudly about his overwhelming thirst.

Leeli hadn't yet ventured into town since the Sea Dragon Festival, and she was anxious. But the sun was bright and the townspeople seemed their usual selves, so her spirits soon lightened and she took to humming while she limped along behind her brothers. They waved at the Blaggus boys who were pushing a wheelbarrow full of garden tools they had just acquired by spending the morning filling out a stack of Tool Use Forms.

The Fangs were at their usual place in front of the jail, laughing wickedly with one another and sneering at the Glipfolk who passed.

Janner was relieved to see no sign of either Slarb or Commander Gnorm.

Zouzab sat on the roof of Books and Crannies with his legs crossed, juggling three stones and watching the children approach.

"Hello, children," he said in his quiet way. "Have you come to…return something?" Janner and Tink stole a glance at one another. Did Zouzab know that they'd taken the map? Janner told himself it was his guilty conscience. They waved at him, Janner trying to be as pleasant as he could with the strange little ridgerunner, though he always found it difficult. Zouzab's eyes seemed to be studying him in a way that was familiar to Janner, though he couldn't place why.

"We've come to see if Leeli here can borrow a few books," Janner said.

"I'm sure that will be nice," Zouzab replied pleasantly enough as he slunk backward, out of sight.

Janner watched the ridgerunner vanish and remembered Nicholas, Ferinia Swapleton's cat. It was usually seen lazing in the shade of the front stoop of the flower shop, licking its paws. But sometimes, when a butterfly bounced through the air in front of it, the cat would spring to its feet and watch the insect with a cold, careful intensity. Janner realized that when Zouzab watched him, he felt like the butterfly. He shuddered and hurried into the bookstore to find Oskar in his office hunkered over a huge volume at his desk.

"The Igiby three! Come in, come in." He spread his arms wide and waved them in. His expression turned to one of horror, however, when he saw Nugget padding along beside Leeli. "Oh! No dogs, lass. First thing you know, he'll be gnawing on some old one-of-a-kind book of mine." He shooed Nugget out the back door to Leeli's disappointment. Noticing, Oskar's expression softened, but only a little. "As the great animal trainer Yakev Brrz wrote, uh, let me see…how did that go…" Oskar closed his eyes with a finger in the air. "Ah! That's it. 'Like it or not, the dog stays outside.' A wise fellow, Yakev was."[1]

Leeli motioned for Nugget to wait for her beside the loading door in the back, where the crates full of books had been.

Oskar then escorted Leeli through the store to find the section on music.

Janner and Tink wandered through the maze of shelves for half an hour before Tink found the loose panel just below the shelf labeled ITCHY RASH REMEDIES AND ANECDOTES. The snot-wax candle was still in its place.

---

1. Yakev Brrz abhorred all manner of animal abuse, most of all the habit of referring to pets as "baby" and attributing to them human characteristics. Yakev's first wife, Zaga, esteemed her two Beckitt Terriers so much that she insisted they sit at the table with them at dinner and that they sleep at the foot of their bed. Yakev, whose communication skills with all manner of animals was unmatched, failed to convince Zaga that her "babies" detested the eating practices of humans and would much rather have not worn the matching lavender lace pajamas to sleep in their human bed. Late one fateful night when Zaga was fast asleep, Yakev tiptoed to the foot of the bed, gathered Schpoontzy and Kiki carefully in his arms, carried them outside, drew from his sleeve a sharp knife, and put them out of their misery. Which is to say that he cut the lavender lace pajamas from the oppressed dogs and set them running free in the moonlight, never to return. It's said that once word of the dogs' deliverance at the hands of the mighty Yakev Brrz spread among dog-kind, wherever Yakev passed, all breeds of dogs yowled and respectfully rolled onto their backs. Nothing more is known of Zaga.

"Is he nearby?" Tink asked, looking up and down the aisle. Janner walked to the end, peeked around the corner and shook his head.

Tink wiggled the panel loose, pulled the map from his sleeve and slipped it beneath the shelf. As he replaced the panel, they heard a quiet voice above them.

"Drop something?" Zouzab said. He was perched on top of the high shelf above them, smiling.

Janner and Tink tried to smile back. Tink told him that he'd seen a woodmouse scurrying about and was trying to catch it before it ruined any of Oskar's books.

"Oh, yes, I see woodmice in here all the time," Zouzab said. "I just"— quick as a flash, Zouzab scurried down the shelf and pretended to snatch at something—"sneak up and grab them before they even know what's happened."

Tink and Janner smiled uncomfortably, still not sure what to think of Zouzab Koit.

Zouzab scurried back up the shelf and disappeared again.

Janner elbowed Tink and nodded toward the entrance. For another fifteen minutes they took wrong turn after wrong turn, trying to find Leeli and Oskar.

They eventually found Oskar, very pleased with himself, holding a stack of at least ten large volumes, all on the subject of the whistleharp.

"Where's Leeli?" Janner asked.

"Eh?" Oskar said, peering down at them through his spectacles. "Oh! She went to check on that little dog of hers a while ago."

Janner's heart skipped a beat. Their first time into town since the incident that nearly killed them, and already he didn't know where she was. He told himself that he was overreacting, but the sick feeling in his stomach sent him running and calling her name, leaving Tink and Oskar standing there speechless.

Janner darted to and fro through the maddening twists and turns of the narrow aisles, trying to find his way back to the office. He rounded a corner and skidded to a stop right in front of Oskar and Tink, who had not moved. He was back where he started.

"I have to find Leeli!" Janner exploded.

Oskar blinked, shocked at Janner's tone of voice, but he dropped the books to the floor in a heap and shuffled forward, leading the way as fast as possible with Tink in the rear. Janner moved past him when he saw the office ahead and burst through the back door, praying that Leeli would be sitting there in the grass scratching Nugget's belly.

But she was nowhere to be seen.

The area behind Books and Crannies was empty except for the stack of old crates piled there two days prior. Beside the crates lay Leeli's new LIZARDKICKER crutch.

Janner felt his insides quake. He couldn't believe that already he had failed to protect his sister, and he had the sinking feeling that this time they wouldn't get out of it unscathed. He was dimly aware of Tink yelling Leeli's name as loudly as he could and Oskar shuffling around the corner of the building, calling for Leeli too.

Janner dropped to his knees, on the verge of tears. He was cycling through feelings of anger towards Leeli for stepping outside alone, anger toward Oskar for leaving her for even a moment, and guilt for once again failing Podo, Nia, and most importantly, Leeli.

Oskar came back around the corner. "She's not here," he said, worriedly adjusting his spectacles.

Suddenly, Nugget appeared, favoring one leg and whining.

"Nugget!" Tink cried, and he ran over to the little dog. "Where's Leeli, boy? Leeli?" Nugget pointed his nose across the field behind Oskar's shop and barked.

"There," said Zouzab from above them. He was standing on the roof again, pointing north toward a cluster of trees. "I can see something moving...there."

"Is it her?" Janner demanded, scrambling to his feet.

"It appears to be a Fang...and...yes, it's carrying something. I believe it's her," Zouzab finished, with a note of sadness in his voice.

With a roar, Janner leapt to his feet and ran as fast as he could for home. His only thought was that he had to find Podo because Podo would know what to do.

Janner and Tink both screamed his name the whole way up the lane to the cottage, and Podo, who had been hoeing in the garden, dropped his hoe and ran, stump and all, to meet them.

"WHERE'S MY GRANDDAUGHTER?" he bellowed.

Between breaths, Janner told him what happened, and in the middle of the story he started crying. He felt stupid for it, but he couldn't hold back the tears any longer.

Tink stood beside him awkwardly, staring at the ground and praying that Podo wouldn't be too hard on his big brother.

Without a word, Podo wheeled around and dashed to the barn.

"Grandpa, what do we do?" Tink called after him.

Podo emerged from the barn, suddenly astride their old carthorse Danny—but both Podo and Danny looked different. Danny was galloping like a war-horse, his mane whipping around like it was on fire, and there on his bare back sat Podo, wild white hair flying, his back hunched forward as he urged the horse on.

Janner thought his grandfather looked ten years younger and twice as strong.

"Stay here," Podo growled.

"But—" Janner said.

"STAY HERE!" Podo roared. The veins stood out on his neck, and his face turned red as a plum. He galloped away down the lane toward town, leaving his grandsons staring after him in awe.

27

A Trap for the Igibys

Leeli was having a miserable time. She had been slung over Slarb's shoulder like a sack of trullie roots. From her upside-down position she was able to see little other than her blond hair bouncing above her head and the grayish green scales of the Fang's shoulder and back.

Slarb's cool skin was smooth and damp, like leaves in the late morning, only the wetness on his scales surely wasn't anything as pleasant as morning dew. He stank, a sharp smell that reminded Leeli of the compost pile beside the garden, where she was often sent with vegetable peelings and scraps of food.

As unlikely as it might seem, Leeli actually found herself feeling sorry for Slarb. He probably had no friends, she thought, and no matter where he went he had to smell himself, unless of course he got used to it, but she dismissed that idea as impossible.

Any compassion she felt for the Fang vanished, however, as soon as she spoke to him.

"You'll—never—get—away—with—this," she said in between the bounces. "My—brothers—and—grandpa—will—"

Slarb snarled and squeezed his clawed hands tighter around her legs until she cried out. Leeli said no more.

The boys would soon notice she was missing, and Nugget hadn't let her down yet.

After a while she began to think that dying would be preferable to the awful stench.

She could tell that they had moved gradually uphill in the direction of Glipwood Forest, but there was nothing for her to do. If she somehow got free, she couldn't run away; she had dropped her crutch when Slarb grabbed her, and even if she had it, there was no chance of outrunning a Fang.

Finally they stopped. Slarb had been striding through the fields for half an hour and the only sound he had made was to growl at Leeli when she tried to speak to him. He stopped in a cluster of trees at the beginning of the forest, sniffing the air.

Leeli kept quiet and waited to see what he would do. Surely he wasn't planning to take her into the forest. Even Fangs knew that entering Glipwood Forest meant a fool's death.

Slarb chuckled to himself, a sickening sound, and threw Leeli to the ground. The fall jarred her and she bit her tongue hard enough to draw blood. She could taste it in her mouth as she fought back the tears. But Leeli brushed her hair out of her eyes, and looked up fiercely at Slarb.

The end of his tail flitted and rustled around on the leafy ground, the only sound that Leeli could hear other than his ragged breathing. His black eyes looked down on her without emotion.

"Your brothersss will be along shortly, I think," he said, and he slunk over to a nearby tree and leaned against it, a smirk on his scaly face.

Leeli lay on the ground thinking hard. She knew Slarb was right. She knew her brothers and that they'd come for her, but this once she didn't want them to. If Slarb didn't kill them, then there was a good chance that the creatures of the forest would. She didn't want them walking into a trap. Leeli looked around and saw a large gnarled glipwood tree a few feet behind her. She scooted back to lean against it.

Slarb heard her movement and he whipped his head toward her and hissed. His long, forked tongue slithered out of his mouth and over his fangs.

Leeli eased back against the tree. She knew Slarb didn't need much reason to kill her so she moved carefully. "I'm not going anywhere, Mister Fang, sir, I'm just leaning against the—"

"Sssilence!" he barked. "The only thing worse than the sssmell of you humans is the screech of your voices."

Leeli nodded, her heart pounding.

During the several minutes that passed, Slarb was silent, listening. He leaned against a tree, seemingly prepared to wait for days if need be.

Leeli's mind was still racing, but try as she might, she could think of nothing she could do. One thought kept coming to her mind. *Get out of here. Hobble as fast as your twisted leg will let you. Don't sit here and wait to watch your brothers die.* It was useless, but she couldn't bear to do nothing.

Leeli eased forward. Slarb took no notice. He had cocked his head to the side, listening to something. Just as Leeli summoned the courage to turn and try sneaking away, she heard a crash in the underbrush off to her right.

No! she thought. Leeli was certain that it was Janner and Tink, come to find her. Slarb slunk into the woods in the direction of the sound. Using the tree trunk for support, she got to her feet as quickly as she could.

"Run!" she screamed. "It's a trap! Run!" Then she turned and lurched through the brush, hopping along as swiftly as she could, waiting for her brothers' screams behind her. *Maybe they heard me in time,* she thought. *Maybe they were able to escape, or maybe they were able to hide long enough to cause Slarb to wander off in the wrong direction.* But maybe they were already dead.

Leeli burst from the cluster of trees and hobbled southward in the direction from which Slarb had carried her. Behind her, she heard a frustrated snarl and then the sound of Slarb coming after her, crashing through the brush. She pressed on, thinking only that she had to get away from the beast behind her. She cursed her twisted leg and the Fangs and the tall grass that slowed her down. Her dress caught on the limb of a duckflower bush, and it jerked her to a stop. Frantically, Leeli worked to loosen the snag and looked back in time to see Slarb flying toward her with his yellow fangs bared. She curled herself into a ball, squinted her eyes tightly shut, and prayed to the Maker that it would be over quickly.

28

Into the Forest

The boys ran to the cottage without a word. Nia flung the front door open and ran to meet them.

"Where's your grandfather? Where's Leeli?" she demanded.

Between breaths, they told her what had happened. She gave Janner a quick look of disappointment that cut to his heart. His stomach felt hollow and cold; there was nothing to do but wait.

Nia said as much. Janner could tell she was worried from the way she stood with her back straight and her shoulders squared. The more frightened she was, the tougher she looked.

Nia led the boys into the house, her hands on their shoulders. The brothers sat on the couch in front of the empty fireplace without speaking for a long time. Janner's eyes roamed the room, and everything he saw reminded him of his little sister—Nugget's pallet on the floor by the hearth, Leeli's whistleharp on the mantle. He thought with shame about the many times he had been frustrated at his sister for slowing him down, as if it were any choice of hers to have been born with a twisted leg. He thought about the times he had teased her for making such a fuss over Nugget, the dog who had done a better job of watching over her than he himself had. He imagined her pretty voice filling the house with music, and he missed her.

Janner slouched back in the couch and stared at the timbered ceiling, trying hard not to cry.

Slarb flew through the air toward Leeli, fangs bared in a vicious snarl. Too frightened to move, Leeli forced away the thoughts of the Fang's long teeth sinking into her, the poison coursing through her veins; in that heartbeat she thought of the warm cottage, the only home she'd ever known. She was sad that she'd never get to see it again.

Leeli imagined Janner, Tink, Podo, and Nia standing on the front lawn waving to her. And she thought of Nugget. She hoped that Janner and Tink would remember to feed him, and scratch his belly once in a while.

Suddenly, Slarb's growl was cut short. Trembling, Leeli opened her eyes and saw the Fang's claws clutching desperately at an arm locked tight around his throat.

She couldn't see the person's face, only a tuft of white hair sticking up from behind Slarb's shoulder—but the arm around Slarb's throat had a dirty knitted sock pulled up to the elbow.

Slarb's black eyes wheeled in their sockets as he scratched and dug into the socked arm, but it did no good. The arm held firm. Slarb staggered backward and turned away from Leeli, revealing lanky Peet the Sock Man, who was either brave enough or foolish enough (and maybe both) to attack a Fang barehanded, or *sock*-handed, as it turned out.

Peet's eyes were squeezed shut as he hung on desperately to the thrashing Fang. Slarb's teeth were bared and oozing with yellowish venom, but his movements were slowing down.

Leeli began to hope that just maybe she would live to see her family and Nugget again. Peet was grunting, straining to keep his grip on the twisting beast; though blood was soaking the sock where Slarb's claws were digging into Peet's forearm, he showed no sign of pain.

Slarb spun around, so fast that Peet's feet flew out behind him. The Fang lurched this way and that, his tail whipping the underbrush. Finally he fell first to one knee and then to the ground, unconscious.

Peet lay on top of Slarb, gasping for air. After a moment, he loosened his grip and carefully slid his arm out from under the creature's neck. When Peet saw Leeli he relaxed and stood up, brushing himself off as if embarrassed. Leeli was still crouched down in the brush at the edge of the trees, looking warily at her rescuer.

"Thank you," she said timidly. "That was very brave."

Peet watched her without speaking, still winded from his struggle.

She felt like she was talking to a scared animal, and her heart went out to him, much as it had gone out to Nugget when she'd found him as a puppy. Something about his face looked familiar—a thought that had never occurred to her before. She'd seen him bouncing through town, but she'd never really stopped and looked at the strange man before. She knew that he was prone to speaking gibberish to lampposts and attacking street signs, but she had never spoken to him. No one did. The Glipwood Township ignored him like a stray dog.

Leeli felt like she should have been scared, but she wasn't. Not only was there a Fang that was still alive, lying just a few feet away, but she was at the edge of Glipwood Forest. She was also in the presence of a man who, though he had just saved her life, was supposed to be as crazy as the Dark Sea was dark.[1] Somehow, though, she felt a peace that surprised her. She hobbled from behind the brush. Peet shrieked and scrambled backward.

"It's okay," Leeli said, again feeling as though she were calming a frightened puppy. Peet's eyes darted to and fro like a trapped animal. She stopped in front of him and smiled up at the tall, ragged man. "Is your name really Peet?"

His wild eyes finally settled on hers. She saw the jittery fear gone for a moment and detected a sorrow in his gray eyes that she hadn't noticed

---

1. From Stawburn's *The Wide Terrain*: "The Dark Sea of Darkness was no darker than any other ocean I ever sailed over. So I'm not sure where it got its name, unless maybe it's because of the feeling you get when you're out there in the middle of it. You feel like you might be guzzled up by any one of giant critters what live beneath the surface. It could get its name from all the storms that whirl up out of it and kick you and your ship around like a kid with a ball. Every night there's a fog that swallows up the stars and leaves you floating blind out there in the darkness. You get to feeling like you'll never make it home and that even your best mates on the ship don't really know you or want to, like they'd never notice if you toppled over the gunnel and plopped right in. Come to think of it, maybe the water *was* darker than normal."

before. He reached out a socked hand to touch her wild hair, and Leeli suddenly felt afraid again. She hopped back a step, tripped over Slarb's tail, and fell hard to the ground. Peet withdrew his hand and gasped as if he had touched a hot coal. The wildness crept back into his eyes.

Slarb groaned and strained to push himself up from the ground. One of his black eyes fluttered open and focused on Leeli.

She cried out and scrambled away, but Slarb wasn't going anywhere yet.

Peet kicked him, hard, slamming his scaled face back into the ground and knocking the Fang unconscious again. Then in one sweeping motion Peet stepped over to Leeli and scooped her into his arms. But she saw with horror that Peet the Sock Man wasn't carrying her home. He was taking her deeper into Glipwood Forest.

Podo reined up his horse at the edge of the trees. He hadn't entered Glipwood Forest since he was a boy, when hunters and rangers had kept the dangerous animals in check. Now here he was, an old man with one leg and no weapon to speak of, and the forest teeming with all manner of hungry beasts. Nugget was panting, staring fiercely into the shadowy wood.

Slarb's trail had been easy to spot. It led out of town, past several homes and farms. The closer Podo, Danny, and Nugget got to the border of the forest, the more the properties were run down and abandoned. Old fences slouched. Sad husks of homes stood charred and forlorn in the fields, where families once worked and lived and loved. These abandoned homes stood like gravestones scattered across the prairie. As he drove Danny northward, Podo thought back to his fine, green years as a boy in Glipwood, long before anyone had heard of Gnag the Nameless.

The memories stung him and filled him with rage.

"Aye, Nugget, she's in there." Podo nodded in the direction of the dark trees and patted Danny the carthorse's shoulder. "I reckon we ought to go get our girl." He clicked his tongue and Danny snapped into a gallop.

Though dusk had settled on the Igiby cottage, no fire burned in the hearth. No lanterns were lit. Janner, Tink, and Nia sat without speaking in the darkening house, waiting, as they had for hours.

"Mama?" Janner said finally. Nia looked up at him from the chair where she'd been sitting with her head bowed. "I'm sorry. I'm sorry I lost her again." Janner couldn't continue without crying, so he looked away.

Nia crossed the room and lit a lantern. She placed it on the windowsill, then sat down beside her older son.

"Hush, now. It'll be all right. It does no good to worry over what's already happened. What matters is now. The past and the future are both beyond our reach."

"I'm afraid she might not come back," Tink said.

"You have to think hard about the very thing before you, dear. Nothing else. To think too long on what might happen is a fool's business. Right now, for your Podo, the thing before him is to find Leeli, not to think about how it happened or who's to blame. And the thing before us is to wait in this old cottage without giving up hope. Even if hope is just a low ember at night, in the morning you can still start a fire."

Janner couldn't hold his tongue. "Is that why you and Grandpa never talk about our father? Because 'the past is beyond our reach?'" Tears filled his eyes. "If Leeli never comes back, will we just pretend like she never existed, the way you do with—Esben?"

Nia stiffened.

Janner stared at the floor and fidgeted with the hem of his shirt. He hated the tension he felt in the room, but he couldn't apologize. He knew Nia was right about hope. He felt it in his bones. But he couldn't bear the way his mother and Podo had buried the memories of his father, whoever he was.

"Janner."

He looked up at his mother. She was a picture of strength. Her elegant jaw was set, her head was erect and her posture firm. But her eyes were churning with conflicting emotions. She looked like she might at any moment burst into tears of either sorrow or anger. "I know it's hard for you, but you have to trust me," she said. "There are things you don't understand."

He rolled his eyes and looked away, but she took his chin in her firm hand and turned his face to hers. "One day you'll know why we don't speak of your father. You both will," she added, looking at Tink. "But he's been dead many years, and your sister yet lives…I hope." Nia looked out the window into the near dark and put a hand to her mouth. "Someone's coming."

Janner leapt to his feet and flung open the door. He saw the shadowy form on horseback making his way up the path to the house. No one dared to breathe. Finally Janner saw that it was, indeed, Podo on old Danny's back and Nugget trotting along beside them, but he couldn't tell if Leeli was there. Janner had a dreadful feeling that earlier that day at Oskar's was the last time he would ever see his sister.

Tink ran to meet his grandfather and the others followed. When he was still a stone's throw away they heard Podo's voice call out in the fading light.

"I've got her," he said. "She's fine."

Tink whooped with joy and ran to help Leeli from the tired horse.

Janner nearly collapsed with relief. He looked over at his mother, who was standing in the doorway with her hands folded tight at her chest. Her eyes caught the last light of the evening, glowing like embers smoldering long into the night.

Cave Blats and Quill Diggles

Inside, each Igiby fussed over Leeli and helped her to sit with a very happy Nugget. Janner set to making a fire. He and Tink showered Podo and Leeli, who was giggling, with questions about the details. But Nia told them to give their poor sister and grandfather time to rest.

Podo eased himself into his chair with a groan and propped his one leg up on the footstool while Nia herded the boys into the kitchen to help her prepare dinner.

In a short while they brought out steaming bowls of henmeat soup on a tray. They sat around the fire and sipped the broth, the boys in anguish from having to wait so long for the story. Podo cleared his throat, and the room was silent but for the crackling of the fire.

"I never found the gut-sucking Fang that took 'er," Podo began with a sigh. He savored the anticipation and slurped his soup, grunting with pleasure and nodding appreciatively at Nia. "But little Nugget here." He patted Nugget's head. "Nugget found the stinker's tracks, didn't ya, boy?"

Nugget wagged his tail and yipped.

"It was Slarb," Leeli said, and all eyes turned to her. "He snatched me from behind Mister Oskar's and took me to the forest, hoping that you'd all come after me."

Nia looked sharply at Podo, who told about how he had come to the edge of the forest and found signs of a scuffle and two sets of tracks leading away from each other. He chose to follow the human tracks, and they led deeper into the forest than he'd ever been.

Janner thought about the horned hounds and shuddered.

Tink asked if Podo had seen any toothy cows. "No, lad, and thank the Maker I didn't. But a cave blat attacked me. Tall as a tree if it was an inch," Podo declared, "and claws like knives. But ol' Danny the carthorse kicked it square in the jaw, and the blat yelped and scurried off."

Tink asked how something as tall as a tree could "scurry," but Podo continued as if he didn't hear.[1]

"The going was rougher the farther I went. At first it was only a few wee gullies and ol' Danny could get down 'em without much trouble, but after a while I was thinking twice before I spurred 'im down there. Deep they were, and I've only got one leg, y'know," he said with a frustrated swipe at his stump. "And then I heard a noise," he said in a whisper. They leaned in close, even Nia.

"We were—" Leeli began, but Podo shushed her.

"Hold on, honey; ye gotta build suspense, see." He paused for effect, and Leeli tried not to laugh.

"Oh, get on with it," Nia said.

"Can I tell the story here?" Podo asked, offended.

"Well I don't know," Nia said. "*Can* you?"

"I can if I don't have any more interruptions," Podo growled, mumbling something about people these days not knowing a good story if it stung them in the rump. "So anyway, I heard someone singing—but it weren't our Leeli here. Now that's enough to scare an old fella half to death, hearing a song in the belly of a dark wood when the only thing he's heard for the last hour is the snort of a horse and his own toots."

Nia rolled her eyes and put her face in her hands.

"So I start looking all around, thinking I must've heard wrong, when it comes again: a voice singing. All of a sudden, Nugget here barks a fury,

---

1. The presence of cave blats in Glipwood Forest may come as a surprise to the diligent reader, because of the usual lack of caves in a proper forest. Cave blats received their names because their large gray eyes and jowly countenances are so unpleasant to behold that it is common, upon seeing one, to think, "I wish that blat were in a cave somewhere, so that I might not have to look at it."

and I look at 'im and he's barking up a tree. At first I think, *Now ain't the time to be fussing over thwaps!* But right then a quill diggle the size of a goat comes out of nowhere and starts baring its fangs and circling. Its quills were raised, and it started screaming like a hawk, and I thought, *Well, it's a good thing I brought my fork from the house, otherwise I wouldn't have anything to fight with at all.* So I knew I didn't have much time before the diggle's quills came flying, and I threw my fork as hard as I could—" He stopped, looking down dramatically.

"And?" Janner asked, taking the bait.

Podo looked back up, relishing the suspense. "And I missed," he said with a shrug, leaning back in his chair. "The fool thing stuck in the ground about a foot in front of the critter. 'Brilliant,' says I, wonderin' what to do next. That critter hissed and jumped back and turned to sling its quills. But just before it did, I saw the last thing I ever expected."

Podo enjoyed a long, noisy sip of cider while the Igibys waited on the edge of their seats. "Swinging on a vine from somewhere come that crazy fella from town, Peet the Sock Man." Janner noticed Nia's and Podo's eyes meet at the mention of Peet, as if they'd had a whole conversation in that one moment. But Podo continued so smoothly that Janner wondered if he hadn't imagined it.

"He saved me," Leeli piped in, speaking fast. "He fought Slarb and took me to his house in the forest. It was wonderful, even though he smelled like a rotten onion berry."

"So back to the quill diggle," Podo said impatiently. "Peet the Sock Man swung down with a staff and smacked that diggle so hard it turned inside out, and while it was scurrying away, he took a stone out of a pouch and threw it at least a mile and hit it square in the head."

Janner's jaw dropped. "It was Peet!" he said. "It was Peet who threw the rocks at the Fangs that attacked Leeli before, wasn't it?" They all looked at him.

"Well, it might have been," Nia said, "but no one saw him, so we can't know for sure, can we?"

"Well, no, but who else—"

"What happened next, Papa?" Nia said curtly.

Podo cleared his throat. "So, as I was saying, we were standing right underneath a tree house way up in the top of a glipwood tree and sure enough, there was little Leeli, safe and sound, wavin' down at ol' Podo like she was on holiday."

"So the Sock Man didn't try to hurt you?" Tink asked. "He always gives me the weirds."

"No!" Leeli said. "He fought that Fang all by himself and took me to his tree house. He has lots of books and a rope ladder, and he just needs some friends. Mama, can we bring him some food? All he eats is animals from the forest. He kept the diggle and said he was going to eat it later— and it wasn't really inside out, by the way—but I just thought that maybe we could help him—"

"We'll see," Nia said, with a wave of her hand. "Enough talk about this Sock Man character. I'm glad he saved you, dear, but it's plain that he's not right in the head. Now it's time you children get ready for bed. You need rest."

Nia peeked her head through the door to the children's bedroom. She listened for a moment and heard the deep breathing of sleep coming from all three. Only Nugget stirred. Snuggled tightly beside Leeli, he raised his head, cocked it to one side, and wagged his tail slowly for Nia. Nodding to Nugget, she smiled and pulled the door closed.

Podo was nearly asleep in his chair with his leg propped up on the footstool. He had unstrapped his peg leg and the wooden stump lay on the floor beside him.

"Fire's getting low, lass," he said with a yawn.

Nia sat down on the couch and yawned too. She stared at the flames and thought long before speaking.

"He can't come near them, Papa."

"Eh?" he said, scratching his head and stifling another yawn.

"Peet."

"Ah." Podo roused a little and stared into the fire as well. They were silent for a long time again.

"Tomorrow morning I'll have a talk with the children," Nia said. "I'll forbid them to ever speak with him again." She sighed and let her hair down from the bun. "These last few days have been the longest I've lived through since we came here, Papa, and I pray to the Maker that the danger passes soon. If my maggotloaf is good, and if we can last until that Fang, Sloop—"

"Slarb."

"—is transferred to another village, I think we'll be all right. At least we'll be together. And we'll be alive."[2]

"Aw, but this ain't life, lass!" Podo said. "Not as it's meant to be. Do you see the way the people's heads bow? Do you see the fear that leaks out of 'em and sits on this town like a fog on the sea? Bah! They've forgotten what it is to live anymore. But yer Podo hasn't." He smiled at the fire and closed his eyes. "Today when I was ridin' through the wood I remembered what it was like to have the wind in me hair and the world unrollin' before me eyes." Podo looked hard at Nia. "If Esben was still kickin', he'd have a thing or two to say about these Fangs breathin' their venom down our necks. He'd have somethin' to say about that Carriage rattlin' up these hills to carry off the youngsters—"

"Enough, Papa. He's not here. And that recklessness is exactly what got him killed."

"No, lass," Podo said. "The Fangs is what got 'im killed."

"But if he had run, if he had come with us and laid low, then he'd be

---

2. Though the Skreeans weren't sure why, the Fang soldiers were rotated from town to town regularly, and each regiment sailed from Fort Lamendron back to Dang for a few weeks each year. Fangs returning to Skree would boast of having been "rested up plenty" and were meaner than usual for the first few months.

here now—" Nia cut herself short. She was on the verge of tears. "He'd be here now," she repeated to herself.

Podo put one of his weathered old hands on her arm.

"It's all right, lass. And don't you worry about having any long talk with the bitties about ol' Peet the Sock Man. You know as well as I do that for young lads, a warning is about the same as an invitation. They'll not be able to stop thinkin' about 'im if you do that. I say just let it go." His voice grew dangerous. "And I'll take care of ol' Peet. Don't you worry about him coming near the children again. I'd say he's done quite enough."

Nia said nothing as she stared sadly at the dying fire, struggling to burn.

30

The Untimely Death of Vop

As Nia and Podo bade one another good night, Slarb limped back to the jail with a swollen face and a large bleeding wound on his leg. He had woken in the forest clearing with an awful headache and a ratbadger chewing on his leg. Slarb had snatched it up, sunk his fangs into its neck with a growl, and tossed the limp creature into the woods. Several seconds had passed before he even remembered what he had been doing there in the forest. But as he staggered back toward town, Slarb imagined himself eating the Igiby children one by one, along with their little dog.

The *clop* of hoofbeats coming toward him interrupted the reverie. Slarb dropped into the high grass just in time to spy Podo Helmer trot by in the direction from which he had just come. When he saw Nugget beside the horse, Slarb nearly sprang from his cover. By now, his hatred for the indestructible little dog equaled his hatred for the children who had humiliated him so.

But the humiliation for Slarb the Fang was just beginning.

The Fangs of Dang, it was widely known, were rarely injured. They certainly weren't in much danger from the Skreeans, who had no weapons and who seemed to have very little courage. The only time a Fang was ever hurt was when a fellow soldier inflicted the wound during a scuffle over a gold bracelet or a bowl of booger gruel.[1]

---

1. The recipe for booger gruel, according to sources in Dugtown, is simple: two cups of flour, a teaspoon of crushed basil, and one gallon of viscous nasal matter from any animal on hand. Stir over low heat until thickened. (The method of collecting said mucus is unclear.)

Slarb limped up the steps to the jail, hoping to find a bandage for his wound. The other Fangs stopped what they were doing and gaped as he passed. Slarb's face was horribly swollen, he was covered with dirt, and his leg was bleeding steadily from the ratbadger bite. The Fangs burst out laughing and asked him what had happened.

Slarb the Fang sat in the front room of the jail and dressed his wound beneath an onslaught of scorn from fellow Fangs. He could only bear the derision for so long, however. He finished applying the bandage to his leg, and without warning he lashed out at the closest Fang, a brute named Vop.

They tumbled and snarled and broke every piece of what little furniture there was in the front room of the jail. They rolled on the floor, punching and scratching and biting one another while the others watched and cheered for Vop.

With a yell, Vop flipped Slarb over his head and slammed him into the wall at the target where the many throwing daggers were stuck. Several daggers clattered to the floor.

Slarb pulled himself to his feet, insane with anger, and grabbed one of the daggers. He flung one at Vop, who was receiving congratulations from the watching soldiers for winning the scuffle. With a sickening crunch, the knife buried itself in Vop's back. The Fangs stopped laughing and watched in shock as he fell lifeless to the floor.

Slarb stood alone, breathing hard with a smirk on his face.

The Fangs disliked Slarb already. Now he had stabbed one of them in the back.

"He killed ol' Vop, he did," said one, looking down at Vop with surprise.

"Vop was a fine Fang to have around for a good chuckle," said another.

"An' he didn't exactly ssstart the tussle either," said Brak, who narrowed his eyes at Slarb. "It was Slarb what started it, and ol' Slarb there went an' got 'im when he weren't lookin'."

"I've knowed Vop sssince we come over from Dang," said one, sniffing.

"We burned lots of villages down together, me an' him. Tossed me first kid ssscreamin' into the Carriage with him, I did."

"Commander Gnorm took a ssspecial liking to ol' Vop. Said he was like the nephew he never had," said another, sliding his sword from its sheath.

The more they glared at Slarb, the more he stared at the door. The gang of angry Fangs took a collective step toward him, hands outstretched, weapons drawn, as Slarb sprang for the door. But it was too late. The Fangs groped, but Slarb wriggled, screamed, and in a moment was shocked to find himself bounding down the steps of the jail amidst a hail of insults and curses.

Slarb ran and ran, out of Glipwood and up the long road toward Torrboro, though he didn't know where he was going. He no longer felt the rat-badger wound on his leg or the bulge on the side of his head where Peet the Sock Man had kicked him. He knew that Commander Gnorm would order his execution when he returned to find Vop stabbed in the back. But Slarb no longer cared about that either.

The cold, white moon shone on him with disdain as Slarb ran, grinning madly, his twisted mind thinking of nothing at all.

Except, that is, for his hatred of the Igibys.

31

Khrak's Medallion

Over a breakfast of bacon and fried totatoes the next morning, Janner had a feeling for the first time in a week that everything was going to be all right. The breakfast was good, the sun was shining, no one was hurt, and he had three new books to read. Hopefully, Slarb had gotten the message that interfering with the Igiby children wasn't a good idea. In the past few days, as far as Janner knew, Slarb had been knocked unconscious by a rock, clouted by Commander Gnorm, and nearly strangled by Peet the Sock Man. He may even have been eaten whole by some hungry beast of the forest.

Still, Podo and Nia had decided everyone should stay close to the house for a few days until the dust settled. It had been an eventful week, and neither Podo, Nia, nor Leeli even knew about Janner and Tink's encounter with the horned hounds and the weapons in the cellar of Anklejelly Manor.

Podo was pleased to have collected and delivered five more garden thwaps for his old rival, Buzzard Willie. It was as if the pirate had found a new purpose in collecting and redepositing thwaps in his old age. Though he had repented of his wild days at sea, he cackled with glee while he snuck around to Willie's garden to set loose the thwaps.

The children, under Nia's tutelage, were hard at work on their T.H.A.G.S.

Janner was toiling over a poem Nia had instructed him to compose. The subject matter was the Sea Dragon Festival, and he sat trying to think of something to rhyme with "festival" other than "best of all."

Tink, barefoot and lounging in the crook of an old tree, was sketching a fazzle dove that had nested in the hollow of a nearby oak. It was his third attempt at getting it just right, and he squinted at the drawing and cocked his head this way and that.

Just outside the back door of the cottage, Leeli practiced her whistle-harp while Nugget dozed at her feet.

Life at the Igiby cottage seemed to be returning to normal.

"Ah, 'Dougan's Reel,'[1] an ancient tune from the Green Hollows," Oskar N. Reteep was pleased to inform Leeli from around the corner of the cottage. "Splendid."

He had come over to check on Leeli and offer profuse apologies for allowing her out of his sight. He carried her little crutch under his arm.

"In the words of the famed shoe burglar Hanwyt Moor, 'I'm so sorry. It won't happen again.'" He held out the crutch. "And you must be Lizard-kicker, I presume?"

Leeli hugged Mr. Reteep around his sizable waist.

"May I still come over and borrow books sometimes, sir?" she asked.

"Of course! Of course, young princess! More than ever now."

---

1. Dougan dol Rona of the Green Hollows. The Hollowsfolk are known primarily for two things: fruit and fighting. The Green Hollows is a country of rolling vales and vineyards, tended to with affection by its citizens. The fruit of the Hollows is fatter, juicier, and tastier than any in all of Aerwiar, partly because the ground is so fertile and partly because of thousands of years of fruiting lore known only by the Hollowsfolk. The Green Hollows is also known for its annual festival of games, called the Fynneg Durga. The men of the Hollows are notoriously boisterous, willing to wrestle as soon as laugh, and they consider a punching contest entertainment of the highest order, especially if it means a lost tooth or a broken nose. The women of the Hollows are famously beautiful and wise, which is probably the ancient cause for the culture of fighting among the men. Any outsider wishing to marry a woman of the Green Hollows was subjected to violent (but good-natured) ridicule and was obligated to participate in an especially brutal version of the games, the Banick Durga, to win the woman's hand. Whether or not the contender passed the trial, he was awarded with copious fruit. Dougan dol Rona of Dorminey asked for the hand of Meirabel Lannerty of the Hollows and was forced to compete in the Banick Durga for her hand. Amazingly, he bested the men of the Hollows in all the ten bouts, but quite accidentally killed Meirabel's brother in a boxing match with an ill-placed blow to the temple. The tune "Dougan's Reel" (composer unknown) captures in song both Dougan's sorrow that he would never marry Meirabel and the speed with which he ran for his life from the Hollows men.

Nia smiled and welcomed in Oskar for a cup of cider.

Just as they were sitting down, Podo returned from his errand at Buzzard Willie's garden, and he greeted Oskar stiffly.

Oskar squirmed beneath Podo's gaze.

"Podo, you must know how sorry I am," Oskar said, his eyes downcast. He nervously pressed a stray lock of white hair across his forehead. "Had I known…had I known that the Fang was nearby, I never would have…" He trailed off, trying to think of an author to quote.

Podo softened and shrugged it off with a wave of his hand as he sat down at the table beside Nia. "No harm done," he said, with what he meant to be a light punch to Oskar's shoulder. It jarred Oskar so that his spectacles were left dangling off one ear. Podo didn't notice.

"The word at Shaggy's Tavern is that Commander Gnorm is back from Torrboro and that he ain't happy," Podo said. "Blaggus said that he heard 'im yelling at the top of his lizard lungs about somethin' having to do with Slarb. Said he heard that Slarb killed another Fang."

Oskar rubbed his shoulder and straightened his glasses. "A dead Fang? I don't believe I've ever seen one of those."

"They're not much to look at," Podo said. "All dust and bones."

Oskar raised an eyebrow.

"Or so I've heard," Podo added.

"And Slomp?" Nia asked.

"Slarb, dear," corrected Oskar.

"Well, that's the odd bit," Podo said. "Shaggy says he ain't been seen since he killed the other fella. Said he ran off and never came back. I reckon if he did come back Gnorm would kill 'im as dead as the other one." Podo looked out the window. "I have a feelin' we might be rid of that stinker once and for good."

"Until we're certain, I don't want the children going into town alone," Nia said.

"Aye, we'll lie quiet for a few days," Podo agreed. "But there's no sense hidin' like cave blats for the rest of our lives, lass. Besides, now that the festival is over all but a few of 'em will be heading back to Torrboro. Things'll be back to normal soon enough."

"And I assure you," said Oskar earnestly, "the children will be safe at Books and Crannies—should you choose to trust me with their company again." He looked at his hands.

"Ol' geezer, didn't ye hear what I said? No harm done! And that's that." Podo leaned over with a smile and playfully whacked Oskar on the shoulder again, this time sending his glasses clattering to the floor.

Hoping to avoid any further displays of friendship from Podo, Oskar bade them farewell. He stepped out of the cottage and found Tink leaning against the tree drawing on parchment. Oskar waved Tink over to him and whispered, "And this is for you, lad. I found it very helpful, myself."

He slipped Tink a small book and cleared his throat. With a sympathetic pat to Tink's head, he strolled down the lane.

Tink looked down at the book in his hands. *Homemade Rash Remedies: A Study in Discomfort.*

General Khrak was tired of meeting with Fang commanders. All week he had suffered their impudence, their whining, and their groveling, though the groveling pleased him and eased his suffering considerably. The sun was getting low in Torrboro, and he was staring at the rain out the high window of the Castle Torr, ignoring Commander Plube, a Fang with a habit of laughing at his own jokes. Khrak was considering having him executed for his bad sense of humor.

"So this human walks into a tavern and says to the two-headed hogpig, 'Who let out the goats?' And the hogpig, he says, 'I did, and what of it?' And so the human, he says, 'Oh, nothing,' and he takes the hogpig by the tail and—"

Plube stopped midsentence as Khrak rose from his throne and descended the steps, fixing him with an alarming gaze. The chamber was empty but for General Khrak and Plube. The greasy smile on his face melted away as Khrak approached until their noses were nearly touching. Plube was quivering in his armor. Never once during one of their meetings had Khrak left his throne, much less climbed down the steps.

Plube closed his eyes and awaited the death that was sure to come. He had always fancied that Khrak enjoyed his jokes and stories. In his opinion, they made reporting on his boring precinct of Skree much less drab, and Khrak always seemed so humorless. He was only trying to help.

General Khrak said nothing. He merely stared, waiting for Plube to open his eyes. One eyelid eased open, then the other. Plube relaxed a little, chuckling warily.

"Go. And I don't ever want to hear another story about a hogpig in a tavern. Ever."

"Y-yesss, lord," Plube stammered feebly as he backed away. He tripped over himself in his haste, and when he fell, General Khrak laughed for the first time all week. The door thudded shut behind him and Khrak yawned. He was hungry.

"SSSlave!" he said, and an old woman in tattered clothes shuffled into the room, bowing all the while. "Have a bowlful of ratbadger-tail salad brought to my chambers. And make sssure the lettuce is perfectly brown this time!" She bowed out of the room in a flurry of mumbles and apologies, and the Fang made his way through filth-strewn hallways to his chambers.

He slunk into a chair and waited for his meal. He would be leaving the next new moon for the Castle Throg, and he always had to prepare his mind for that journey. Gnag had summoned him, which meant that he would spend four weeks crossing the Dark Sea of Darkness; then a long, dry trek across the barren Woes of Shreve to the Killridge Mountains, where the Nameless One made his home. He dreaded the journey. Here in Skree he was General Khrak, ruler of the land; but in the Castle Throg, he was the one groveling, he was the slave. No matter. It was a small price to pay for the power he wielded in Skree.

Gnag had plans to widen his kingdom, to build a larger army, and if Gnag remained pleased with his service then it would be he, General Khrak, who led the great army into the Far West. He closed his eyes and reveled in the destruction he would visit on the peoples beyond the maps. He wanted that command. He was a Fang of Dang, made for war, yet here he was in Torrboro wasting his days with fools like Plube.

True, he enjoyed the food and the fine filth of the place, and he enjoyed the groveling he received. But he felt that if he had to spend much more time listening to precinct commanders babbling on about the humans in their measly towns, he would gnaw off his own foot. Khrak stood up and paced. If only he could find the Jewels of Anniera. That would change everything. Gnag would let him do whatever he pleased.

The old woman entered with a bowl of still-wriggling ratbadger tails on a brown, slimy bed of lettuce. The ratbadger tails were like living, hairy noodles, as fat as fingers. Khrak grabbed the bowl, held it to his face, and breathed in the rank aroma.

"And your favorite sweat sauce, lord," the woman said, her voice quavering slightly. That Khrak had let her go without injury was a sign that he was pleased with the meal.

Khrak sat and slurped up his first ratbadger tail and sighed, slouching back in his chair again.

Out of habit, his hand wandered to the medallion hanging around his neck. His newest piece of jewelry, courtesy of…who was it? Ah. Commander Gnorm, the fat one, a few days earlier. From Glipwood.

Khrak dipped another tail in the sweat sauce and chewed on it thoughtfully while he toyed with the medallion. He looked at it closely for the first time, admiring the rubies that adorned its edges, caressing it with his scaly fingers. He gobbled another tail while he flipped the medallion over and examined the back—and choked.

Khrak leapt from his chair and spat the ratbadger tail to the floor. He moved across the room to a lantern that burned in a sconce on the wall and held the medallion up to the light. There, engraved on the back of the medallion, was a dragon with wings.

The Seal of Anniera.

Could it be? he wondered, his mind whirling. *In Glipwood? After all these years?*

General Khrak laughed for the second time that day.

32

The Making of a Maggotloaf

As trouble escalated with the Fangs, Nia knew it was time to turn her attention to preparing Gnorm's maggotloaf.

She laid two slabs of henmeat on the compost pile, where bugs were sure to find them. When she checked on the meat the next day, it was putrid and sweating. She nodded to herself and tried to think of other repulsive ingredients.

At dinner she announced that all members of the Igiby clan were to cut their fingernails and place them in a bowl by the kitchen door for the remainder of their lives, or until Gnorm was transferred to another town. Nugget sniffed out a firebug nest at the base of a tree, and Nia made a thick paste by mashing a bowlful of the bugs with a rock. She would never have admitted it, but she was enjoying trying to make a meal as disgusting as possible.

Then it rained for two days. The rain kept the children inside and miserable, so they had no choice but to work on their T.H.A.G.S. for hours at a time. But Nia was glad for the rain because it bade worms from the ground. She had Tink and Janner collect bowls full of the crawlers and added them to the firebug paste.

On the third day, the rain blew over and the sun shone hot again. Nia donned a pair of gloves, wrapped a scarf around her face, and gathered the spoiled henmeat from the compost pile. The meat was whitish, moist, and to Nia's relief, teeming with maggots. She baked it all into a plump, moist loaf and garnished it with a dash of Nugget's fur.

Nia placed the oozing loaf on a platter, covered it with a rag, and she and the children set out down the lane for town. A foul odor trailed out behind them like a black cloud and summoned flies to follow. The children were to wait in Oskar's bookstore while she delivered the loaf to Gnorm at the jail.

"If, and only if, I discover that Slarb hasn't returned, may you be permitted to stay at Oskar's for the afternoon," Nia said, holding the maggotloaf at arm's length. "Whatever you do, stay clear of the Fangs. And stay together."

She looked at Janner, who nodded. He wouldn't let Leeli or Tink out of his sight again, no matter what.

They walked the rest of the way without speaking, the only sound the buzzing of flies that floated from beneath the cloth.

Once in town, Janner herded Tink and Leeli into Books and Crannies, where they watched from the window. Zouzab dangled upside down, spiderlike, from a rafter and peeked out as well. Boldly, Nia walked up the steps of the jail and with the slightest bow presented her sordid meal to Commander Gnorm.

Janner, Tink, and Leeli shifted to see more clearly. Nia's back was to them and all they could see was Gnorm sitting in his rocking chair, sharpening his dagger, his boots propped upon the porch railing. Nia stood before him for what felt like hours while the children and Zouzab watched in tense silence. Finally, she turned and walked away. She looked directly at the window of Books and Crannies and nodded with a tight smile. Janner, Tink, and Leeli sighed in unison with relief. They could see Gnorm gobbling away in a cloud of flies, his face buried in the maggotloaf.

"It would appear that your mother has pleased the Fang," said Zouzab. He flipped up into the rafters, hopped over to a high shelf, and smiled down at the children. "Perhaps now you'll visit more often?" he said, and without waiting for an answer, he disappeared.

Janner felt a wave of relief wash over him. The nod from Nia meant that Slarb was gone. Life just might return to its normal slow pace, and to Janner's surprise, he was glad. But he had questions—and many of them about the lanky fellow with the socks on his arms now rolling head over heels down the dusty street before them. Janner studied Peet like never before. Used to be Peet only came to mind when he was skipping through town with a stick in his mouth or juggling buckets by the cliffs. Now Janner couldn't help watching for him and wondering about him.

"Tell us about his tree house," Janner said, staring after Peet.

"And his smell," Tink added.

"And his books," Janner said.

Leeli looked annoyed at her brothers.

Janner pulled her and Tink to the floor near the window, where they could hunker, watchful of Peet in the distance. Outside, Nugget wagged his tail and stared at the door, patiently waiting for Leeli.

"Did he say anything the whole time you were with him?" Tink wanted to know between bites on a length of tumtaffy.

"No, I already told you," Leeli said. Her defensiveness about Peet reminded Janner of the way she was about Nugget before he learned not to lift his leg indoors. "When he got me up the rope ladder and into the tree house, he said I was safe. Other than that he just sat in the corner like he was afraid of me. I tried to talk to him but he just sat there, wrapping and unwrapping a piece of string around his wrist. He started rocking back and forth and humming something, and I think it was the most beautiful song I've ever heard. It made me sleepy, so I curled up against the wall. I guess I fell asleep. Like I said, the next thing I heard was an awful screeching sound."

"The quill diggle," Tink said.

"Yes, and that's everything. I called to Grandpa when I saw him, then Peet carried me down. Grandpa doesn't seem to like Peet very much, but he did tell him thanks. Then we got out of the forest as fast as we could."

"But what kind of books were they?" Janner pressed.

Leeli huffed. "I couldn't tell. They had leather covers with designs on them. There was an old chest in the corner and a pile of junk. I wasn't there long before I fell asleep." She smiled to herself. "And when I woke up he had put a blanket on me."

After a moment Tink whispered, "Do you think you could remember how to get to his tree house again?" Leeli looked at him like he was crazy. "Even if I could I wouldn't tell you. Grandpa was on a horse, and he was still attacked by a blat and a diggle. What if he'd been attacked by a toothy cow? It's miles into the forest. Don't be silly."

"I didn't say I was going out there," Tink said, taking another bite of tumtaffy.

"Well then, why did you ask?"

Tink shrugged.

Janner was quiet, staring in the direction of the forest.

"What are you thinking about?" Leeli asked.

Janner thought for a moment before he spoke. "That makes twice now that Peet has come to our rescue—first with the rocks in the alley, then with you in the forest. I think he's looking out for us."

"You don't know that it was Peet who threw those rocks," Leeli said, glancing at the ceiling. She lowered her voice. "It could have been Zouzab. It could have been anyone."

Janner looked out the window to see Peet rolling around the corner at J. Bird's barbershop. "All I'm saying is it's a little strange."

"Leeli, how far away was that snapping diggle when Peet threw the rock at it?" Tink asked.

"I don't know, maybe…from here to…" Leeli squinted at the building across the street. "Here, to the jail."

"There's something I haven't told you," Janner said, voice lowered. "The night we got out of jail I overheard Ma and Grandpa talking—talking like they knew who threw the stones, and they didn't want us to know."

"Look." Leeli pointed out the window at their grandfather making his way up Main Street.

Podo stomped along at a steady pace with his arms swinging and a nasty scowl on his face. He stopped and looked up and down the street before turning up the narrow alley at J. Bird's, the same alley where Peet had just gone.

"What's he doing?" Janner asked, as he peered above Tink and Leeli.

A few moments later, Peet the Sock Man flew around the corner, weeping like a child and bleeding from his lip. He was running like a frightened animal, and Leeli's heart broke for him.

Podo reappeared at the corner and brushed himself off before marching back in the direction of the cottage.

"What was that all about?" Janner wondered aloud. "Did Grandpa just hit him?"

"I'm following him," Tink said, looking in the direction that Peet had run.

"No!" Leeli said.

"I'm following Peet," Tink repeated, wiping taffy-covered hands on the front of his shirt. "You can stay here if you like, but I want to know where he's going." Before anyone could stop him, Tink stepped away from the window, opened the front door, and started down the street.

"Tink," Janner yelled. "Tink!"

But Tink kept walking.

"Come on," Janner growled. "We have to get him."

"What about Mister Reteep?" Leeli asked.

Janner stopped. "Just wait here." He shot down the aisle that he thought might lead to Oskar's desk and came back a few minutes later, out of breath. "Let's go. I just told him we finished and we were leaving. He didn't even look up from his book."

"But—"

"I know it's ridiculous, but I can't just let Tink go by himself. We have to stay together." Janner handed Leeli the crutch and held the door for her. "Feel free to try to talk him out of it, but you know Tink. He's following Peet, whether we come or not."

When they caught up with him, Tink was peeking around the corner of The Only Inn.

"I thought you guys would never make it," he said with a wink.

"This isn't a good idea," Leeli said. "You know, Mama said—"

"There he goes," Tink whispered, looking over Leeli's shoulder, and he was gone.

Leeli watched Tink jog north, up Vibbly Way.

Nugget whined, eager to run.

With a sigh of resignation, Janner held out an arm to his sister. "After you."

33

Bridges and Boughs

Tink raced up the slow rise of the land, past the last houses of Glipwood, with Janner, Leeli, and Nugget just a few paces behind. Now and again Tink would catch a glimpse of Peet's white hair dashing through a field, and he would speed up to keep the Sock Man in sight.

Janner didn't like how close they were getting to the forest. They weren't as far from town as Anklejelly Manor, where the forest was older and wilder, but the trees here were thickening, and they made Janner nervous.

After several minutes Tink stopped before a run-down house, roofless and charred, standing in a cluster of mossy oaks. Janner and Leeli caught up to him and the three of them stood, panting in the middle of the dusty road.

"You see him?" Janner asked, hoping that they'd lost Peet.

The three Igibys peered through the boughs that covered the way to the building.

"We probably should turn back." Janner nervously eyed the forest. "I think you're forgetting our little incident with the *you-know-whats* at the *you-know-where*."

"What are you talking about?" Leeli asked.

"At the manor?" Tink asked, scanning the yard for signs of the Sock Man. "Aw, this is nothing like that. Besides," he looked at Janner, "if you're so sure Peet's looking out for us, we shouldn't have anything to worry about, right?"

Leeli thumped her crutch on the ground. "*What* manor?"

"I'll tell you later," Janner said, and she huffed, crossing her arms across her chest.

"Look!" Tink said. A short distance to their right, Peet was running through the trees behind the old house. But as suddenly as they had seen him, Peet disappeared.

"Now how did he do that?" Tink wondered aloud.

Silence, except for the songs of a few strange birds and an occasional growl from Tink's stomach.

"Let's go," Janner whispered, though he too was scanning the area for Peet. "There's no telling where he went. Now come on."

Tink stared into the treetops, paying Janner no mind.

"Fine, then," Janner said. "Come on, Leeli. Let's go home."

Leeli didn't argue.

Janner took her hand and they turned to go, hoping Tink would give up and follow once he saw they meant to leave. But within ten paces, Janner realized the threat of leaving Tink alone wasn't working.

Tink was still scanning the trees, still looking for Peet.

"Tink, I'm serious," Janner said.

"Don't be such a ninny," Tink said over his shoulder, never taking his eyes from the trees. "I just want to see if I can figure out how he disappeared like that. He might have a tunnel or something. I'll be right back."

And without a word, Tink was running. Again.

"Tink, *no!*" Janner cried.

Janner watched from the side of the old house as Tink tiptoed between the twisted roots and trunks of the trees. He turned and waved at Leeli with a wide grin as Janner shook his head and motioned him to come back. Tink moved toward the trees, closer to the forest's edge.

With a frustrated sigh, Leeli plopped down beside Nugget.

Suddenly, Nugget tensed and raised his hackles. He looked at the woods and growled.

"Oh no," Janner moaned.

Something was coming, and from the sound of it—something big.

Janner and Leeli waved frantically, trying to get Tink's attention without making any noise. Janner wanted to run and grab him but was afraid to leave Leeli alone.

Tink, hunkered over, paid them no mind. He was investigating something on the ground, but then he heard it too.

A crashing noise came from the forest, the sound of something large and moving fast. Leeli and Janner were too terrified to move. They saw through the knot of trees a dark creature the size of a horse—bounding directly toward Tink.

Janner had heard Podo speak of toothy cows, and he had read a description of one in one of Oskar's books.[1] Janner knew from the creature's size and speed that the dark beast now only a few yards away from his little brother was the same.

Tink had no way of outrunning it.

He whipped his head around in time to see the fearsome cow bearing down on him, its long teeth bared, its girth trembling.

Janner, Leeli, and Nugget sat frozen with fear, unable to move and yet unable to take their eyes away from the sight of Tink's impending death. Leeli started to scream but Janner clapped a hand over her mouth and pulled her to the grass, behind the wall of the house. He didn't want her to see, and Tink was simply too far away to be helped. If she screamed, the toothy cow would make quick work of all three of them. Not even Nugget would make it home.

So they lay in the tall grass, hearts pounding, waiting with dread for Tink's final scream.

---

1. Rumpole Bloge's *Taming the Creepiful Wood* (Torrboro, Skree: Phute & Phute & Co., 3/112), a riveting autobiography detailing his years of ranging Glipwood Forest in the early days of the Third Epoch. In it, Bloge describes the cows as being "squarish in frame, with a moist snout and eyes that at first appear dull as a bowl of mud. But woe to that man who considers not the lethal potential in that bovinial thrump! In those yellowish sabers that protrude from its lippy mouth! How I wish my dear Molly had not spurned my warnings of the toothy cow's cunning and thew, ere that toothéd brute devoured her!" See page 288 in Appendices.

But it never came.

They heard the cow skid to a halt, followed by a scraping, snuffling sound. Then came a low grumble that wasn't at all the sound one would expect from a monster feasting on a boy. Janner closed his eyes and tried to sort out what he was hearing. He didn't want to risk being seen by the creature, but the faintest hope that Tink might be alive fluttered in his heart. He could stand it no longer. Janner held a finger up to his lips and moved ever so slowly to peek around the corner.

The beast was standing on its hind legs, scratching and nosing at the tree.

Toothy cows, it seemed, were not good climbers.

Janner breathed a long sigh of relief. "He's okay," he whispered. "I don't know how he did it, but he's okay. He climbed the tree before it got him." Leeli sighed and smiled at Nugget, who licked her face and wagged his tail. "Stay quiet," Janner whispered. "We have to wait until it leaves."

Janner peeked again and saw the toothy cow give one last swipe at the trunk of the tree before lumbering back into the woods with a moo of discontent. A long moment passed. Janner scanned the tree line, praying to the Maker that Tink was unharmed.

Suddenly, Tink's head appeared upside down from the upper branches of the tree. He waved at Janner, who waved in return, unable to repress a smile.

"He's okay, Leeli. Look."

Leeli erupted in giggles at Tink dangling from the tree. It was hard to stay mad at Tink for long.

"I guess his fear of heights isn't so bad when something's about to eat him," Janner said. He motioned for Tink to come down, but to his amazement, Tink shook his upside-down head.

"What is he doing?" Janner muttered, remembering how angry he had been at his brother just moments ago. "He almost got killed and he's still acting like a fool."

"Maybe he found something to eat up there," Leeli suggested.

"That cow could still be around. We need to get out of here while we can." Janner eyed the trees suspiciously.

Tink whistled from the tree and beckoned again for them to join him.

Unable to believe that he wasn't running like mad for home, Janner pulled Leeli to her feet, and they moved carefully toward the trees. He marveled at Tink's ability to coerce him into bad situations. They stood at the foot of the tree, looking up at Tink, but the canopy was so dark, they could barely see his figure in the branches above.

"Look around on the other side," Tink whispered, brimming with excitement.

At first, Janner saw nothing but a vine-covered tree trunk. Then he realized that the leaves and vines were disguising a rope ladder dangling against the tree trunk. Janner's stomach fluttered at the discovery, and again he was torn between his responsibility and his undeniable urge to find out what was up the ladder, hidden in the leafy branches. He looked, worried, at Leeli.

"Do you think you can climb?"

Leeli didn't reply but answered by leaning her crutch against the tree and patting Nugget on the head. She shinnied up the ladder like she had six good legs, not just one.

"I'll be back in a minute, boy," she whispered down when she had reached the limb where Tink was standing.

Janner followed after, muttering to himself. "Always causing problems...just once...wish...he'd use his brain..."

Tink was delighted, standing on a limb about thirty feet in the air, completely unbothered by the height.

"Tink, aren't you scared?" Leeli asked.

"Why?"

"You're in the top of a tree!" Janner said.

Tink blinked at his brother, looked down, and went as white as a cloud. He hugged the nearest branch and closed his eyes tight.

Leeli shook her head. "Well done, Janner."

Immediately filled with regret, Janner tried soothing his brother's shattered nerves. "Tink, it's okay. You climbed all the way up here without a problem. We just have to climb back down. Remember the cliffs last week? Remember when you heard the dragon song and you weren't afraid at all? Be brave like that again. Let go."

At the mention of the dragon song a slight change came over Tink—and Janner glimpsed a stronger, different Tink, like Janner had seen at the cliffs. Tink peeled himself from the tree and took a steady breath. He even looked down at the ground and forced a laugh.

Leeli and Janner exchanged glances.

"All right," Janner said. "I'm sure you're proud of your discovery. Now let's get down from here and go home."

Janner turned to descend the ladder.

"Wait!" Tink smiled again. Before Janner could protest, Tink edged out farther onto a fat limb and pushed a leafy branch out of the way.

"Take a look at this," he said as he stepped aside.

Beyond the leaves swayed a bridge of wood planks suspended by ropes stretching to the next tree. Through the branches they could see yet another bridge leading from that tree to the next one, and so on, deeper into the shadowy leaves of Glipwood Forest.

"This is how he gets to his tree house without having to worry about the forest critters," Leeli said.

"This must have taken years," Janner said slowly, with awe. Janner and Tink gazed at the bridges, aching to explore the forest from the heights of the trees. But not with Leeli. Janner didn't see how she could cross the bridges with a crutch even if she wanted to come, which he doubted.

"Leeli—" Janner said, but she cut him off.

"I'll need my crutch."

Her brothers looked at her with surprise. "Well, I can't go traipsing through the forest without it, can I?"

Breaking into a grin, Tink scurried down the ladder, retrieved the crutch, and scrambled back up.

Janner didn't like it, but he was once again as curious as his brother. *Why does this keep happening?* he thought.

Gripping the ropes that stretched across what seemed a sea of leaves and branches—and land far beneath, Tink inched out onto the bridge. He reached the drooping middle, bounced a little, and nodded. Janner had Leeli go before him, and she was surprisingly agile and able. Before long all three Igibys were strolling from bridge to bridge, climbing with confidence through the limbs of the trees in between.

Now and then they saw curious fazzle doves watching them pass. Below, the toothy cow, or one like it, trudged through the glipwood trees with a dead cave blat in its maw. The forest was boiling with life, both below and above them. Janner suddenly felt like an intruder, some rude houseguest who had entered without permission.

The bridges zigzagged for what seemed like miles before they came to a fork. Two bridges angled off into the leafy canopy in different directions. Tink stopped high in the arms of a sweeping oak, and Leeli and Janner sat for a moment to rest.

Janner was about to suggest that they start back. Who knew how far into the woods Peet's tree house was? And even if they found it, he was beginning to wonder how Peet would feel about trespassers.

"Leeli, are you sure we can trust him?" Janner wasn't so confident. True, Peet had saved Leeli and maybe saved all of them from the Fangs before that, but he still seemed crazy. "You don't think he'll be upset with us if he finds us…or if we find him?"

"I saw his eyes." She smiled, staring at the memory of it. "He won't hurt us; you'll see."

"Still, I think we've come far enough. We shouldn't even be here," Janner said.

"You guys don't have anything to eat, do you?" Tink asked.

A voice from behind them scared all three Igiby children out of their wits: "Perhaps you could join me for broiled rump of snapping diggle."

There in the middle of the bridge, with the ratty knitted stockings pulled up to his elbows, stood Peet the Sock Man. A skinned diggle carcass dangled from one socked hand.

He bowed low and smiled at the children.

"Would you like to see my castle?"

34

Peet's Castle

The boys stood as still as stones, but Leeli stepped forward. She limped out onto the bridge and stopped in front of Peet. White hair wild, face smudged with dirt, he stood there unmoving, gazing at her. His eyes were deep and blue, and they shone like jewels.

At once, Janner knew that somehow beneath the stench and beyond the strangeness, Peet the Sock Man was full of goodness. His eyes were so deep and so peaceful, Janner even began to believe that maybe Peet wasn't crazy at all.

The rope bridge creaked in the silence as they stared at one another.

"Hello, Mister Peet," Leeli said after a moment. "I'd love to come to your castle again." She reached out to his face and he stood frozen, a skittish animal about to spring. "Did something happen to your lip? It's swollen."

Peet shook his head slowly, staring blankly at her.

Janner cleared his throat.

Peet blinked and looked up with surprise. "Yes, well then. Hello. Follow me patee-tee-teeee." He whirled around and strode away, leaving the Igibys no choice but to follow in stunned silence.

After six more creaking bridges, they saw the tree house where Podo had found Leeli four days earlier. It was cradled in the boughs of the largest tree they had yet seen, towering twenty feet higher than the bridge that led them to it. The structure looked to have been made from the old lumber of fallen houses that littered the meadows near Glipwood. The planks were of mismatched grains and shapes, but arranged and nailed together neatly. Green-leafed branches cast quiet shadows on the sides of the little building and made it look to Janner as sturdy and welcoming as The Only Inn. There were even windows in Peet's tree castle.

The last bridge led to a thick, winding limb that was worn from much traffic and had no rope railing. Peet ambled across the limb without a thought, but it was too precarious for Leeli to cross with her crutch.

Peet turned back and noticed this, gasping. He bounded back, swept up Leeli, and carried her across in one fluid motion. Neither Tink nor Janner received such service, but they crossed without trouble.

Another rope ladder on the other side of the trunk led up to a trap door in the floor of the tree house through which Peet was already helping Leeli. The boys scrambled up and into Peet's castle in the trees.

Peet was humming as he tore the diggle carcass into pieces and dropped them into a pot.

Leeli made herself at home and sat cross-legged on the floor against the wall.

"Come in, young men, come in. Diggle cooking, rumple eating, diggle diggle rump food," he said in a singsong voice.

Tink and Janner climbed into the tree house and sat next to Leeli, who wore a very satisfied expression on her face. She looked up at Peet and gestured to her brothers. "Mister Peet, these are my broth—"

"Janner and Tink, Tanner and Jink, Jinker and Tan, Janker and Teeeeen," Peet said without looking up from the pot.

"But—how did you know our names?" Janner asked.

"Small town, boys. Crazy people hear lots of things, Wigiby," Peet said.

"It's Igiby," Tink said.

Peet shrugged and lit a small bundle of sticks and moss that sat in a crude fireplace beneath the pot. The fireplace was lined with stones, and above it he had fashioned a chimney of sorts from some kind of hide sewn together to make a tube.

Janner was impressed by Peet's ingenuity—that is, until the tree house filled with smoke. Peet didn't seem to notice.

Tink coughed. "Mister, uh, Peet the Sock Man, sir, aren't you worried that your house will catch fire?"

Peet fished a leather pouch from a small box beside him and sprinkled some of its contents into the pot. A delicious smell rose from the pot and mingled with the smoke.

"Worried? Not at all, young Wingiby." He pointed through the nearest window and the children could see three nearby trees whose branches were charred and leafless in places. "I've burned down my castle three times before, and I've always survived. I'm not borried a wit. Worried a bit." He went back to stirring the pot. "But this time I think I figured out the problem, see, problem, see, problem, see," he sang with a wink. "Rocks. See these rocks? They don't catch fire. Nope." He coughed and for the first time noticed the smoke filling the room. "Eeep!" he cried. Peet tugged on a piece of twine that dangled from the chimney tube, and the smoke slowly cleared. "Open the flue, open the flue, open the flue for me and for you."

Janner began to rethink his opinion of Peet. He was as crazy as a moonbird.

Peet dropped the diggle carcass into the boiling water and turned to the children. He sized the three of them up, particularly the brothers. His lips were moving, and he was absently scratching his flurry of hair with one socked hand. The pot began to steam and Tink's stomach rumbled.

Peet looked at him, and a flash of pain came over his face. "Hungry, are you, Tink?" he murmured. "Of course, you are."

Janner could see the stack of leather-bound books Leeli had mentioned beside an old trunk against the opposite wall. Something about them tickled at the back of his mind.

"So...do we call you Peet?" Janner asked, fishing for more answers to his mounting questions. "Is that your real name?"

The Sock Man stirred the boiling pot with a long wooden spoon and didn't answer.

The Igibys stared at him in an awkward silence.

"What's a real name?" Peet said finally. He pointed the spoon at Janner. "Is Janner Igiby *your* real name?"

"Yes sir."

"Is it?" Peet said, turning back to his cooking.

Tink could think of nothing but food. After several minutes of watching Peet fuss over the stew, he cleared his voice. "Is that almost finished, sir?"

Peet raised the spoon to his lips and tasted the broth. He nodded, then produced four wooden bowls from a crate and ladled the stew into them, smacking his lips. They ate in a silence punctuated only by Tink's and Peet's occasional grunts of pleasure. Janner was surprised to find that snapping diggle was delicious.

"Now, little Dinglefigs—"

"Igibys," Tink corrected again, through a mouthful of meat.

"—Iggyfeathers, whatever." Peet grew serious and sat up straight. "I thank you for your kindness and your visitation." His face darkened. "However, I must ask that you never, never, ever come here again." His voice cracked and he sank to the floor. "You cannot visit me. I tell smerrible. I smell terrible. You sweet birds could be eaten by a dapping sniggle—snapping diggle, flapping figgle, Igibys. Or a toothy cow! Oh, the horror. And I might be dangerous—I hight murt you—might hurt you without meaning to, you see. I—"

Peet stopped short and cocked his head to one side, listening. He shrieked and leapt to his feet, but his head smashed into the low ceiling. Unsteady from the blow, he staggered, a socked hand lifted to his head.

"Something…*outside!*" he breathed, and collapsed in a heap. The children stared with shock at the figure on the floor, all lanky limbs and white hair. Then they heard a whine from below them.

"Nugget!" Leeli cried, and she scrambled over to the trapdoor. Nugget was looking up at her from the foot of the tree, wagging his tail. "He found us!" Leeli said, then panicked. A creature of the wood could have gobbled him up! "We have to get him up here!" she insisted.

With a careful scan of the forest below, Janner climbed down the ladder and managed to carry up the little dog under one arm.

Peet was still unconscious but didn't look hurt. In fact, he appeared to be taking a happy afternoon nap.

Just let him sleep," Tink said. "He wanted us to leave anyway." Tink slurped up the last of his bowl. "Snapping diggle stew," he declared. "Who could have guessed it would be this good?"[1]

Janner crept past Peet to the pile of books in the corner.

"I don't know if that's such a good idea," Leeli said.

Janner shushed her. "I just want to have a look."

He crawled over to the pile and slipped out one volume. He opened it, and Tink and Leeli saw him gasp and look at Peet with wonder.

Peet stirred.

Quickly, Janner slid the book back into place and scooted back to where he had been sitting.

Tink and Leeli questioned Janner with their eyes, but he shook his head, then cleared his throat and said loudly, "We should go."

---

1. During the Second Epoch, Tombilly, Chief of Ban Rona in the Green Hollows, fell ill to a malady for which the medicians of the Hollows could find no cure. Their chief was wasting away and could eat no food, though his wife cooked for him a new meal daily. The wise men searched the land over for a meal that might cure his sickness. When old Ma Vorba, the seed catcher, suggested stewing a snapping diggle, she was ridiculed for a fooless, but she cooked the diggle with greenions and totatoes and served it to Chief Tombilly when his wife was away. The chief's health returned. For years the diggle was believed to have healing powers, until it was discovered that the chief's poor wife was but the most dreadful cook Aerwiar had ever known, and Tombilly was starving himself rather than eat another bite of her food. To this day, a traveler eating a fine meal in the Green Hollows might still hear someone exclaim, "Ma Vorba, that was tasty!"

The Sock Man groaned and sat up, rubbing his head.

"Bye, Mister Peet." Janner was extra polite. "Thanks for the food."

"That's what? What's that? Food?" Peet's eyes widened. "Something's out there!" he shrieked. He leapt to his feet and crashed into the ceiling again. "Ouch!" He staggered about with a socked hand on his head.

"It's all right, Mister Peet," Leeli soothed. "That was just my dog, Nugget. Remember little Nugget?" Leeli scratched the dog's chin.

"Nemember little rugget," he said, wincing and looking at the dog with confusion.

"We have to go," Janner said.

"Yes, you do," said Peet, plopping back down. "And don't come back. I'm so sad to say it, but don't come back." He touched his swollen lip. "You mustn't come back." His head drooped. "Good-bye, Wingiby Igifeathers."

Peet carried Leeli across the high limb and placed her gently on the bridge while the boys followed. After they crossed the second bridge, Janner turned to wave good-bye. Peet was back in his castle, watching them from the window. Janner couldn't be sure, but it looked like Peet was crying.

Janner didn't speak the whole way back. Several times Tink asked him what he'd seen in the book, but Janner didn't answer. The Igiby children wound their long way over the bridges until the trees began to thin out again.

The only sound was Nugget whimpering as the little dog scrambled across the bridges, more afraid of falling than of a whole gobble of toothy cows. Janner marveled as Tink tried to reassure Nugget that heights were nothing to fear.

Halfway back Janner and Tink heard familiar, chilling howls that made them and Leeli freeze in their tracks. Several dark shapes emerged from the tangle of brush below them.

From their perch on the tree bridge, the Igibys watched silently as a pack of horned hounds passed through the trees below like a gray fog. When the hounds had gone, the leaves on the forest floor directly beneath the bridge rustled, then the ground bulged like a pot of boiling cheesy chowder. Out from its burrow popped a warty, brown digtoad as big as a goat.[2] At the same time, to Leeli's horror and her brothers' fascination, an oblivious fazzle dove lighted on the ground not far away, pecking at worms in the dirt. Without warning, the digtoad's tongue shot out and *sklotched* the bird into its mouth, leaving a cloud of gray feathers floating in the air where the bird had been.

Leeli squeaked and covered her mouth. The digtoad turned up its black, bulbous eyes and regarded the children for a long, terrible moment. Finally it let out a blatting croak and half-walked, half-hopped away. Just as the sound of the digtoad's departure faded, a smaller creature with black, matted hair skittered into the area.

"A ratbadger," Janner whispered to Tink and Leeli.

The ratbadger twitched its large, pointy ears and sniffed around the forest floor until it found the digtoad's hidden burrow, where it slunk inside without a sound. A moment later, the large rodent appeared with a yellowish egg held carefully in its mouth.[3]

With what Janner could only assume was an angry croak, the digtoad returned, its tongue darting out as it pursued the fleeing ratbadger.

In seconds, the forest was quiet again. Janner marveled at the way the forest could hide things. It could seem so innocent and harmless, even beautiful, while beneath its surface prowled such ruthless, deadly creatures. Why was so much in Janner's world not what it seemed? He thought about his mother, about Oskar, then about Peet the Sock Man. They all had secrets.

"It was a journal," Janner said, breaking the silence.

"And?" Tink said.

---

2. The bumpy digtoad has been known to attack humans, though never yet fatally. Victims of a digtoad attack complain of the "squishy, flootchy feeling" of having a sticky tongue violently flapped upon them. Since the bumpy digtoad has no teeth, its bites are said to feel to the victim like being "gummed like a dumpling in an old man's mouth."

3. The ratbadger is dangerous not just because of its long claws or jagged teeth or because of its feisty disposition. The ratbadger's greatest weapon is its eggish flatulence.

Janner looked at Tink and Leeli. "On the front was a picture." Janner looked intently at Tink. "A picture that we've seen before."

"What was it?"

"A dragon, with wings."

Tink's eyes widened. "The same as the Annieran journal? The one we found at Oskar's?"

Janner nodded. "And there were lots of them in the tree house. At least twenty! How would Peet have gotten his hands on Annieran journals?"

"Maybe they're his," Leeli said.

"I don't think so. The first page said, 'This is the journal of Artham P. Wingfeather, Throne Warden of Anniera.'"

Tink frowned. "What's a Throne Warden?"

"I don't really know." Janner shrugged. "I haven't read much about Anniera or its history. Oskar doesn't have many books on the subject."

"Sounds important," Tink said, looking east through the dark foliage of the forest.

"Anniera." Janner repeated the name to himself. The word felt good on his lips, like laughter or a pretty song. Standing in the middle of the swaying bridge, he suddenly was lost in thoughts of faraway green lands, of dragons with wings, and of their mysterious sock-handed new friend. Neither Tink or Leeli said anything, but Janner knew they were thinking of Anniera too.

Their thoughts were interrupted by the clicking chatter of a cave blat lumbering across the forest floor below them.

Without another word the Igibys made their way back to the edge of the forest.

Janner paused to be sure no toothy cow, cave blat, quill diggle, horned hound, or other manner of beast was prowling, then scooped up Nugget to carry him down the rope ladder. At the bottom, he set the grateful dog on the forest floor and waited for Leeli. Tink came last, with Leeli's crutch under his arm. With one last look at the swaying bridge high above them, they made for town as fast as they could.

But back in Glipwood, breathless, Janner was struck with some sense that something was wrong. The streets were empty. A hot wind blew and licked up dust and leaves. Where Commander Gnorm usually lazed on the front steps of the jail, there was now an empty rocker, creaking ominously in the wind.

Janner turned northeast, and his stomach knotted and dread seeped into his bones.

A plume of angry smoke billowed from the trees in the direction of the Igiby cottage.

35

Fire and Fangs

Tink!" Janner pointed toward home, and Tink squinted into the distance and moaned.

Leeli was already hopping along the lane, her blond curls whipping in the wind. Nugget let out a series of desperate barks and tore ahead, up the lane to the Igiby cottage.

Without a word, Janner and Tink ran. Janner's mind raced faster than his feet, picturing a thousand nightmarish things the Fangs could be doing to his mother and grandfather. *Was the maggotloaf not vile enough for Gnorm's taste? Had Slarb returned?* At the edges of his fears lurked the possibility that the Black Carriage had come and stopped at the Igiby cottage, where Podo certainly would not have gone quietly.

Soon Janner could think of nothing but the stitch in his side and the air he couldn't catch. He was at Tink's heels, grunting with every desperate breath. The smoke they'd seen from town filled their noses.

The boys sped up the hill and through the trees to find the barn behind the cottage a swirling storm of fire. Janner felt the heat from it on his face even before he passed the fence gate. Through the gray air he saw a whole company of Glipwood Fangs slithering about, some with torches, others with swords drawn. A cluster of them were bent over something, jabbing at it with the butts of their spears, and Janner saw with horror that it was Podo. The old man wasn't moving. Janner heard a roar and turned in time to see Tink rush straight for the Fangs that were standing over Podo.

"Tink, NO!" Janner cried.

Tink flew into the huddle of Fangs as the air split with the sound of Leeli's screams. A Fang had materialized from the smoke and seized her from behind. All around Janner raged smoke and screams, fire and Fangs. Podo was bleeding and unconscious, and Leeli was being dragged by the arm to where Commander Gnorm was standing, overseeing the chaos with a smug look on his face.

Nugget leapt at Gnorm's leg, and Janner watched helplessly as the little dog was run through by a spear. Nugget yelped and went limp while the Fang who stabbed him put a foot to his flank to jerk out the spear. Nugget lay still, bleeding from his side.

Janner prayed that in the smoke and confusion Leeli didn't see it happen. But he felt sick, and for a moment he considered running, though he didn't know where he would go. He could go to Oskar or Peet the Sock Man, but he couldn't think how either could help his family.

Just then two Fangs appeared from the rear of the house, dragging Nia, her hands bound. Janner felt a wave of relief amid the panic—*at least we're all still alive.*

His eyes met Nia's through the haze of smoke. She pursed her lips and shook her head, indicating that he wasn't to fight or flee. It was too late anyway—Janner had been spotted.

Three Fangs, swords drawn, were marching his way. Not taking his eyes off his mother, he held up his hands and let himself be taken.

The Fangs herded the Igibys to the grass, where they were lined up, kneeling with their hands tied behind their backs. The barn had been burned to the ground and a pall hung in the air, stinging their eyes. Podo was delirious from a head wound, but he was conscious enough to curse and taunt the Fangs that surrounded them.

"Ye'd better tie ol' Podo better than that if ye want to save yer rotten snakeskins," he slurred, his white hair matted with blood.

"Papa, hush," Nia said through clenched teeth, glaring at Gnorm.

Tink huffed and glowered at the Fangs. Leeli was still and silent, staring at the heap of black fur on the ground behind Gnorm. Nugget hadn't moved. Janner wondered bitterly what had brought this upon them. Ever since the Dragon Day Festival their lives had been turned upside down.

"Was my maggotloaf not satisfactory, Commander?" Nia asked in a calm, strong voice.

Gnorm smiled his hideous smile and scratched his jowls. "To the contrary," he said, taking a step closer, "that maggotloaf is all that's keeping you alive." Gnorm waved his hand in Nia's face, flaunting the gold rings and bracelet she had given him in exchange for her children's freedom. "I was willing to overlook the fact that you had hidden these jewels from Gnag the Nameless because you swore that you had no more hidden away. That, and the promise of the maggotloaf, of course." He burped and a fly buzzed out of his mouth. "But I just received an interesting message from General Khrak in Torrboro."

Gnorm unsheathed his long dagger and toyed with it while he spoke. "You see, there is a treasure that the Nameless One has sought all these years, a treasure beyond imagination. And General Khrak, my superior, has just sent a message saying that he believes you know where it is. He's waiting for us at Fort Lamendron. Now I've been wondering to myself, 'Why would that Igiby woman lie to me when she knows I could eat all three of her scrawny children?' Hmm? Why would you do that?" Gnorm leaned over, his whitish belly dangling over his belt. He held Nia's face in a scaly hand. With his snout just inches from Nia's unflinching gaze, he hissed, "Where are the Jewelsss of Anniera?"

The Jewels of Anniera? Janner stole a glance at Tink. Maybe their mother didn't know anything, but he and Tink knew about the weapons at Anklejelly Manor. The map had said something about the Jewels of Anniera. Whatever these mysterious jewels were, they must have something to do with the weapon room. But what was so special about these jewels that Gnag the Nameless himself would go to such trouble to find them?

Nia jerked her head from Gnorm's grip and stared back at him defiantly. "I swear to you, I gave you all the gold and jewels I had," she said, her voice level and cold.

Gnorm considered her a moment. "So. You're going to make this difficult, are you?" He slapped Nia with the back of his hand, knocking her down.

Podo lunged forward, straining at the ropes that bound his hands, cursing Gnorm with all the breath in his lungs.

Nia managed to get back to her knees while Gnorm smirked at Podo, then sheathed the dagger with a snap. "Fangs," he ordered, "search the house!"

Greedily, the Fangs disappeared into the Igiby cottage, tearing apart whatever they could lay their hands on.

Janner winced at the sounds of glass and furniture breaking. He could see the Fangs moving about inside their cottage, laughing their snarling laughs as they drooled venom, flipped over chairs, kicked through cabinets, dumped out bureau drawers, and tore open cushions. Nia, bleeding from the corner of her mouth, stared coolly at Gnorm until at last the Fangs issued from the house, empty handed.

"Nothin' in there, sir," said one.

Gnorm met Nia's gaze. "Bring them."

The Fangs forced the Igibys to their feet, all but Leeli, who was thrown over one Fang's shoulder, just as Slarb had done.

Janner suddenly felt as tired as he'd ever been. His feet dragged as he walked behind his grandfather, who only a few days earlier had looked like a warrior on the back of Danny the carthorse. Now Podo was hobbling along, bent like the old man that he was. Tink said nothing, but scowled with hatred. Janner's heart felt heavy with dread. Just days ago, when he and his brother and sister were in the jail, their only salvation had been Nugget, Nia, and Podo, and the gold that Nia had hidden away. Now the gold was gone, Nugget was gone, and Podo and Nia were to be locked away with them. This time there would be no stopping the Black Carriage. It would creep into town on its dark errand, and they would be fed into its maw, taken away to meet whatever grisly fate Gnag the Nameless devised for them.

Yet Nia's strength still emanated from her like a candle in a dark room. Janner noticed that she was steady and graceful, and even with blood dried at the corner of her mouth and hair askew, she was beautiful.

Questions, more questions, niggled at him. *Why would my mother have a treasure that Gnag sought?* Janner didn't think that was a possibility. Surely there was some mistake, and as Igiby luck would have it, that mistake had led Gnorm to them.

The day seemed hotter than ever as the Igibys were led, like participants in some grim parade through Glipwood to the town jail. No one walked the streets. The doors were closed and the windows shuttered. The Igibys were thrown into one cell, and the barred door clanged shut. Podo whipped his white hair out of his eyes and glared at the commander.

"Gnorm!" he bellowed. "I'll skin you like a snake if you touch my family! I'll tear you apart with my teeth if I have to!" He strained at his bonds, growled, and threw himself at the cell door as a chorus of laughter erupted from the Fangs who filed back into the front room of the jail.

Commander Gnorm looked in from the doorway and bared all his yellow teeth in a wide smile. "The Black Carriage will be here sssoon, so you'd better get to it, old man," Gnorm said with a chuckle, and he closed the door.

Nia knelt beside Leeli and whispered her name. Leeli still hadn't spoken. Podo paced back and forth, twisting at his bonds with no result. Tink, however, let out a satisfied grunt and held his hands out in front of him. His wrists were chaffed and sore, but the rope that once bound them dropped to the ground.

"I've been working at them," he said as he untied Podo.

"Good work, lad," Podo said.

In moments, Tink had everyone's hands free.

Leeli buried her head into her mother, nestled in Nia's arms.

"Ma," Janner asked, "what's all this about a treasure? about jewels? Do you know what Gnorm's talking about?"

Nia and Podo stared at one another in silence. Flies buzzed around their tired faces.

"As I told the Fang," Nia said after a moment, looking back at Janner, "I gave them all the gold and jewelry I had. There's nothing more hidden in that house." She changed her tone abruptly. "Now. There are more important things to worry about."

"Aye," Podo said. "Like how we're gonna get out of here. The way I see it, there's nothin' we can do until they try to move us to the"—he shuddered—"the Carriage." He tugged at the cell door. "We'll just have to wait here and pray to the Maker that we'll get the chance we need." He sat down beside Nia and Leeli and stroked his granddaughter's hair with his big, callused hand. "It's all right there, lass."

Tink and Janner slid to the floor, and the Igiby family waited.

36

Shadowed Steed
and Shadowed Tack
and
Shadowed Driver Driving

The sun melted over Glipwood, and the cell began to fill with shadows. Janner woke with a start. He looked around the cell with a surge of disappointment when he realized that their situation wasn't part of another bad dream. He thought about the cottage, his bed, the chair by the hearth where Podo always napped.

Podo was awake with Nia's and Leeli's heads resting on him, asleep. Tink was curled up in the corner, facing the wall. Janner couldn't tell if he was sleeping or not. The flies had mercifully dissipated, and now the musty cell had the restless peace of the calm before a storm.

"Janner," Podo said. His eyes twinkled in the dim light.

Janner looked at his grandfather and forced a smile.

"Yer Podo's been in tighter sticks than this one. We'll make it out, no fear."

Something in the seriousness of Podo's voice told Janner that the old pirate was trying to convince himself, and Janner suddenly felt a deep sadness. He was sad that he'd never again see the green garden or the wide, lonesome ocean beneath the cliffs or laugh in the lamplight of a warm meal with his family. He could feel his hope fleeing, and it was the Black Carriage that chased it away.

"Grandpa, what do the Fangs want? Why would they think we know anything about a treasure?"

Podo lowered his eyes.

"Son, the Fangs don't need much reason to terrorize us. Whether there's a treasure or not, it seems as though fate's bent on ruinin' us. Curse fate, I say. We've made it this far, ain't we?" Podo's spirit burned brighter the more he spoke. "They can throw us in the jail, they can tear the house to pieces. They can even try to take my wee Leeli here. But as long as old Podo's got breath in his lungs and a beat in his heart, there's no fate, no Fang, no Gnag himself what can tear up this family."

Janner looked away and shook his head.

"Look at me, boy!" Podo said. "When it comes time to fight, you fight. Even if those Fangs tear us to pieces, we'll meet the Maker knowin' we fought hard for somethin' good. So don't you shake your head like you're givin' up."

Janner's cheeks burned at the rebuke. Still, he couldn't stop thinking about being locked in that black cage, carried off to some grisly, unstoppable death. He was angry that the only life he'd ever known was one with Fangs and Black Carriages and a fear so deep and daily that it swallowed his joy.

Then Tink heard it.

He sat straight up and looked at the high window.

In the shadows Janner could see cold fear on his brother's face.

Leeli cried out and Podo held her and Nia tight.

Far away, coming nearer by the heartbeat, was the sound of hooves and the crack of a whip. Janner felt like his heart would burst in his chest. The Fangs outside called out and cackled. The sounds of hoofbeats and whip crack were joined by the rattle of harnesses, the creak of iron wheels, the flapping of black wings, and the croaking of crows.

The Black Carriage had come.

Podo leapt to his foot, pulling Leeli and Nia up beside him.

"Now listen," he barked. "They don't know our hands aren't tied. So wrap your cords around your wrists and be ready to break free when you see me move. I aim to acquire one of their swords, and I don't plan to fill out a form to do it. Leeli, you stay with Janner, and he'll carry you on his back. Hold on tight and he'll get you there safe. All of ye, run like mad for the cottage. If I don't show up soon, then make for the Diggle Trail. Nia honey, ye remember the hidden nook I showed ye years ago? We'll hide there until we figure out what to do."

Nia nodded.

Tink picked up the cords from the ground and handed them out.

"I'll try to get a sword, too," said Tink.

"No, lad. I know you want to help, but I need you all to run. Don't worry about yer Podo. These old paws still remember how to swing a sword," he said with a wink. Janner again had the awful sense that Podo was trying to convince himself and that their situation was far worse than he was letting on.

"Listen to your grandfather, son," Nia said, this time with a tremble in her voice.

Leeli still hadn't spoken.

"Leeli, are you ready?" She nodded her head listlessly just as the door from the jail office burst open, letting in a flood of light.

A Fang strode to the door, a large key ring jingling in his hand. He smirked at them as he unlocked the cell. "Your ride isss waiting."

Podo went first and the others filed after him, hands behind their backs. All the Fangs were outside, lined up in two rows that formed a sort of corridor that led to the open door of the Black Carriage. Even Podo shivered when he saw it.

Four sleek black horses were harnessed to the carriage, their eyes like empty graves. The steeds' nostrils flared as they pawed at the ground and whipped their manes and tails. Sitting atop the carriage was a ghostly, hooded figure in a long black robe that swayed like a banner in a slow wind. A crow perched on its shoulder. The Fang, or man, or ghost, or whatever it was, sat looking forward with the reins in whitish, bony hands. The bowels of the carriage were fathomless, and around the doorway were slick black stains that ran down like dried blood. A chorus of flies buzzed in and out of the carriage door and the occasional whitish worm wriggled forth, plopped to the dirt, and was gobbled up by one of the many crows fussing about.

Commander Gnorm stood by the iron door, a smirk on his saggy face. The Fangs jeered and hissed at them as they inched their way toward the open door.

Janner could barely feel his feet as he walked, just inches behind Podo, nearer and nearer to the Carriage. Janner fingered at the bonds wrapped loosely around his wrists, anticipating with dread the moment when Podo would make his move. He could hear Leeli behind him, whimpering as she limped along, leaning on Nia for support.

As Podo neared Commander Gnorm and the Carriage, he said in a loud voice, "Ah! A fine day for a ride through the country, eh, lads?"

For a split second, Gnorm lost his smile. Most prisoners were either unconscious or hysterical and had to be forced into the Carriage. He wasn't used to prisoners making jokes as they approached it.

In a blur, Podo freed his hands, lunged forward, and seized Gnorm by his breastplate. Podo spun him around and into the line of Fangs, at the same time grabbing the dagger at his belt.

"Run—" Podo bellowed, and the Igibys broke away with a scream, pushing through the line of startled Fangs. Nia held Leeli with one arm and half-dragged her as she fled with the boys. But Podo's yell was cut short. A Fang clubbed him in the head with the pommel of a sword, and he crumpled to the ground.

In a matter of seconds, Janner, Tink, Leeli and Nia were subdued and tied up again. Podo lay in the dirt, unconscious.

The hissing and cursing of the irritated Fangs was silenced by Gnorm's grating chuckle. "Fools," he said, bending down and wrenching his dagger from Podo's limp hand. "Pick him up and throw him in."

It took four Fangs to lift Podo and hurl him into the waiting mouth of the carriage; he landed with a damp-sounding thud.

Gnorm motioned for Janner to follow. Quaking, Janner stepped slowly to the open door. A sickening smell, the smell of dead and rotten things, oozed from the carriage, and Janner could hear Podo moaning and retching from within. With a last look at Tink, Leeli, and his mother, all of whom were pale and trembling, Janner stepped up into blackness.

"Wait," Gnorm said, grabbing Janner's arm.

The Fang grinned at Nia, his yellow fangs glistening in the torchlight. "I'll give you one last chance, woman. Tell me where the jewels are, and I'll spare your precious children. The old man dies either way, of course."

Nia looked from Janner to Tink to Leeli, tears welling in her eyes.

From the belly of the carriage, Podo moaned, "Nia, no…tell them nothing…"

"But Papa, I don't know what to do!" she cried, trembling. "I don't know what to do!"

Podo's weak voice echoed from the carriage again, "Daughter, tell them nothing! We can't leave them."

Gnorm and the Fangs watched all this with smiles on their faces.

Finally, Nia staggered to her feet, her chest still heaving. She stood up and brushed her hair from her eyes. With a heartbroken look at her children, she said in a strong voice, "We'll be riding in your carriage, Commander. Together."

She glowered at Gnorm, lifted her dress, and stepped into the carriage as nobly as if it were a queen's coach. From the shadows of the doorway, her long, slender hand emerged, beckoning in the children.

Janner took her hand and once again stepped up to the carriage on trembling legs. There was no turning back now. The carriage would take them away to their dark fate.

Unable to breathe, he took the first step.

Suddenly, a piercing cry tore through the air. It sounded to Janner like a giant eagle, or a hundred giant eagles all screaming at once. Seeing the look of confusion on Gnorm's face, Janner turned from the carriage just in time to catch a white-haired blur streaking toward them from Vibbly Way.

37

Talons and a Sling

Running faster than Janner believed possible, Peet the Sock Man bore down on them, mouth open in a vicious cry, wildness in his eyes.

The Fangs watched him come, unable to understand what they were seeing, too shocked to react. Peet leapt into the air with an animal-like grace and spread his socked arms wide, his screech still filling their ears, the crows scattering before him.

Peet fell on three of the Fangs nearest to him in a fury of talons and shrieks. The talons, Janner saw, were Peet's—three long talons, in fact, that tore from within the socks on both arms and shredded them to pieces. The remains of the stockings floated to the ground like feathers. The Fang company stood motionless as their fellow soldiers crumpled to the ground, sliced and bleeding from a hundred wounds. Peet wasted no time. Slashing and spinning, his talons now covered in green blood, he felled two more Fangs before any of them had the sense to draw a weapon.

Tink and Leeli ducked beneath the Black Carriage. Janner followed, unable to believe his eyes.

Commander Gnorm sputtered and growled as he watched his soldiers fall, one by one, to the swift talons of Peet the Sock Man. More than half of the Fangs were either dead or dying. The remaining ones had come to their senses and were advancing in a half circle on Peet, who was backed up against the wall of the jail.

Peet screamed at them, the swipes of his talons keeping them at bay.

"Kill him!" Gnorm bellowed from a safe distance.

The Fangs closed in, jabbing at Peet with spears.

Janner shut his eyes, waiting for Peet's final wail, but it never came. Janner heard Gnorm grunt with surprise.

Podo, covered with grime, had shot from the carriage and was wrestling Gnorm's sword from him. Gnorm's fangs were bared and oozing venom. He snarled and thrashed at Podo, who was trying to hold him down, avoid his fangs, and draw Gnorm's sword from its sheath. They struggled in the dirt while Peet fended off the surrounding Fangs.

"Come quick!" Nia told the children. She climbed out of the carriage, also covered with black grime, and bustled them away from the fight, making for the shadows on the opposite side of the street, beside Books and Crannies. Janner knew that neither Peet nor Podo would last much longer, so with a prayer to the Maker he shot away from Nia.

Gnorm was so consumed with fighting Podo that he didn't notice Janner behind him, lunging for Gnorm's dagger. Janner gripped the hilt, cold in his sweaty hand, drew it out, and ran it deep into Gnorm's side. The fat Fang spun around, his black eyes wide with surprise and rage.

"A boy!" Gnorm yelped, aghast. With the Fang's own sword, Podo finished him off.

Janner stood in shock over Commander Gnorm's dead body.

Suddenly, above the sounds of the battle, a high, steady whistling sound tore through the air. Fang and human alike stopped and covered their ears, but as soon as it started, the odd sound died away. They had no time to wonder about it. Podo howled and engaged the Fangs who had recovered from the noise and were closing in on Peet.

Podo's growl, Peet's screech, and the snarls of the Fangs mixed with the racket of clashing steel.

In a matter of moments, only Peet and Podo were left standing—the pirate and the Sock Man, covered in green blood and gasping for breath, knee deep in a pile of scaly corpses. The two warriors looked at each other without speaking for a long moment.

"You all right, then?" Podo asked gruffly.

Peet nodded. He was out of breath, but standing tall. The sadness in his eyes had been replaced with a piercing, almost noble aspect, though Janner noticed that Peet seemed unable to look directly at Podo.

They turned their attention to the Black Carriage and the bodies of Fangs littering the street around it. The ghostly driver, forgotten in the battle, was still sitting on the carriage, holding the reins. The hooded head turned slowly their way and a chill ran through Janner.

Podo took a threatening step toward the driver, gripping a Fang sword.

"Zounds!" the driver said and whipped the black horses into a gallop. "Zounds!" it repeated, as the carriage sped away.

"No!" Podo cried. "We have to stop the carriage, or that critter driving it'll get reinforcements!"

Podo started after the carriage, but it was nearly out of sight.

Janner heard an odd hissing sound from somewhere above him. He turned in time to see Zouzab Koit on the roof of the jail whirling a sling. The rock flew out of the sling and whizzed through the air, striking the ghostly driver with a dull thud.

The driver of the Black Carriage fell limply from his perch, and the dark horses came to a stop, snorting and stamping the ground at the edge of town.

"It was you!" Janner said, astonished. "You threw the stones at the Fangs in the alley!"

Zouzab smiled his thin smile and bowed his head. "Yes, young Janner. Ridgerunners see many things. It wouldn't do to let the Igiby children get hurt, now would it?" With that, he disappeared into the shadows.

"It was him, it was, it was," Peet mumbled. "I was there too, around the corner, but Zou-runner Ridge-zab slung his rocks first, first..." Peet's words trailed off into murmurs when he realized that the Igibys were watching him. Already Peet's eyes were sad and downcast again, and Janner wondered whether he had imagined the fire he had seen in them moments ago.

A light breeze blew through the streets of Glipwood, where sixteen

Fangs of Dang lay dead, and somehow the Igibys were still standing. Tink broke away from Nia, ran to Podo, and hugged him fiercely. Nia, Janner, and Leeli followed. They huddled in a long embrace while Peet kept at a distance, hiding his taloned hands behind his back, shuffling his feet.

Finally, Nia looked over at him. "It's all right, Peet," she said.

He stopped fidgeting and looked at the cluster of Igibys. Tears filled his eyes, and he looked down at his talons, covered with Fang blood. He wiped them on his shirt as if to make himself more presentable.

"Peet," Nia said gently. "It's all right." She beckoned him to them.

Peet the Sock Man stared at her, eyes wide and shining. He tried to fix his wild, white hair and stood erect as he inched closer to the family. Peet reached out to hug them, still unsure of himself. He looked down again at his strange, clawed hands, and Janner saw a look of anguish pass over his face. His gaze met Janner's. The large, teary eyes moved from Janner to Tink, where they lingered long as well. The Sock Man dropped to one knee and looked lovingly at Leeli, who for the first time since seeing Nugget's broken body, smiled.

Peet broke into sobs and commenced kissing the children's feet in turn, pawing at their legs and mumbling through sobs. "Safe! Jewelbyfeathers! They're safe, praise the Maker."

"That's enough," Podo grunted, toeing Peet away from the children. Podo glared down at the Sock Man. The look on the old pirate's face was a confused mixture of anger and pity.

Suddenly a door creaked open in the shadows across the street. In the dim light they could make out a figure emerging from the entrance of Books and Crannies. Podo took a threatening step toward the shop and raised the crude sword he'd been using.

"Who's there?" he growled, his voice echoing in the deserted street.

"Pssst! Come, quick!"

It was Oskar N. Reteep.

Podo snorted with relief. "Aye, come on children. It's no good standing here in the open with all this filth lying about. Inside, and hop to it!"

But Leeli broke away with a sob and hopped toward the cottage, where she knew Nugget's body lay.

"Lass!" Podo said. "This is no time to—"

But Nia quieted him with a stern look, moved to Leeli, and put a comforting arm around her. Janner couldn't hear what his mother was whispering to Leeli, but he saw his sister nod, stand up straighter, and take a deep breath as she and Nia turned back to Books and Crannies.

The Igibys hurried across the street. Peet scampered along behind them, keeping well away from Podo. Oskar, wild-eyed, peeked out at them, spectacles twinkling in the moonlight. He beckoned for them to enter and opened the door as they approached.

"That's it, now. Inside, inside! What in blazes are you doing, you old pirate!" Oskar said with a laugh and a slap on his knee. "I heard a commotion and looked out just in time to see the last lizard go down! Why, nothing like that's happened since the Great War! Come to think of it, nothing like that happened on this continent even during the war. That may be the most Fangs that Gnag has ever lost in Skree.[1] And young Janner here! And Peet!" What little they could see of Oskar's face showed that he was happier than they'd ever seen him.

"Why, in the words of the Sage of Brivshap, 'Exactly!'" Oskar laughed, clapping his hands. "Exactly, I say! Zouzab! Fetch some water from the cistern for these warriors, if you please. Zouzab!" he called.

No answer came.

Oskar scratched his head. "Now, I wonder where that little fellow's off to?"

---

1. This was true. Before the Great War, the Skreeans had heard rumors of Gnag the Nameless, rumors that snakelike creatures and trolls and other imaginary monsters from children's scary-tales had conquered the lands of Dang, across the sea, but they couldn't believe that Skree itself was in any danger. In the 442nd year of the Third Epoch, a thousand ships laden with such creatures infested the Dark Sea of Darkness off the coast of Skree. It was said that the war cry of the invading Fangs could be heard as far inland as Torrboro. With few exceptions, the Skreeans surrendered without a fight.

"Outside," Podo said. "He took out the carriage driver with a stone and a sling."

"Did he now?" Oskar said, looking at Podo with surprise. "No matter. Follow me, everyone."

Peet, who stood just inside the door fidgeting with his hair, sneezed, reminding everyone of his presence.

"You," Podo said gruffly, pointing Gnorm's sword at him. "You wait outside."

"But Grandpa!" Leeli said. "He just saved our lives!"

"What was that bowing and kissing our feet about?" Tink demanded. "Did he say something about jewels?"

"Tink," Podo said, "you know the feller's crazy in the head. A crazy old fool, that's all." Janner shuddered at the bitterness he heard in his grandfather's voice. A sniff came from Peet's direction.

Oskar coughed. "Come now, there's no use carrying on in the dark. Follow me. Peet, you too," he said, turning to go.

"No," Podo said in a menacing voice. His face was as hard as rock.

Ignoring her grandfather, Leeli moved to Peet and took his strange, reddish claw of a hand, drawing him past Podo.

In one swift, terrible movement, Podo jerked Leeli away from the Sock Man, seized him by the shoulders, and thrust him out the door. "I said NO! You stay away from these children, do you hear? Away!"

Peet lay sprawled on the ground. The look on his face in the dim light was one of torture, as if he hurt too much even to cry out. Podo slammed the door and leaned his head against it, panting. No one spoke a word. Leeli sniffled, trying to hide her sobs. Janner kept waiting for Nia to intervene, to talk some sense into Podo's unfair treatment of Peet, but she was silent, her expression unreadable in the dark.

"Now let's go," Podo said as he straightened and turned to them.

No one moved.

"Oskar!" Podo barked. Oskar leapt into action and beckoned them to follow.

Through Books and Crannies' front window, Janner caught a glimpse of Peet silhouetted by the lamplight of the street, walking away with his head bowed low. Janner's heart ached for the poor man.

Oskar led them past tottering bookshelves until they detected the soft yellow glow of the lamp-lit study ahead of them. Oskar disappeared for a moment and returned with a pitcher of water and five small clay cups.

Janner was surprised at how thirsty he was. His stomach rumbled, and he realized that they hadn't had food or drink since the snapping diggle stew at Peet's tree house.

He thought about Peet's strange talons—he had never seen nor heard of anything like them. And if he had doubted before whether or not Peet was looking out for them, now he knew for sure, even if he'd been wrong about the stones in the alley. But why? Why had Peet chosen to watch over the Igiby children out of all the other people in Glipwood? Janner was even more bothered by his mother's and grandfather's strange treatment of the Sock Man. *Why is Podo so angry with Peet?*

But more immediate fears pushed those thoughts from Janner's mind. His whole family was in danger. Their home was ransacked, their barn burned, and they had just killed a company of Fangs. They had to come up with some plan for where to hide and where to live.

With a pang of sadness it struck Janner that there was a very good chance that they'd have to leave Glipwood—possibly forever. How could they stay in light of all that had happened? Obviously Gnag the Nameless sought the jewels, wherever they were, and he thought the Igibys were hiding them.

The adults huddled over Oskar's desk and spoke in hushed tones.

Leeli was in a corner sitting on an empty crate, staring at nothing in particular.

Tink, however, was fidgeting, moving about like a shrub in the wind. His cheeks were flushed and he looked angry. "Will somebody tell me what's going on?" he burst out. The adults looked at him with surprise.

"Not now, son," said Nia.

"Why not?" Tink pressed. Janner, trying to save his fiery little brother from trouble, laid a hand on his arm. Tink jerked away. "Why not now? Why did Grandpa drive away the man who just saved our lives? I want to know where the jewels are and why Gnag the Nameless thinks we have them. What's so special about those jewels anyway? And who is Artham P. Wingfeather, and why does Peet the Sock Man have his journals in his tree house?"

"What?" Podo and Nia said at once.

Oskar stared at Tink, wide-eyed.

Tink's head dropped and his eyes met Janner's apologetically.

Nia folded her arms and glared at Tink. "How do you know what's in Peet's tree house?"

Tink didn't look up or answer the question, so Janner spoke.

"We followed Peet there today. We didn't, uh, mean to, but..." Janner's voice trailed off.

"It was my fault," Tink said quietly.

"Lad," Podo rumbled, "ye'd better be glad there are more pressing things afoot, or I'd tan your hide. What are you thinking, going off into the forest alone? Haven't you ever heard of toothy cows? Of horned hounds and snapping diggles and cave blats? Right now, since you've shown that yer not responsible enough to be treated like a man, yer gonna keep quiet and let the elders in the room figure out what's to be done. And that goes for the lot of ye," he finished, looking disappointedly at the three of them.

A loud banging on the back door of Oskar's store made everyone jump.

Oskar shrugged at Podo, who pressed a finger to his lips. Podo gripped Gnorm's curved sword and eased over to the door.

The banging came again, louder this time.

Podo took a deep breath, hefted the sword, and wrenched open the door.

38

An Unpleasant Plan

What do you mean, bringing this trouble down on us?"

"You Igibys will be the ruin of us!"

"What do you suppose will happen to this town now you've gone and killed a passel of Fangs?"

A crowd of Glipfolk gathered at Oskar's back door, and no one looked happy. Podo hid the sword behind his back and held a calming hand out to them, but the people were pushing forward and getting louder by the second.

"Easy now, Alep. We'll figure somethin'—"

"Jouncey as a two-ton bog pie!" Charney Baimington declared, and several Glipfolk agreed.

"Just what do you plan to do with sixteen dead Fangs, Mister Igiby? Answer me that!" shouted a plump woman waving a broom.

"Ferinia, calm down. That's just what we're doing is coming up with a plan."

"A plan! I've got a plan! We should run the Igibys into the Dark Sea of Darkness, that's a plan!" Mayor Blaggus shouted from the back.

It was all Podo could take. "ENOUGH!" he roared, and the townsfolk went as still and silent as statues. "The only thing going into the Dark Sea of Darkness tonight is bird droppings. Now listen to me, folks. We didn't ask for this to happen, but it's happened. It is what it is, and we'll figure out something. Now if you'd be so kind as to let me and Oskar here have a few minutes to think, we'll get this sorted out and be with you directly." Under

Podo's glare, the crowd grumbled and muttered but finally dispersed. He closed the door and sighed. "Now, to business."

Janner and Tink sank to the floor and listened while Podo and Oskar hunched over the desk and talked in earnest.

"The town will be set to the flame," Podo said gravely.

Oskar adjusted his spectacles and thought for a moment before nodding. "True. There's little to be done about dear Glipwood, I fear. It's only a matter of time before the Fangs at Fort Lamendron realize something's amiss."

"Aye, and Gnorm said he was under orders from General Khrak himself. He'll be expecting Gnorm and the carriage in a few hours. When it doesn't show, they'll send forces here."

"I've heard the Fangs can run like lightning when they've a mind to—faster than a horse," Oskar said, pushing a wisp of hair behind one ear. "If that's true, we don't even have until morning before more Fangs arrive. Fort Lamendron has hundreds, maybe even thousands of the beasts. They'll come here angry. They need little reason to terrorize us." Oskar sighed. "This is no little thing."

"Blast it all," Podo said, driving his fist into the table. "There's not much the Glipfolk can do. Either they fight or they run. Even if they had weapons, the townsfolk wouldn't have a flabbit's chance against a regiment of Fangs. They'll have to run. The roads to Torrboro should be clear enough, yet. They can hide there, and by morning the Fangs will find Glipwood as empty as a ghost town. Maybe then there's a chance it won't burn. And after we're gone for a while and the dust settles, the townsfolk might be able to come back."

"Some will stay, you know."

"Aye," Podo said after a long moment. "Some will refuse to leave." He punched the table again. "Me bones want to stay and fight those cursed lizards!" He glanced at the children and Nia. "But we have no choice. We're running, and running far."

"The Ice Prairies?" Oskar looked grave.

"Aye. It's the only place the Jewels will be safe anymore."

Janner and Tink looked at one another, their eyes wide. They both had questions but were afraid to incur Podo's wrath again, so they sat in stunned silence. There really were jewels, and Podo and Nia had them.

"There's no time to dally," Podo said. "I have to get to the cottage and gather what I can for the journey. We won't be coming back for a long time." Podo breathed a weary sigh and added, "If at all."

Janner and Tink looked at one another again with wide eyes. *We're going to the Ice Prairies?* [1]

"We'll need supplies, old friend," Podo looked at Oskar. "Real weapons, not these flimsy things." Podo looked with distaste at Gnorm's blade.

"Anklejelly Manor, of course," Oskar said with a nod.

Janner felt his cheeks redden.

"You'll find more than enough of what you need," Oskar said.

"Good. I'll take the boys with me to the cottage to gather what we need. Can you keep Nia and Leeli safe until we get back?"

Oskar winked and bustled over to a crook of the study, where he stooped and pulled up a corner of the rug. Beneath was a trapdoor. "There are lanterns, blankets, and enough dried food to last a good while down there, just in case. In the words of Aman Putan, 'We'll hide them there until you return, at which point you'll head out for safer lodging.' I'll have the map and key to the weapons chamber when you get back."

"Boys, come with me," Podo ordered, and they leapt to their feet.

While Nia and Leeli stepped down into Oskar's secret basement, Janner and Tink followed their grandfather outside, where the small mob of Glipfolk waited impatiently.

Podo cleared his voice and the chatter ceased. "We've considered our options, friends, and none are easy." Podo looked hard at the Glipfolk—

---

1. The Ice Prairies lie north of the Stony Mountains. Few humans have settled there, and what villages do exist are notoriously difficult to find because there are no roads. In fact, some who dwelt in the Ice Prairies visited the warm climes of lower Skree on holiday and were never able to discover their homes again. See map, page xiii.

people he'd worked with for years, some he'd known since he was a boy. He took a deep breath, reluctant to say what he had to say. "We'll have to run."

No one spoke.

"You can either stay here and burn with the town, or you can flee. A regiment of Fangs from Fort Lamendron will head this way as soon as they get a whiff of what happened here tonight. They'll be here before sunrise, we figure. When they get here, they'll probably tear down the place out of spite, and destroy you with it. So if you want to avoid a mean death, you should get what you need and head north, to Dugtown or Torrboro. By morning, I fear Glipwood will not exist."

The wind moaned in the treetops. Podo waited for a challenge to his verdict, but none came. The people saw the truth of what Podo had said. Wordlessly, they dispersed, casting rueful glances at Podo as well as at the boys.

Janner felt the scorn of people who had only ever smiled at him, and he wanted nothing more than to make things right. But how? What was done was done, and there was no undoing it.

Shaggy the tavern owner plopped into a rocking chair on his nearby front stoop and lit a pipe. It was clear that he meant to stay. A scraggly old man approached, big tears running down his face and into his scruffy white beard.

"Buzzard Willie," Podo nodded in greeting.

"Oy, old mate. I never told you proper I'm sorry I stole Merna Bidge-holler from ye back when we was lads. Been meanin' to tell ye that fer years, you rascal." He sniffed.

Podo chuckled uncomfortably and clasped his friend's shoulder, embarrassed about the many, many garden thwaps he'd dumped in Buzzard's yard.

"Merna? I tell ya, Willie, I'd plumb forgot about that. Mostly, anyway," he added under his breath. "Water over the falls, that's all it is. Water over the falls. Now you get on to Dugtown and stay with yer grandkids, eh? I'll see you one of these days, ol' mate."

Buzzard Willie nodded and drew his sleeve across his weepy face. "Oh, and sorry about yer barn burnin' down. Looked like them Fangs really tore up things. I went out there earlier to give ye a little somethin' from me garden, courtesy of meself. Left it on yer porch. A gift, for Merna's sake."

"Aw, now Buzz," Podo said. But his old friend was already moving across the street toward his house to gather up his wife and belongings.

Podo looked at his grandsons. "Well, lads," he said, changing the subject, "that went better than I expected. It looks like they're all leavin'. All but Shaggy and the Shoosters, that is." He said this with a hint of pride for his friends who were sitting on the stoop of The Only Inn, raising a toast to their town and waving good-bye to neighbors and friends. Glipfolk who were leaving had friends and family elsewhere and hurried to make it safely to their refuge without being caught.[2] But for some, like Shaggy and the Shoosters, all they had and all they ever wanted was right there in Glipwood. They had nowhere to go and aimed to die fighting for their home.

"Come on, boys," Podo said, and they followed him to the jail where Fang corpses were scattered about, shriveled and dried as if they'd been decaying for years, not minutes. All that was left were crackled snakeskins, dusty bones, and armor.

Podo pulled a sword from one of them and the clawed hand crumbled to a pile of dust that drifted away on the wind.

"Go on and grab two more swords," Podo said, as he collected a few daggers, including the one that Janner had buried in Gnorm's side. Podo

---

2. The road to Torrboro was well traveled, both by menfolk and Fangs. Fang troops traveling to and from Fort Lamendron marched north and west from the coast, through Glipwood, and followed the road along the edge of Glipwood Forest until it met with the River Blapp. The evening curfew was well enforced, so the Fangs did little to patrol the road at night. Glipfolk traveling through the night to Torrboro had little to worry about until they reached the city itself, and by then the morning would have come anyway, so they wouldn't have raised suspicion. Of course, the road's adjacency to the forest presented difficulties of its own, and several of the travelers were likely to be set upon by Skree's usual array of night creatures. See map, page xiii.

blew the dust from the weapons, walked to the tavern, and offered them somberly to Shaggy and the Shoosters. Janner and Tink heard a few murmured words between them, before their grandfather embraced his old friends, each in turn.

Then in silence Podo and the boys walked briskly out of the township of Glipwood, where for a thousand years people had come for the Dragon Day Festival and been glad. Janner could hardly believe that in a matter of hours it would be rubble.

"That's it, young Leeli," Oskar said as he helped a despondent Leeli Igiby down the wooden steps into the dank basement. "Down you go."

He sat her down on the dirt floor next to Nia and lit a lantern. It illuminated a tiny room with a few crates against the far wall. Oskar busied himself with arranging the crates and checking the supplies, and when he thought all was right, he turned his attention to the mother and daughter. He peered down at them through his spectacles.

"I know it's not the most comfortable accommodation, dear. In the words of Burley the Pow, 'This place is indibnible. And dank.' But you shouldn't be in here for long, depending on how much time Podo takes fetching the supplies. It's just best if we keep you hidden, in case something should go wrong."

Oskar cast a longing glance up at the warm light of his study. "I'm afraid there'll be no time to save my books. All my maps and tomes and volumes and volumes of lore, lost forever. And this was the last of it, dears. All the books left in all of Skree were kept safe here. But no longer. No longer." He blinked and came to himself again.

"Ah, but the jewels. What use are books if the Jewels of Anniera are lost to us?" He winked at Leeli. "I'll be packing what little I can afford to bring. And where is that little ridgerunner? I could use his help," he said to himself.

"I'll close this until it's time to go. In the words of Adeline the Poetess, 'Get some rest. It's for the best.'"

Nia squeezed his hand. "Thank you, Oskar. You're a good friend."

Oskar closed the hatch, and they were in darkness but for the single lantern atop a crate. Leeli cuddled up close to her mother, who could feel her daughter shivering.

The barn behind the Igiby cottage had burned down to smoke and ashes, but the cottage still stood. Janner tried to grasp that he was seeing his home for the last time, and as much as it saddened him, he felt an undeniable thrill. He had often dreamed of seeing what lay beyond the great trees of Glipwood, but he always thought he would have to wait until he was much older to do it. Here he was, twelve years old and on his way to the Ice Prairies, a place he only knew by its name on an old map.

"You boys hurry on in and set to packin'," Podo said. "Not much. Just get a few tunics and britches each and tie 'em up in a bedroll. Do the same for yer sister. I'm off to round up Danny from the north field where the poor old beast's been hitched to the wagon since the Fangs showed up. I just hope he's still got the fire to tow us far enough tonight. I'll be along in a minute to fetch what else we need." Podo strode off into the darkness to the pasture.

"I can't believe we're really leaving," Tink said as he and Janner approached the cottage under a bright moon. "Where are the Ice Prairies, anyway?"

"All I know is that they're north, over the Stony Mountains. A long way from here."

Janner found in the dark the lantern and matches that were kept on the porch near the door. He lit the lantern and the two brothers pushed open the front door and stood looking at the mess made of the cottage during Gnorm's reckless search for the jewels.

If it hadn't been for the smell of smoke in the air, perhaps they would have detected the lingering, vile Fang odor. And if they hadn't been thinking about the long journey ahead, they might have noticed the sound of breathing or seen the long, serpentine tongue flitting hungrily from behind the door.

39

Buzzard Willie's Gift

Leeli and Nia looked up at the ceiling of their hiding place, alarmed at the commotion they heard.

Footsteps. Many footsteps, running, pounding, shuffling.

A scuffle, followed by a loud crash, sent dust floating down on them. Leeli started to sneeze but Nia clamped her hand over her daughter's mouth. Nia could only guess at what was happening above them, and it couldn't be good. She felt like a trapped animal. There was nowhere to turn, and she had no weapon with which to fight. She held on to Leeli, and they backed as far into a corner as they could and waited, praying. The footsteps clunked slowly toward the hatch, and Nia breathed a sigh of relief because it sounded like Oskar when he had busied himself in his study earlier. Maybe he had accidentally knocked over a shelf in his rush to salvage some important books.

But then she heard a voice, and it wasn't Oskar's.

Nia squeezed Leeli tight.

The trapdoor was drawn slowly open, and they squinted up at the bright light streaming in.

Nia's eyes adjusted, and she saw the slight silhouette of Zouzab, twirling his odd little whistle around his finger.

"Oh," Nia sighed, "Zouzab, it's you. Oskar was just—"

Nia's breath caught in her throat when beside him another slight figure appeared—another ridgerunner. They both smiled at her in a way that made her blood run cold.

"Here they are, sergeant," Zouzab said, and a Fang leapt into the chamber as Zouzab and the other ridgerunner scurried up to the top of a bookshelf.

The cottage door slammed behind Janner and Tink as Slarb the Fang emerged in the lamplight and shoved them across the room. The boys crashed into one another and went sprawling to the floor, atop the burble-skin rug. The air was knocked from Janner's lungs and he doubled over, water streaming from his eyes. He was dimly aware of Tink moving beneath him. When he was able to open his eyes, through the blur and stars in his vision, he beheld Slarb slowly moving their way, a long curved sword in his scaly fist.

Slarb was ragged and thinner than before; dirt was caked between his scales, and his skin, rather than the usual cool green, had a ghostly pallor, like old lettuce lying in a gutter. A stench surrounded the Fang like a cloud of insects. To Janner it was the smell of madness, of murder. Slarb's scaly skin hung from his frame like an ill-fitting costume. His time in the wild had changed the evil creature, if possible, for the worse.

"Igibysss," Slarb rasped. "Going to the Ice Prairies, are you? Going to try and escape with the jewels? Oh, don't look so surprised. I watch and lisssten. I hide in the shadowsss. I know that the Igibys have the jewels, and now that Gnorm has failed, I will do the work that he could not. I will bring the Jewels to Gnag the Nameless, won't I?" Slarb pointed the sword at Tink and looked at Janner. "Because if you don't tell me where the jewels are, boy, I'll think of something horrid to do to your dear brother, see? I know you came here to fetch them, and I know where you're planning to run." Slarb's voice grated like stone on stone as he watched the boys with glowing, hungry eyes.

Tink had recovered from the blow and scrambled to his feet as Slarb took another threatening step closer. Janner was thinking hard for a way out. Slarb was blocking the front door, and the way into the kitchen was just to the right of the Fang. To the left was a window. It was possible that one of them could make it through before Slarb could strike, Janner thought, but only one of them. Even if they did somehow scramble through, Slarb would run them down in a matter of seconds. Janner could see nothing nearby that could be used as a weapon, unless the Fangs had an unknown fear of burbleskin rugs. There was nothing they could do. Janner's legs were trembling like leaves in a windstorm. *Where's Grandpa?* he thought desperately. *How long could it take to get the wagon?*

Agile as a cat, Slarb lunged forward, grabbed Tink's hair, and threw him back to the floor. In the same motion he seized Janner's arm and wrenched him close, pointing the tip of the sword between the boy's eyes. Tink cried out and struggled to move, but Slarb had one clawed foot on his back, pinning him down. Janner labored not to breathe the sharp odor that enshrouded the creature.

"Where are the Jewels of Anniera?" Slarb whispered, breathing so close to Janner's face that his hair moved. Janner could hold his breath no longer and gagged. Slarb twisted his foot on Tink's back, and Tink cried out again. "If you want your brother to live, tell me where the jewels are hidden, boy!"

Janner looked wildly around the room, too afraid to pray or fight or think.

Then came the rattle of the wagon approaching the cottage. Janner drew in his breath to cry out, but Slarb clamped a cold, moist hand over his mouth.

"Not a sound," the Fang said, lowering the tip of his sword to rest on the back of Tink's neck. Janner waited in agony as he heard Podo grunt his way down from the wagon and *tap-clunk* to the front door. The footsteps stopped. They heard a shuffling sound just outside, then Podo grunted like he was lifting something.

"Janner? Tink?" Podo called, entering the cottage with a large wooden trunk in his arms. He stopped dead in his tracks when he saw Slarb standing over Tink.

"If you move, old man, I'll kill them both," Slarb said, eyeing the trunk greedily. His tail flitted about on the floor beside Tink. The Fang hissed and steaming glops of venom dripped, sizzling, onto the floor. Tink whimpered. Podo stood frozen. Through the haze of fear and the stink of Slarb's hand over his mouth, Janner managed to wonder dimly where the trunk in Podo's arms had come from.

In one motion, Slarb whipped Janner in front of him and wrapped an arm around his neck, using Janner as a shield from Podo.

"What's in the trunk, old man?"

"Don't know," Podo said, his voice level. "Now you let the lads be and we'll settle this, you and I."

Slarb laughed and squeezed Janner tighter. "The only way to sssettle this is for you to give me the jewels, old man. So I'll ask you again. What's in the trunk?"

"It's a gift from Buzzard Willie, back in town. I don't have a notion what it is, lizard."

"You're a bad liar, old man."

Podo lowered his voice. "You'll not live past this night if you hurt either of me lads. You've not seen my wrath when it's stoked proper, nor do ye want to." Podo took a step closer.

Slarb growled and twisted Janner's head sideways, baring the side of his neck. The Fang opened his jaws wide and drew his dripping teeth closer. A look of defeat came over Podo's face, and he drew back a step.

"Please, no. I beg ye," Podo pleaded. "Don't."

Slarb smiled a hideous smile.

"Good. Now put the trunk down and move away."

Podo did so, and Slarb edged across the room, still clutching Janner from behind.

Tink got to his feet, and he and Podo watched helplessly as Slarb crouched down to unlatch the trunk. Janner was wondering what Slarb would do when he didn't find the jewels in the trunk. The look of worry on Podo's face was what scared him the most. If Podo didn't know what to do, what could possibly be done? The latch on the trunk clicked open, and Janner strained to see.

"And now we'll see these jewelsss that have caused so much trouble." Slarb smiled a wide, sickening smile as he lifted the lid.

Thirty of the angriest, hungriest garden thwaps ever to breathe the air of Aerwiar poured out of the box like a furry plague. Janner wrenched himself away and tumbled to the floor. The thwaps covered Slarb from head to foot, chattering and squealing in such cacophony that Janner and Tink held their ears. Slarb looked like a giant furry burble doll careening about, crashing into walls, lunging to and fro. Podo snatched up Slarb's blade and drove the Fang through the door and into the kitchen. The brothers listened anxiously to the riotous sounds of Podo's battle cry, Slarb's shrieks, and the thwaps' squeals.

At last Podo emerged, out of breath and spattered again with the green Fang blood. He saw that Janner and Tink were unharmed and he smiled, his eyebrows lifting in a happy way that gave Janner hope that they'd make it out of Glipwood alive. One of the angry thwaps scurried out of the kitchen, but Podo growled and booted it back.

"Remind me to thank ol' Buzzard Willie, eh? That rascal." Podo disappeared into his room while the boys busied themselves, gathering extra clothes and rolling them up in a blanket. Janner was glad he didn't need anything from the kitchen. He didn't want to see Slarb's bony corpse in the room where he'd had so many glad meals with his family. The boys made bedrolls for Leeli and Nia and carried them along with their own to the wagon.

Immediately, Janner sensed something wrong—a smell in the air, or some subtle sound on the wind that he couldn't quite place. He looked down the lane toward the town and saw in glimpses the orange glow of hundreds of torches at the edge of Glipwood Township.

"Grandpa!" he cried. "Come quick!"

Podo bounded out of the house with a bundle over his shoulder. "What is it?"

Janner pointed. Now he could make out hundreds, maybe thousands, of torches in two columns snaking off into the dark distance, moving toward Glipwood from the east—from Fort Lamendron.

"So soon?" Podo whispered. "Maker help us."

40

Betrayal

With a fierce look in his eyes, Podo threw the bundle into the back of the wagon and mounted it without waiting for the boys. They scrambled in as Podo said, "Hya!" to Danny the carthorse, who whinnied and tore toward Glipwood.

Janner's eyes watered in the wind as he watched the sweeping boughs of glipwood trees whiz by. He prayed to the Maker that Leeli and Nia were still safe. He wondered how they possibly would escape with Nia and Leeli, if indeed the Fangs had overrun the town. He looked up at Podo, at the white hair flying out behind him, bluish now in the moonlight, and felt better. Maybe Podo didn't have a plan, but knowing that his grandfather was with him, even in the face of the Fangs of Dang, made Janner feel like he could be more than he was. He drew strength from the old man, like water from a well, and rested in it. And he looked admiringly at Tink, who had found a Fang sword among the remains in the wagon and was holding it in two fists, clenching his jaw.

Podo reined up the horse when they could see the torchlights among the buildings in the distance. "Whoa, Danny boy. Easy now," he whispered. He motioned for Tink and Janner to follow and disappeared into the brush beside the road, fast as a thwap.

From where they stopped they could dimly see the lampposts on Main Street and they could hear a mixture of chatter, laughter, and movement that was oddly familiar. Janner realized with a shudder that the last time he had heard such volume was when the town was full of hundreds and hundreds of visitors to the Dragon Day Festival. Could there really be that many Fangs in Glipwood? Janner grabbed a sword of his own from the wagon. Like the weapons in Anklejelly Manor, it was heavier than he expected. He felt his youth in its weight. He tried to look confident for Tink, but his little brother was already moving into the shadows beside the road after Podo.

"All right, lads," Podo whispered from a leafy cover. "Listen up. I need you to be men, do you hear?" They both nodded. "There's strong blood in yer veins, and if ye trust me and let the Maker guide ye, we might live to see the sun lift this mornin'. I'm makin' this up as I go, so you follow me close and do as I say. No questions. If we get separated, then we meet at a place called Anklejelly Manor."

Janner and Tink instinctively glanced northward.

Podo raised an eyebrow. "I see ye know where I'm talkin' about. And ye've probably been there from the look of it."

Janner looked down.

"Hmph. There's a lot that we need to talk about when this all blows over, I reckon. But don't you fret about it now. Ye know I love you boys. And I love yer mother and sister too. Besides, they're a right bit prettier than you louses. So we've got to get 'em back, hear? We're gonna get 'em and make like mad for Anklejelly Manor. Other than that, we'll just see how the leaves fall. You clear?"

"Yessir," the brothers said in unison.

Without a word, Podo again vanished into the shadows.

Janner and Tink followed through the gardens and fields behind the buildings facing Main Street. They hopped a fence, and Janner was again surprised at Podo's nimble speed.

They halted between two buildings and had their first clear glimpse of the street.

Fangs were everywhere. Some stood in formation while a ranking officer bellowed orders at them. Others milled about drunkenly, laughing or fighting with one another. Some sat and dozed in the very alley they were looking through, only a stone's throw away. It was clear that the Fangs had just arrived and were out of order.

Janner's pulse quickened and he felt the danger anew. One noise, one Fang looking in the wrong direction at the wrong time, and they would be found out, caught like flabbits in a snare. Two fences ahead lay the field behind Oskar's shop. Podo vaulted over another fence and beckoned the boys on. With a last look down the alleyway, to be sure no Fang was watching, Tink and Janner followed.

They made it to Oskar's yard without incident and hunkered down with their backs to the trunk of a fat tree. Podo peeked around the tree while the brothers fought to catch their breath and calm their nerves.

"Oskar's door is open and the lantern is still burning inside," he whispered. "I can't see other than that. We ought to be able to make a run for the rear of the building, then it's just a matter of sneakin' around the corner and through the door. You lads ready?"

The bright moon made the open distance across to the building precarious; there were even more Fangs loitering in front of and between Ferinia's Flower Shop and Books and Crannies than there were in the first alley.

Podo didn't wait. With another glance down the alley, he dashed across to the building. Janner took a deep breath and set to go. But just as he took his first step, Tink jerked him back behind the tree. A Fang lumbered toward them along the side of the building. Janner and Tink held their breath and clutched their swords, their backs to the tree. But the Fang lost interest in whatever he was doing and his footsteps receded. Janner snuck another peek and saw that the way was clear.

They sprinted to the safety of the shadows at the rear of Books and Crannies. Podo nodded at his grandsons with a proud wink. He looked around the corner and down the alley. After a few seconds, he motioned for the boys to follow. With a last deep breath, they turned the corner and darted through Oskar's back door.

Podo's growl told Janner that his mother and sister had been captured. The trapdoor stood open and black like an empty grave. Podo stood over the hole, breathing hard and rumbling in a way that made Janner fear he might actually explode.

"I'm sorry," came a weak voice from behind them. They whipped around to see Oskar N. Reteep lying on the floor beside his desk with a bleeding wound in his chest. He was pallid and feeble, his glasses hanging askew on his round face. He coughed.

Podo knelt at Oskar's side and grabbed his limp hand. "What happened?" Podo gently pushed a damp swath of Oskar's stringy hair out of the old man's eyes.

"Zouzab...betrayed us. In the words of Chonk," Oskar breathed, "'I should've known.'"

Podo bowed his head, half in rage, half in sorrow.

"He signaled to Lamendron...with his whistle...during the battle..."

Janner remembered the shrill sound they'd heard just after Commander Gnorm died.

Oskar winced and coughed again. "Only another ridgerunner could've heard it at that distance. All these years, he's been watching, spying. He only stopped the Black Carriage with his sling so that we would think we had more time."

"But he saved us with the rocks in the alley," Tink said.

"Yes, he did...because he suspected—" Oskar's eyes drooped and his voice broke.

Suspected what? Janner thought.

"How do you know all this?" Podo asked, his rage getting the better part of his sadness.

"Zouzab told me," Oskar rasped. "He told me after the Fangs...took Nia and Leeli. He knelt right where you're kneeling now...and told me everything." Oskar faded with every breath. "I'm sorry, old friend. The jewels...keep them with you. Hold fast to them!"

"I will. By the Maker, I will," Podo said, squeezing Oskar's limp hand.

Oskar's eyes widened and focused on something above and behind Podo. Janner looked up in time to see Zouzab vanish into the labyrinth of bookshelves.

"It's him!" Janner cried.

With a roar, Podo bounded after Zouzab, books toppling over in every direction.

"Janner, Tink. Listen," Oskar said weakly. They bent over the old fellow and strained to hear him over Podo's mad search for the ridgerunner. Oskar gripped Janner's arm. "It's too late. He's too fast…in a matter of seconds Zouzab will have already informed the Fangs that you're here. You have to go now. Run! Run!"

Janner's heart broke for his mentor. He couldn't imagine leaving him to die, leaving Podo to be captured by the Fangs, or leaving Leeli and his mother to whatever fate Gnag had for them. His mind was a flurry of memories of old Mr. Reteep, who had taught him to love books, who had given him his first journal. Tink stood quietly behind Janner and bowed his head.

"Run!" Oskar breathed, his weak eyes pleading with them.

Choking back tears, Janner turned to go—and collided with the hulking, smelly body of a Fang.

41

A Rumble and a Screech

It was as if Janner had run into a blur of hissing, claws, teeth, and pain. He felt his wrists tied, then the world turned upside down as he first was shoved to the ground and then jerked to his arms and feet by cold hands. He could hear Tink screaming. But all Janner saw was a sea of scaly faces and black, red-rimmed eyes. He felt the flick of forked tongues and smelled the rot of Fang flesh.

The air was full of howling and snarling.

Then he realized that the sound was coming not just from the Fangs, but from someone else too. He strained his neck to see out Books and Crannies' front window, where his grandfather's white hair whipped about in the center of a circle of Fangs. Podo was in the middle of the street waving a sword and keeping a host of surrounding Fangs at bay. The Fangs seemed to be enjoying it, cackling and jabbing at him with the butts of their spears.

Janner was carried outside and thrown to the ground, relieved to find Tink, Leeli, and Nia lying beside him. The sense of comfort at their presence, even in a sea of evil, was more than his heart could take, and he cried. Janner wished his hands were unbound, not so he could run but so that he could embrace the ones he loved.

Then, without warning, Nia was jerked from the ground.

"Enough! Or the woman dies!" called a lithe Fang who appeared to be in command. He lifted up Nia by her waist and drew his sword. Podo's fury disappeared like the snuffing of a candle. He looked across the sea of scaly heads at his daughter and his bushy eyebrows trembled. The only sound was of the old pirate's heavy breathing. At his feet lay several dead, already-decomposing Fangs.

"No," Podo breathed, his voice cracking.

"Lay down your sword, then, old man, or sssay good-bye to the woman."

Podo, full of sorrow, looked long at his daughter. Nia was silent, her jaw set and her eyes closed.

"General Khrak," one of the Fangs said.

"Not now, you fool," said Khrak, lowering his voice. "Can't you see I'm lifting this human? This is harder than it looksss."

"Nia girl? Are ye okay?" Podo called.

"General Khrak," the lesser Fang repeated.

"Silence, worm!" Khrak snarled.

"Yes, Papa," Nia said. Podo's face softened. He lifted his sword above his head in a gesture of submission, about to lay down his arms.

"General Khrak."

"*What?*" Khrak said, and he turned on the soldier as he dropped Nia to the ground again.

"Something coming, sir."

"Eh?"

"Something coming this way. Look." The Fang pointed.

Khrak looked, and every eye in Glipwood followed. Something certainly was coming—a speeding, bounding shadow across the field, and no one had the slightest notion what it was—but it was big. And in the light of the fat moon, they could see that someone was riding it.

Two sounds split the air and sent a shiver of panic through the whole regiment of Fangs. A rumble like the explosion of close thunder, together with the soaring cry of a bird of prey, crashed over the Fangs of Dang like a mighty wave.

Podo's jaw went slack at the sight before him.

Peet the Sock Man, arms wide and talons bared, was riding on the back of a giant black dog the size of a horse.

"What in the deep...?" Podo breathed.

The last Podo had seen of Nugget was a motionless mangle of fur with a spear run through his side near the cottage when they'd first been captured. The beast that bounded toward him, however, was like nothing he'd ever seen.

Thirty Fangs were flattened to the ground like weeds in the wind when Peet and the giant Nugget creature slammed into them. The Fangs were so transfixed by the huge black thing in their midst that Podo was able to push his way through in an instant to the children and Nia.

Even Khrak was immobile, gawking at the wild-haired Sock Man who was tearing into his army with talons and a giant dog.

"Crawl!" Podo said. "I'll cut you loose when we're clear of the Fangs!" They wriggled and wormed their way between hundreds of Fang legs while the soldiers emerged from their surprise and began an attack on the beast and its rider. By the time General Khrak noticed they were gone, the Igibys were climbing into the wagon at the edge of town, giddy at the very breath in their lungs.

Podo turned the wagon north toward Anklejelly Manor and urged Danny the carthorse, "Like lightning, Danny boy!"

"What was that, Grandpa?" Janner asked as they jostled north past the Blaggus Estate.

"Was that Peet doing all the screaming?" Tink asked.

"Aye," Podo called back from the front of the wagon.

"What was the other noise?" Janner asked. "The growling, I mean."

Podo hooted and slapped his knee. "Leeli girl," he called over his shoulder. "You ready for this?" Podo turned and leaned close to Leeli's face. He took her chin in his old gnarled hand. "It was Nugget. That little dog of yours is *alive*. Aye, and he may be more than that."

Leeli's face was a perfect picture of wonder. Tears rose to her wide eyes and her mouth hung open and begged to smile. "But...how? All those Fangs! How can you be so sure he's alive?" she asked, feeling deep inside her that what Podo said was true. The deep roar she'd heard had sounded wonderfully familiar to her.

Janner smiled to hear Leeli's strong voice come back to her.

"Oh, I'm sure Nugget's fine," Podo laughed. "There's not much a Fang could do to him now, I tell ye. Wait and see, lass. I reckon Nugget'll pick up our trail and be with you shortly."

As Danny the carthorse pulled the wagon along at a trot, the Igiby children began to feel the weariness of their travails. So much had happened since they had followed Peet the Sock Man to his tree house in the forest, and it didn't appear that any rest was in sight.

Leeli leaned on Janner and was soon fast asleep. He put an arm around her, then felt a weight on his other shoulder. Tink had fallen asleep too, his head unconsciously resting on his brother. Janner thought with a smile how horrified Tink would be to know that he had snuggled up to his big brother.

Nia leaned forward and kissed Janner on the head.

As they climbed the long, steady slope north, away from Glipwood and the cliffs over the Dark Sea of Darkness, they could see the warm lights of the town's streetlamps twinkling in the distance, an irony in light of the evil that swarmed the streets there.

Janner said a silent prayer for Oskar, then for Peet, who had once again swooped in out of darkness and saved their lives when all was lost. Janner wondered why Podo hated him so much. What secret history did they have, and how could Podo not replace that anger with gratitude when Peet had not once, but three times, rescued them?

"Mama?" Janner could stand no more silence.

"Mmm?"

"Where will we go?"

Nia looked troubled. She brushed at her dress and looked up at the moon. "I really don't know, son. The Ice Prairies, for now. Oskar told us that the Fangs are sluggish in the cold and they avoid it when they can. He told us there's an outpost of rebels there, those who would drive the Fangs back across the sea to Dang. Oskar said he knew some of them, so your grandfather plans to seek refuge there. But getting there…"

"Is it far?"

"Very far. But we first need to live through this night. Don't worry. Your grandfather has a plan." Nia laughed, a welcome sound in the dark. "Or at least he's in the process of making up one." Nia stroked Janner's head. "You should rest your eyes now. We won't be there for a little while yet."

His mother's voice soothed Janner and his eyes drooped.

A thumping in the darkness behind the wagon startled Janner awake. He braced himself as a dark shape approached the wagon, moving faster than a horse at full gallop.

Podo, hearing Janner's gasp, raised his sword in one hand and held the reins with the other. But when he saw in the moonlight what was approaching, his manner lightened and to Janner's surprise he reined up Danny the carthorse.

The wagon stopped, and Leeli and Tink stretched and rubbed their eyes. A black shadow bounded toward them—a shadow oddly familiar to Janner. Astride it and covered in dark patches of green Fang blood was the white haired, lanky figure of Peet the Sock Man.

With sleepy eyes, Leeli peered into the moonlit night, trying to understand what she was seeing. She leaned over the edge of the wagon as the dark creature approached and Podo climbed down with open arms.

The creature let out a deep, happy noise—like a bark, only much, much larger.

"Nugget, lad," Podo said, reaching up to scratch the creature behind a big floppy ear.

Leeli's eyes widened, unbelieving.

Peet slid off Nugget's back, slinking away from Podo, who hadn't even acknowledged the Sock Man's presence.

"Nugget?" Leeli ventured timidly, afraid to believe this was really him.

The giant dog yipped, if it could be called that, as it was a sound that shook the air and made birds scatter half a mile away. Leeli let out a happy squeal and tumbled out of the wagon. She crumpled to the ground, forgetting in her elation that she had only one good leg.

Nugget bounded over to her and set to licking her with a tongue nearly as big as she was. She squealed with delight and disbelief. She was sure she had seen a Fang kill her dearest companion, and now he was alive and as big as a horse. Nugget crouched his bulk low to the ground, and Leeli laughed as she climbed onto his back. She sat astride her dog, burying her hands deep in his soft fur. Nugget stood there panting, tail as long as a broomstick and wagging dangerously.

From the tall grass several paces away, Peet the Sock Man cleared his throat.

Janner wanted to run to the strange man and hug him, but he was wary of it. Podo had made it plain that Peet was to stay clear of the children, and Janner was afraid of bringing more of his grandfather's wrath down on the poor man. He was also unsure of the lethal talons that served as Peet's hands.

Had Leeli not been so enraptured with Nugget, she would have reached out to him with her typical compassion and typical disregard of Podo's gruffness. But as it was, the family stood in a cluster around the giant dog, and Peet stood alone.

"Peet," Janner asked with a cautious glance at Podo. "How did Nugget get so big? How was it he came back to life?"

"Nuggy and I made it out," Peet said, ignoring the question. "But only barely, bonely. The snakes. They're coming. Coming fast. You've got to hide the pewels, Jodo. Jewels, Podo. You can't let them fall to the Fangs."

"Don't tell me what I've got to do," Podo growled. The children were startled. Even Nugget whined and buried his face under his giant paws. "I reckon I know how to keep things safe better than *you*."

"Father," Nia said, placing a hand on Podo's arm. He glared at his daughter and seemed about to retort, but with a great will he held his tongue and stomped away to the wagon.

So the jewels are here somewhere, Janner thought. He tried to imagine what the jewels were and whether or not they were wrapped in the bundle Podo had brought with him out of the cottage, the bundle lying in the wagon just behind his grandfather.

"Back in the wagon," Podo said, trying to speak calmly. "Somebody's led the Fangs right to us." He seemed ashamed at the unfairness of his own remark. "Either way, we've got to get a move on. The manor is just ahead, and it's our only hope of making it to mornin'. Now listen. Ye children are gonna wait inside while I try to find the weapons Oskar told me about. He never had a chance to give me the map." He looked back down toward the glow of town where he had last seen his old friend.

"We know where they are, Grandpa," Tink said.

"Do you now?" Podo said, his eyes narrowing. "You boys have been right busy, I'd say." Tink started to respond, but Podo cut him off with a quick cut of his hand.

A Fang silhouette appeared in the moonlight over a rise not an arrow's shot away.

"Here they are!" the Fang cried.

Peet the Sock Man lost no time. He shrieked and bolted across the meadow toward the evil lizard.

The Fang scurried off, waving its arms and yelling to the rest of the soldiers that he had found their quarry.

"Onto the wagon! Now!" Podo commanded.

Nia and the boys clambered into the back, and Podo snapped Danny into motion.

Leeli clung to Nugget's neck as he galloped along beside Danny the carthorse, who was quite unsure about the happy beast beside him.

42

Good-bye, Iggyfings

The foreboding, skull-like face of Anklejelly Manor materialized out of the darkness as they approached. Illumined with ghostly moonlight and framed by the dark wall of Glipwood Forest, the sight of the ancient manor sent a shiver straight down to Janner's toes and set him sweating. He tried not to think about the horned hounds or the ghostly moan that had oozed out of the tunnel that led to the weapons.

Behind them, another of Peet's screeches echoed over the wide meadow. He raced toward them and away from the Fangs at full speed, hundreds of soldiers coursing up the field behind him. Podo drove the wagon through the dilapidated gates, past the odd statues and the overgrown fountain until the upturned cobblestones and rubble proved too much for Danny.

Podo leapt to the ground and quickly worked the harness and tack loose. Once Danny was free, Podo slapped the horse's rump. "Now git! Git!" Danny whinnied and was off, galloping along the edge of the forest and away from the coming battle.

Anklejelly Manor had been frightening enough during the day. Now it was deep night, with a horde of Fangs fast approaching. The forest wall loomed an arrowshot away, teeming with unseen creatures that would put fear even into a Fang.

It seemed to Janner that there was nowhere left to run—none of the options seemed safe, not running into the forest, into the Fangs, or into Anklejelly Manor.

At least in the manor they would have an army's share of weapons. What good some swords would be to an old one-legged pirate, a woman, and three children, he didn't know, especially against an army of Fangs. But at least they had Peet and Nugget. Still, formidable allies that they were, Peet and Nugget couldn't defeat hundreds of Fangs.

Janner began to despair. Even if his grandfather had a talent for improvising in dangerous situations, sooner or later he was sure to run out of ideas. That time seemed to have come. He watched Podo helping Nia out of the wagon while only a few minutes away stormed the Fang horde.

"Janner!" Podo said. "You know where the weapons are?"

"Yessir, Tink and I do," Janner said. "Inside, under the cellar."

Podo nodded. "Good. Janner, you lead the way. We've got to get down there, and fast."

"But, grandpa, we'll be trapped!" Janner said. "There's a long tunnel, and there are horned hounds, and there's a ghost down there, and—"

"A ghost, eh?" Podo said, tossing the bundle from the cottage over his shoulder. "Well, would you rather face your imagination or a Fang blade?"

"But we heard it!" Tink insisted. "We heard the ghost and it chased us out of the tunnel!"

"That sound is nothing but the wind. It's just something Oskar rigged up to a shaft to scare off folk that weren't supposed to be down there—like you and yer brother, for example. Now, you need to trust yer Podo and get to it."

"What do you plan to do with more weapons anyway? There will still be only five of us!" Janner said.

"JANNER!" Podo bellowed.

Janner's mouth clapped shut.

"Leeli, come on down from there," Podo said gently. "Nugget's gonna have to take care of himself now. There's not much in all of Aerwiar that he needs to fear anymore, and he can't follow where we're headed. He'll be fine come sunrise, you'll see." Leeli protested and hugged Nugget tight as Podo pulled her down. The dog whined and nuzzled her gently.

"Tink, help your sister," Podo ordered.

Suddenly Peet materialized out of the darkness. His breathing was ragged and he staggered wearily.

"I wanted to say good-bye, young Iggyfings. I'll fight for you as long as I can." Peet looked at Podo with a new boldness. "I'll fight for them."

But without a word of thanks or even a glance, Podo stepped up the stone stairs and into the black mouth of the manor.

"I won't follow," Peet called after the old man. "I'll stay away from you all, like you said. But I *will* fight for them." Peet turned to the children and bowed low. "Good-bye, Iggyfings," he said, then he turned and strode through the gate and toward the ocean of Fangs, his arms spread wide and his talons bared.

Tearing his eyes away from their protector, Janner took a deep breath and followed Podo into the darkness of the manor.

"Nugget," Leeli cried over her shoulder. "You go someplace safe. Find me when this is all over. Go!"

But Nugget stood there, his giant head cocked sideways, his ears perked up expectantly.

"Mister Peet! Will you take care of him?"

"Yes, princess," called Peet from across the moonlit lawn.

Nugget whined again as Leeli was led by Tink through the doorway, swallowed by the darkness.

Nia was last, and as she entered, the first of the Fangs poured through the gates of Anklejelly Manor, a hissing riot of snakes and snarls.

43

A Ghost in the Wind

All was darkness.

Janner tried to remember which doorway led to the room with the missing stairs. It had been dark enough last time they were in the dilapidated mansion, and then it had been the middle of the day. Now it was night, and he was scared out of his wits.

His eyes adjusted and Janner was able to detect signs of bluish moonlight sneaking through cracks in the ceiling and puddling on the floor. He could just make out the wide staircase that led to the upper floors. Podo's hand was on Janner's shoulder, and Tink, who was helping Leeli, had a hand on Podo's back. Nia held on to Leeli's elbow.

Janner turned left and the train of Igibys entered a black hallway.

"Lad, I don't mean to rush you," Podo whispered. "But that noise you hear outside is Fangs coming fast."

Janner wasn't certain, but this felt like the right hallway, the one lined with doors on either side. If this was the case, he just had to find the third door on the left. He scooted his feet forward carefully with his hands outstretched until he felt the first doorway. The train of people behind him grew more frantic by the second.

"I wish I had some light," he muttered.

"Aye, son. Me too. But even if we had some fire, there's nothing the horned hounds like more than a good blaze. Them and a great passel of other critters in the forest are drawn to it, especially at night. We don't need toothy cows *and* Fangs after us, now do we?"

"No sir."

"You can do this, lad."

"They're getting closer," Nia said from the back.

Janner felt his way to the second, then the third doorway. "This is it."

Like a gust of wind, the fear of the ghost of Brimney Stupe whooshed into Janner's heart. All the other horrors visiting them now seemed harmless. Here he was about to descend into the dark, stairless cellar and crawl into a tunnel where a ghost kept watch. Podo had said the sound was nothing but the wind, but Janner's imagination was strong and working hard. Death by Fang seemed better than facing the groaning ghost of Brimney Stupe, imaginary or not.

Sensing the silent urging of his family behind him, Janner edged forward, kicking little stones and debris as he did so. He fully expected to see Brimney Stupe's ghastly form rise up from the cellar door and set to eating his brain right out of his head.

Then he reached the dark doorway that dropped off into the cellar.

"We're here," he breathed. He shook his head with frustration at himself for kicking the rope and plank back into the cellar when he and Tink had escaped last time. "There are no stairs, so we have to jump down." He tried to hide the tremble in his voice.

"You first then," said Podo. "I'll help lower down yer ma and sister."

Janner thought to protest but kept silent. In his mind he saw a faceless figure standing at the bottom of the cellar, waiting to wrap its cold arms around him and gobble him up.

It's not real, Janner told himself. *It's only the wind. Only the wind. There is no ghost of Brimney Stupe.* He sat on the ledge, turned onto his stomach, and scooted himself over until he was hanging by his fingers against the cellar wall. He closed his eyes and willed himself to drop. *Only the wind. Trust Podo.* With a prayer to the Maker, he let go.

The ground wasn't so jarring this time, now that he was expecting it and he wasn't jumping from the full height. He got to his feet.

"I'm okay. It's not too far down," he said.

"Well done, lad," Podo called down.

Then, from out of the darkness, Janner heard the moan.

AAAAAAAAAAAAAHHHHHHH

It rose up out of the tunnel and swirled around the room. Janner smacked his hands over his ears and screwed his eyes shut. His mind grew numb with panic, and he tried to convince himself that if he opened his eyes he wouldn't see the glowing eyes of a hungry ghost. He scoffed that he ever believed Podo that a sound so horrible could be the wind.

"Janner!" He could hear Podo's voice faintly, cutting through the ghostly groan. "It's the wind, lad! There ain't no ghost!" the old man cried.

AAAAAAAAAAAAAAHHHHHHHHHHHH

Time and time again Podo had proven trustworthy, Janner told himself. Why shouldn't he trust him now? Janner clenched his jaws tight and prepared himself to see Brimney Stupe and then the Maker.

Finally, Janner opened his eyes. Darkness.

Podo thudded to the floor beside him and pried Janner's hands from his ears. In the blackness Janner sensed his grandfather's face close to his and felt his warm breath when he spoke.

"It's all right lad. Just the wind. Feel my hands. These are real."

Janner nodded. At the touch of Podo's big callused fingers, the moaning shrunk in his mind and was replaced with shame. He was thankful that in the darkness his face was hidden.

"Sorry," Janner said.

"No time for that," Podo said, ruffling Janner's hair. Just as he reached up and called for Leeli, the thump of footsteps and a snarl floated through the house above them.

The Fangs were inside.

Shadows moved over shadows in the manor as the Fangs spread like smoke through the house. Janner no longer heard fighting outside, which meant that Peet and Nugget were dead or had finally fled. Janner was angry at himself that he had been more afraid of the imaginary ghost than of the Fangs. He had cost them valuable time.

"Nia! Pass Leeli down!" Podo hissed.

Nia took Leeli's hands and lowered her into his waiting arms. She did the same for Tink, then Nia dropped Podo's bundle down and came last. When she scooted off and thudded to the ground, there came a grunt of surprise from the room above them. Suddenly the dim outline of a Fang appeared in the doorway, peering down.

The Igibys froze. A breathless moment passed, during which Janner was sure Podo had made a grave mistake leading them here. Though they could not see it, a slow smile spread across the Fang's face.

"I can ssssmell you," the Fang hissed. "General Khrak!" he called, then disappeared from the doorway, and they heard it call again, "General Khrak! I've found them!"

44

Following Podo

Tink!" Podo wasted no time. "Where's the tunnel?"

Tink remembered the matches and lantern he and Janner had discovered the last time they were there. He felt his way to the corner of the room near the pile of wood planks and grabbed the matchbox, but—the lantern was missing. Tink's heart shriveled till he remembered that he had dropped it at the foot of the steps in his terror at the moaning of Brimney Stupe.

With a deep breath, Tink rushed down the steps. His foot struck the lantern and he snatched it up and bounded up the steps. One strike of the match and the cellar was full of yellow light, illuminating the mouth of the tunnel and the stairs leading down to shadows. Tink lit the oil lamp and held it high.

"Tink, no!" Janner yelped. "The light attracts—"

But Podo cut him off. "Too late for that. In you go, quick!" Podo bustled Leeli and Nia down the steps. The air grew close and damp, and suddenly the manor above them seemed far, far away. It was difficult for Janner to walk Leeli through the low-ceilinged passageway, but after it opened up they were able to scoot along at a quick pace.

"Tink, they're coming!" cried Podo from the rear. Janner turned the corner and saw Tink staring at the old doorway. At the look on Tink's face, Janner felt a thud of despair. How had they forgotten? The map was the key to opening the door, and it was still at Oskar's shop.

"What's the wait?" Podo said as he rounded the corner with Nia.

"The map—it had a key. Holes that showed which of these buttons to push. Tink, do you remember which ones?"

"It was in the shape of a W," Tink said, jabbing the buttons. He turned the latch and—the door didn't budge. Tink rattled the handle frantically. Now they could hear the Fangs behind them, probably in the cellar.

"I don't know what's wrong!" he cried. "Janner! Isn't this right?"

"Hurry lads!"

Janner stared at the rows of buttons on the door.

Podo looked around the corner. "They're in the tunnel!" His voice was urgent. "Have you got it?"

Janner closed his eyes and went over it again and again in his head. The buttons had been in the shape of a W, centered on the door. He was sure that was right. Why wouldn't the door open? Tink pressed all the buttons in again, firmly, and tried the handle. Still the door wouldn't budge.

"Wait—the corners!" Janner said. "Press the corners in!"

"That's it!" In a frenzy, Tink clicked buttons in again, this time with the four corners pressed. The door swung open, and the Igibys tumbled into the room full of dusty weapons.

Podo wasted no time in choosing a shield and spear from a pile. "There'll be no room to swing a sword in that tunnel," he said to himself as he moved back to the iron door.

"Grandpa, you can't go back out there!" Leeli said.

Podo didn't seem to hear her. He stopped and looked at Tink, who was using the lamp to light a torch on the wall.

"Janner, find a blade and follow me with that lantern. Tink, you arm yourself and stay here with Nia and Leeli. If we fall, you hold this door shut till these Fangs die of old age, hear?" Then he turned and reentered the passageway.

Janner stood at the doorway his grandfather had just exited, thinking that he was seeing the kind of courage that he had only read about. Who knew how many armed Fangs clotted the very passageway his old, one-legged grandfather had just dashed into? Janner wanted nothing more than to own that kind of courage, but there he stood shivering in his skin and feeling as useless as a dead leaf.

He heard a rattle behind him and turned to see Tink rummaging through the weapons and armor. Nia hefted a short sword from the pile, then gave Leeli a long dagger and pulled her close. They stood in the center of the room, Tink now in front of his mother and sister with a shield and sword.

Janner took a deep breath, grabbed the nearest sword, and followed Podo into the tunnel with the lantern, barely able to keep his legs under him. The sound of steel on steel that echoed from the passageway was nearly drowned out by Podo's roar.

Janner could see nothing but the damp stone walls, the end of his sword, and Podo's rear. Beyond Podo he heard the enraged Fangs and caught glimpses of scaly fists and bared teeth. Podo stood his ground in the low tunnel, barring the way with the great shining shield. Whenever he saw an opening he jabbed the spear with all his might. The Fangs wailed and growled, and Podo managed a few steps forward. Janner nearly tripped over something and saw with disgust that he was stepping over the body of the Fang Podo had just slain.

He wondered what he was supposed to be doing. He couldn't fight from his position behind Podo, not that he would do much good if he could. If Podo fell, Janner wouldn't last a minute. And why had he brought the lantern? Podo was blocking all the light that might've done him any good. Janner considered putting the lantern down so that maybe he could squeeze beside Podo and get in a jab or two. But then he heard Podo's voice in his head.

Just trust me, boy, and do as I say.

Podo had wanted him to bring the lantern. That was that. Janner grimaced as he stepped over yet another dead Fang. Why were they forcing their way back up the tunnel? It made much more sense to him that Podo should have made his stand in the armor room. They could lock the door and hold it shut, and if the door was breached they could at least slay the Fangs one at a time as they entered the chamber. Either way, Janner figured they seemed hopelessly trapped.

Trust me, boy.

Podo killed another two Fangs and forced his way further up the tunnel. Janner could see that they were getting closer to the cellar. What then? He didn't know, but he grew more and more panicky the closer they got. Perhaps Podo planned to die gloriously with Janner in the cellar, making their final stand on the woodpiles—

The woodpiles. *"There's nothing that attracts the beasts of the forest like a good blaze,"* Podo had said.

Janner suddenly understood. And the prospects terrified him.

Podo advanced again, and suddenly he and Janner were climbing over more dead Fangs and up the steps to the cellar. They burst into the dark room to find two more lizards poised to attack. A third Fang leapt from the high doorway and more were coming. Podo set to waving his spear around wildly, forcing them back.

"Janner!" he bawled, jabbing at a Fang who had stepped in to thrust.

"I know! The woodpile!"

Janner edged along the wall toward the heap of old timber, keeping a close eye on the Fangs, but they were preoccupied with the mad one-legged ex-pirate bellowing at them. He held the lantern over his head, clenched his eyes tight, and hurled it down onto the stack of old, dry lumber. The oil in the lantern splattered across the wood, staining it with liquid fire that whooshed along the dried planks. In a matter of seconds, the blaze shot higher than Janner's head and inched upward to the ancient wood of the cellar ceiling, the same ceiling he and Tink had pelted rocks through for light.

Podo risked a glance at the flames and paid for it with the first real wound he had received in many long years. One of the Fangs stabbed him in the belly. The others were so surprised that the old warrior had actually been hurt, they stood for a moment in shock. With a roar, Podo ran the Fang through and flung his spear at the others. The spear skewered one of them, and even before its body crumpled to the ground Podo had gathered Janner before him and was bounding back down the stone steps.

The other Fangs, unconcerned with the rising blaze, awoke from their shock and gave chase.

Janner ran with all his might. He burst into the weapon room to a surprised Tink who was ready to strike the first thing that came through the door.

"Grandpa's coming, and the Fangs are behind him!" Janner said breathlessly, skidding to the ground. Tink rushed over and stood with his back to the wall beside the door. He gripped his sword in two hands and clenched his teeth.

With a loud cry, Podo tumbled through the doorway and collapsed, bright blood covering his hands and the front of his tunic.

Two Fangs were close behind. They trampled over his body as if he were already dead, howling with victory. Tink swung his sword with all his might as the first one burst into the chamber. The blade cut the creature cleanly in two, though it continued running toward Leeli and Nia as its bottom half and top half slid apart and sunk to the floor within inches of them.

The second Fang received a lesser blow from the same swing, but a crippling one. It howled at the wound in its side but still advanced toward them, its blade aimed right at Leeli.

Janner found his feet and struck the charging Fang's blade upward with his sword. But the Fang flew into Leeli and Nia, and the three of them crashed to the floor in a heap.

In unison Janner and Tink cried out and rushed to the pile to discover the tip of Nia's sword protruding from the Fang's back.

"Grandpa!" Leeli cried, wriggling from beneath the creature.

All eyes turned to Podo as Leeli scooted to him. Moaning, on his back just inside the doorway, Podo was on the verge of losing consciousness.

More Fangs were coming, and with them, heat and the smell of smoke.

45

A Long Night

Quick!" Janner said to Tink, and they dragged Podo out of the doorway. They slammed and locked the heavy door just as the pursuing Fangs crashed into it. Janner and Tink braced the door with their shoulders as the snake men pounded on it bodily.

Tink looked at his brother. "I don't know how long we can hold 'em."

Before Janner could answer, the sound of panic seeped through the anger in the monsters' voices, and orange firelight flickered through the crack under the door.

Janner and Tink stood bracing the door, exhausted by the Fangs who clawed and pounded on the door.

Podo lay on his back and moaned. Leeli held his head in her lap as Nia pressed a wad of his tunic to the wound.

"Do you hear that?" Janner said, cocking his head sideways.

"Besides the Fangs on the other side of the door?" Tink said, sweat dripping from his brow.

"Horned hounds," Janner said.

A bone-chilling howl worked its way through the rock and fire. Then another howl, and another.

Podo had been right once again. The firelight had drawn the hounds from the bosom of Glipwood Forest.

For hours they stood that way, Janner and Tink's backs to the door, holding it fast against whatever might be on the other side. The piercing howls of the horned hounds mingled with the snarls of Fangs, who struggled ever more violently to get in. Janner thought many times that the old iron door would surely break from its hinges and the weapon chamber would become their unmarked grave.

But the door held. Eventually the pounding ceased, though far above them the howls continued, and then different sounds—terrible mewling, gurgling sounds.

Podo's breaths grew more and more raspy and shallow. His face was sweaty and ashen, and he had fallen unconscious. Leeli laid her head on his shoulder and fell asleep. Nia sat beside her father and held his hand. Her eyes were closed and she hummed an old whistleharp tune that echoed in the chamber. Janner felt his eyes drooping. A long time had passed without any signs of disturbance from the opposite side of the door. All he could hear was the roar of the blaze and the occasional crash of falling timbers.

"You should rest," Janner told his brother.

Tink wiped his brow and shook his head. "I'm fine."

They had survived much longer than Janner thought possible. He knew they would sooner or later have to emerge from the chamber, and what would they find? Fangs? Horned hounds? Walls and floors of the manor burned to the ground, leaving them with even fewer places to hide?

Though his head spun with worry, Janner's eyelids drooped. The sleepier he got, the less he cared about the Fangs, or whatever monsters had been trying to get at them. He shook his head to keep himself awake, but seeing the sleeping forms of Nia and Leeli in the waning torchlight made it difficult.

"I don't know how much longer I can…stay awake," he mumbled to Tink, whose answer was a long, loud snore.

Tink had slid to the floor with his back against the door, fast asleep.

The last thing Janner knew as he drifted off was the low groan of the ghost of Brimney Stupe. It filled the chamber and whipped the torch flame in an unseen breeze.

Nothing but the wind, Janner thought, and then he slept.

Janner woke with a start and leapt to his feet. The chamber was completely dark. He thought for a moment that he was in the Black Carriage, that he could still hear the cawing of crows, the remnants of a dark dream clinging to him like cobwebs. Tink's familiar snore brought him back to the underground chamber. *The torch must be spent,* he thought—*but the Fangs! The hounds!* Janner put his ear up to the cold iron door and listened.

Silence.

No horned hounds howled. No Fang snarled or hissed. All was still.

Janner nudged Tink with no success. He groped in the dark and could feel Tink's figure, curled up and sleeping a few feet from the door.

He thought about opening the door without waking the others. He could do it quietly, just to see if the sun had yet risen and whether by some miracle of the Maker the Fangs were gone or at least distracted. He put a sweaty hand on the door handle, hesitated for a moment, and turned it. The click echoed in the room and Janner flinched, afraid he would alert the monsters outside and above.

With a deep breath, he pulled on the great door and it creaked open. His eyes had so adjusted to the darkness that the faint light trickling down the tunnel stung. As Janner shielded his eyes, his mouth dropped open at what lay before him.

A pile of shriveled Fang corpses clogged the passageway. They were so decomposed it was impossible to tell what had killed them, but by their tangled positions, Janner could see their deaths had been woeful.

He stepped over the threshold and made his way past the pile of armored skeletons, vainly trying to avoid touching them. He toed one of the dead Fangs. The leather armor made little noise as the bones collapsed in clouds of dust. Janner turned the corner and squinted again as stronger light shone on him, down the passageway from the cellar.

Still he heard no sound, but as he tiptoed up the tunnel steps the smell of smoke increased, and he could see through the entryway bits of flame fussing weakly about on hunks of charred wood.

Janner emerged to peer up at a sky so blue and placid that his chest heaved a tearless sob. Anklejelly Manor had burned to the ground, and many of the Fangs had burned with it. Bits of charred armor lay strewn across the cellar floor. The ceiling was gone, the walls were gone, and much of the stonework had collapsed as the ancient timbers tumbled down. He couldn't see much above the rim of the cellar, which was now just a rectangular hole in the ground, but he knew somehow that the Fangs were gone. So, too, were the hounds and whatever manner of beasts had been drawn to the flames. The wind blew, embers sputtered, and Janner found himself smiling wide at the pristine sound of cooing fazzle doves.

A mournful wail split the air.

Janner nearly tripped over himself trying to dart back into the tunnel. His heart pounded as the wail grew closer by the second. *It was some kind of trap,* he thought bitterly. He should've known it was too good to be true that their enemies were destroyed.

Then he stopped.

He recognized something in the sound and felt the urge to laugh. Only Peet the Sock Man could make such a sad racket. Janner stepped back into the open.

"Peet?" he called, still timid about making too much noise. "Peet!"

The wailing stopped abruptly and Janner grinned. He heard a scrambling sound followed by the sudden appearance of a white plume of hair at the edge of the cellar.

At the sight of Janner, Peet's reddened, teary eyes grew wide with disbelief, then joy, laughter, and then disbelief again.

A thunderous *woof* sounded, and Nugget's giant head appeared next to Peet's.

"Igiby! Praise the Maker, it's an Igiby!" Peet laughed and leapt down to the cellar. He wrapped his arms around the boy, lifted him up and spun him around.

Janner noticed that Peet was wearing new knit socks on his arms. The two laughed together beneath the blue, blue sky.

Peet put him down and held Janner's shoulders, with foreheads nearly touching. "Leeliby? Tinkifeather? Are they safe? Safe?"

Janner nodded eagerly.

Nugget whined at the lip of the cellar, wanting to jump down but afraid of the drop. Janner held out a hand and told him to stay, worried that if Nugget did jump in, they would have a heap of a time getting him back out.

"Come on," Janner said, leading Peet down the tunnel.

Janner opened wide the door to the chamber, and light fell on his family. They looked so peaceful he didn't want to wake them. But when Peet's eyes fell on Leeli and then Tink, he gasped with joy and said, "Heee!"

All at once, Leeli, Tink, and Nia stretched and squinted and yawned, confused at what they were waking to. All they could see were the silhouettes of Janner and Peet in the doorway.

"Janner?" Nia called. "Is that you? Are the Fangs…gone?"

"All dead, dead, scooch and tail, tooth and scale," said Peet.

"Yes, Mama," Janner said with a smile. "Tomorrow came."

"Grandpa?" Leeli said, scooting over to where he lay on the floor.

Blood had soaked the cloth on Podo's wound and gathered on the floor in a puddle around him. Nia held his face and spoke his name with a trembling voice. The old pirate's breathing was shallow and watery. Hard as they tried, they couldn't rouse him.

Podo was going to die.

46

Water from the First Well

The light had grown stronger in the weapon chamber, and a light breeze was moving the long cobwebs that dangled from the weapons and armor. The moaning of the wind continued, but in the daylight it had lost its ghostly tenor. The family stood or knelt around Podo, unsure of what to do. He had always been in charge, and they felt helpless without him barking orders at them. With a deep breath, Nia gracefully assumed that office.

"Janner, Tink. Help me move him into better light. I need to see the color of his face." Podo moaned as they dragged him closer to the door. Nia's face was grave when she looked at her father.

"Peet," she said. "It's time you told us what happened to Nugget."

Peet averted his eyes and fussed with the front of his shirt.

"Peet," Nia insisted. "My father will die, and I have a feeling you might be able to help him. I know you two have…history," she said with a glance at Leeli, "but he needs you right now. We all do."

Peet nodded but wouldn't look her in the eye.

"How did you heal Nugget?" Nia asked. "I've read about similar things in the old books, but I've never seen anything like that before."

Peet cast anxious glances at the door and shifted his weight from foot to foot, as if he wanted to run away. After a long moment, he spoke.

"Water from the First Well."

Nia's eyes widened. "What?" she whispered.

"I healed the dugget nog—Nugget dog—with water…from the First Well."

"But—where did you, I mean—"

"What's the First Well?" Leeli asked. She was sitting beside Podo holding one of his big, gnarled hands in her tiny ones.

"The First Well," Nia said, still looking intently at Peet, "is, is…the first well in the world. The first well in Aerwiar. A gift from the Maker to Dwayne and Gladys."[1]

"The First Fellows?" Janner asked.

"Yes. The old tales say that the water was poured into the mouth of the well by the Maker himself. It courses under the ground and is the lifeblood of Aerwiar. Without it, the trees would never blossom and the grass would never grow. All life would wear thin until it finally faded. The Maker gave us the well as a gift, and for long ages it was guarded and used to heal and to restore."

"It was lost?" Tink said.

"Yes. It was lost. Long ago. Long before Anniera even had a name." Nia regarded Peet. "Until now."

Peet was sniffling, great tears once again filling his tired eyes. "Years ago, before I came here, I found it." Peet shuddered at some terrible memory. "I found the First Well, and I brought some of the water here. When I saw little Dugget nying—Nugget dying—I got some from my castle and gave him a drop to drink." Peet flashed a grin at Leeli through his tears. "And it worked."

"Where is the water now?" Nia said with as much patience as she could muster. "Can you get some and bring it here?"

Peet nodded, wiped his nose with one of his socks, and was gone.

---

1. According to Frobentine the Mumn's *The Fall of the First Epoch*, the First Well was hidden near the unwalled city of Ulambria, where Dwayne and Gladys ruled their people with peace, wisdom, and an abundance of cheesy foods. Frobentine places the location of Ulambria somewhere north and east of the Killridge Mountains, in the heart of what is now the Byg'oal Forest. Other sources disagree, claiming that Ulambria lay in the Jungles of Plonst, in the troll kingdom. All scholars agree, however, that Ulambria is a good sounding name for a city.

Janner looked down at his dear grandfather who had fought so hard for them, and he smiled at the thought of him growing three feet taller (and wider) with a sip from the ancient water. Podo was already the biggest soul he knew. But now, Janner thought, his grandfather seemed to be shrinking and his face had gone from pale to gray.

"Please hurry, Peet," Nia whispered, stroking her father's face.

Janner and Tink pulled Leeli from Podo's side and helped her out of the tunnel to see her beloved dog. The Fangs who had perished in the tunnel were all but dust and armor now, and the children stepped easily past them.

Nugget was lying with his snout dangling over the edge of the cellar. The sight of Leeli set him to barking, wagging his tail, and running as fast as he could in ground-shaking circles.

Leeli giggled and clapped. She waved to her horse of a dog and complained that there was no way to get to him yet. But her spirits were lightened, and that made Janner's heart glad.

"I can't believe we made it," Tink said to himself. He squinted up at the sky much the same way Janner had, appreciating perhaps for the first time how wonderful a thing the sky was to see. "We should stay with Mama," he said. "She shouldn't be alone if Grandpa..."

"You're right. Come on, Leeli," Janner said.

"We'll be back," Leeli said to Nugget, who whined in answer.

Nia looked small, all alone with Podo in the chamber. She had his head in her lap and was praying over him, rocking gently to and fro. She looked desperate.

For all Janner could tell, Podo was dead already. The eldest Igiby felt his heart sag in his chest, heavy with sorrow and hardening with anger. He was angry at the Fangs for ever setting foot on Skree. He was angry at

Zouzab for betraying them. He was even beginning to feel anger toward the Maker for creating a world where things like this could happen.

Podo had fought bravely, tirelessly, to protect the ones he loved, for freedom and goodness, and here he lay dying.

"Your father was a good man. A brave man. He fought well and died well in the Great War."

Janner could hear Podo saying that about their father, Esben, and now it was happening to the old warrior too. He had certainly fought well, and soon enough he would die well, though not in the Great War. And it was all for them, Janner thought, for his daughter and his three grandchildren, who had all lived to see the wide, blue sky that morning.

Then Janner remembered the Jewels of Anniera. None of this would have happened if not for those cursed jewels that Gnag and all his minions were so bent on finding. And none of this would have happened if Podo and Nia hadn't been trying to keep them hidden. Janner felt his anger turning toward Podo and his mother for caring more about the Jewels of Anniera than he and his siblings. Why hadn't they just given up the jewels? Were these jewels really worth the price of losing their home? worth dying for? Janner felt the tears rising in his throat, and he turned away so Tink wouldn't see him cry.

But Tink's head was buried in his arm; he was leaning against the wall, muffled sobs coming from him in waves.

It seemed a very long time that they waited while Podo rasped and Nia prayed and all three children shed tears for their grandfather.

And then Janner heard a rustle.

Peet the Sock Man appeared at the door to the chamber. With a socked hand outstretched, he offered a tiny leather flask.

Leeli nudged Peet toward Nia, who held Podo's head. Tink and Janner joined them, gathered around Podo as Peet removed the cap from the flask.

Nia lifted Podo's head and opened his mouth so that Peet could pour a bit of the water down. But Peet shook his head and instead pulled the makeshift bandage away, exposing the wound. It gaped deeper and worse than they had imagined, and Leeli covered her eyes.

Peet poured a trickle of water over the wound, then nodded and recapped the container.

"Are you sure that's all he needs?" Nia searched Peet's face. "He's barely alive."

"I used a bit too much on Nugget, wouldn't you say? We don't need a giant Podo, do we?" Peet chuckled nervously. "I certainly don't." Seeing that no one laughed with him, Peet's face straightened. "The water is strong. It can heal deeper wounds than this." Peet looked down at his socked hands, and the old sorrow came back to his face. He sighed, wiping his hands on his tunic as if he could clean off the talons that were hidden beneath the knitting.

"I'll be outside," he said. "I don't want to be the thirst fing he sees when he rouses."

Peet left the room.

"What I wouldn't give for a pot of flabbit stew about now," said a warm, gritty voice.

Podo lay on the ground looking up into his daughter's eyes and grinning. Overjoyed, the children rushed to him, careful not to jar his wound. Only a pinkish scar remained beneath the dried blood streaked by water from the First Well.

Podo sat up and yawned as if he'd been napping in his favorite chair. He smiled at Janner, Tink, and Leeli with eyes that seemed younger than they ought to have been, and the Igibys wept and laughed and squeezed him as if he'd just returned from a long journey.

After a long stretch, Podo rose and gathered his bundle. A boyish spring was in his step as he walked with his family through the iron door.

They stepped over dusty piles and armor as Janner and Tink recounted the events of the long night: the burning of the manor, the howls of hounds and shrieks of Fangs, and about Peet's water from the First Well.

Nia listened proudly as her boys regaled the old pirate with a tale that would rival one of his own. Podo listened to it all with his eyebrows raising and lowering at each turn of the story.

Leeli nestled under her grandfather's arm while she limped along. Her face brightened as they reached the lip of the cellar wall.

Peet was there, sitting on the edge of the cellar beside Nugget. Without speaking or looking at Podo, Peet threw down a rope. He hefted Podo up first, and then, with another of their silent, intense exchanges, Peet retreated and allowed Podo to pull into daylight the rest of his family.

47

Old Wounds

N ugget yipped (a very loud, deep yip), and Leeli climbed onto his back again. Astride Nugget, she beamed like sunlight.

The sky, however, was beginning to cloud, and in the east over the Dark Sea of Darkness, a black storm gathered. The tall grass of the plain rippled like water, and near its amber shore lay countless bodies of horned hounds. The beasts were scattered across the field and around Anklejelly Manor in clusters, most of them beside telltale piles of Fang armor, from which the lizards' white, dusty remains were blowing away in the steady east wind.

Near the forest Janner spied six dead toothy cows as big as Nugget, and around them was a dense cluster of Fang armor and weaponry. A mighty battle had been fought while the Igibys slumbered in the belly of the manor. Now only flies buzzed around the corpses as the sun beat higher and stronger.

Podo sent Janner and Tink back down to the weapon room several times for swords, shields, and bows with healthy supplies of arrows. After rummaging through the piles of weapons, Tink and Janner both settled on the swords they had used the night before. With a last look at Oskar's secret armory, they pulled the iron door shut and rattled the handle to be sure it was securely locked. The boys passed the weapons up to Podo and clambered up the rope.

"Right, then," Podo said. "We've a long way to go to the Ice Prairies. And it won't be long before someone finds out about what happened here tonight. We'll have all manner of beast after us, looking for the Jewels of Anniera, to be sure."

Janner bristled. He was tired of hearing about the jewels that had ruined their lives. Tired of not knowing what they were and why Gnag the Nameless wanted them so badly. Janner was sick of adults and their secrets, and though he was glad his grandfather was alive and glad they had made it through the night, he had a squall of resentment in his chest that was building into a storm—a storm he could hold in no longer.

"You keep talking about these precious jewels! Everything that's happened to us has been because of them, but no one will tell us where they are! We've lost our home, our friends—and we almost lost you, Grandpa— all because Gnag the Nameless wants these jewels. For some reason, you think these 'precious jewels' are more precious than we are, or you wouldn't have them in the first place, would you? Why can't we just take them and throw them into the Dark Sea so they'll stop destroying everything around us? And now what are we doing? Now we're running away, off to the Ice Prairies, wherever they are, and still you won't tell us what's going on!"

Podo waited patiently for Janner to finish.

Janner took another deep breath and blurted, "So what's going on?"

To his surprise, Podo wasn't angry, and Nia was actually smiling.

"Aye!" Tink added, crossing his arms. "What's going on?"

Now it was Podo who smiled. He looked at Nia and they laughed.

Janner could make no sense of it, and neither Podo nor his mother tried to help.

"We'll tell you all about it tonight," Podo said, turning toward the road, "once we find a safe place to rest." The old man tossed the bundle over his shoulder and took a deep, glad breath of salty air. "Follow old Podo!" he then roared with gusto, and marched off in a southwesterly direction, away from the forest.

"Papa," Nia said.

"Eh?" Podo said, stopping several paces away.

"I think we should go to Peet's tree house. He has food and—"

"Food?" Tink said.

Peet the Sock Man perked up and looked at Nia with a twinkle of hope in his eyes.

"We ain't goin' there," Podo said, his bushy eyebrows bunched together. "We're heading to Torrboro then up the North Road until we find safe passage to the Ice Prairies." He whipped his head around and set out again, but Nia didn't move. Podo turned again, his face red. "Come on, I say!"

"No." Nia's back straightened.

"What?" Podo took a step back toward his daughter.

"I said no." Nia took a step forward. "You've held on to your anger long enough, Papa, and now that anger is becoming a burden you no longer bear alone. It's causing us to suffer with you—you stubborn old fool."

Podo was dumbfounded.

"Peet saved all of our lives," Nia said, "yours most recently. You may feel fine now, but not half an hour ago death was lapping at your toes. And do you know who you should be thanking for the breath in your lungs?"

Peet was backing away sheepishly, but Nia grabbed his arm and pulled him forward. "This man," she said. "He's got provisions and shelter in the forest, where no Fang will want to venture for a long time after what happened here. Now I love you, Papa, but I'm the mother of these children, and I've a mind to put food in their bellies and pillows under their heads. We're going to Peet's tree house and that's final."

Combined looks of bewilderment, embarrassment, and anger flashed over Podo's face. Janner wanted to laugh. Podo sputtered and formed the beginnings of words with his mouth but came up with nothing to say.

"Peet, lead the way," Nia said.

Peet obeyed Nia's order with wide eyes and a nervous smile, marching off in the direction opposite Podo's. Nia and the boys followed.

Leeli rode Nugget to where Podo stood, alone and dumbfounded. She sidled up beside him, leaned over and kissed him on his whiskery cheek.

Nugget followed suit, dragging a sloppy pink tongue up Podo's arm, soaking his shirt. Then they, too, turned away from Podo and followed Peet, moving north and west, in the direction of the forest.

Podo eyed the smoking remains of Anklejelly Manor.

"Hrmph," he said finally, trudging after his family.

48

Shelter

The gray sky had become a river of churning, low-flying clouds that sped along so heavy and close it seemed they scraped the treetops. The Igibys, a giant dog, and Peet the Sock Man walked along the forest border for an hour.

Janner kept a careful eye on the trees to their right, but Peet showed no sign of worry. He strolled along without speaking, his white hair whipping about in the strong wind. Janner took comfort in the odd man's confidence. He had proven himself a good friend and a capable fighter.

Behind them, another white-haired man walked in silence.

Podo hadn't said a word since they'd set out for Peet's tree house, but his eyes showed that his spirit had lightened. He didn't look so angry anymore, and he appeared to be considering some matter that required careful thought.

Leeli rode high like a queen on a royal horse, her face in a perpetual smile. She had her family and her dog, and she no longer needed a crutch as long as Nugget was around. His furry paws were as big as platters, but they made little sound as he padded along.

Nia's arm was around Tink, whose skinny, quick frame was showing signs of fatigue. He leaned into his mother and rested his head on her side.

Janner looked back toward Glipwood, but he could see nothing of the town. They passed a few abandoned farmsteads but otherwise saw no sign of either human or Fang. He thought about their cottage, about Slarb's grisly end with the thwaps, and Podo's swift sword. He shuddered to think how close he and Tink had come to dying at the hands of that mad creature.

But they hadn't died. Even with an ocean of Fangs in pursuit, they had somehow, thank the Maker, stayed alive and whole.

But not everyone had survived. The last Janner had seen of Oskar, he was lying on the floor of his dear bookstore, urging the Igibys to run. He had tried to save them with his dying breath. It was Oskar who had made their refuge beneath Anklejelly Manor, who had lost his life trying to protect Leeli and Nia. *But why did Oskar hide the weapons?* Janner wondered. *And how did he come by them?* Janner remembered that Oskar had spent many years since the war traveling about Skree, gathering books and curiosities. *But weapons? Had he actually been searching for the Jewels of Anniera? Could that be what Podo was carrying in the bundle on his shoulder? Why did his grandfather despise Peet the Sock Man so?* And the biggest question of all: *Why would the Igibys have something that Gnag the Nameless would so relentlessly want to find?*

Janner was consumed with so many questions, he almost didn't hear Peet's announcement.

"Here we are." Peet had stopped in front of the biggest oak tree in sight.

The oak protruded from the line of the forest and spread its thick, sagging arms above and around them, like a mother hen protecting her young. "Rugget will be safe here," Peet said as he swung himself into the lower branches and reached out to help Nia up. Far above them, barely visible through the leaves, was one of Peet's rope-and-plank bridges, dangling between the trees.

"Up we go," he said, still not looking at Podo. He pulled up everyone except for the old man, nor did he offer to help, but turned from Podo and threaded his way up through the branches to the bridge.

Podo passed the bundle up to Janner and scrambled much less gracefully into the tree.

Janner felt a spatter of rain and looked up.

The sky had grown dark, and the rope bridges began to rock in the winds of a burgeoning storm.

Peet, Podo, and the Igibys hurried along the bridges as the storm unleashed its stinging rain, and they were soaked through as they climbed up through the trapdoor and gratefully entered Peet's castle.

To Janner, with the storm blowing outside, the tree house was the finest accommodation in all the land. He helped Peet light three lanterns quickly, and relished the comforting yellow and orange light they cast on the walls and ceiling. Peet snapped the door shut and the howl of the wind was all but gone. Leeli found a spot and sat with her back against the wall, a dry blanket tucked under her chin. Peet pointed out a stack of old quilts beside her.

"Lots of dry blankets for you. It gets very cold here in the winter, see, see."

"Mister Peet, what about the fire?"

"Eh? Ah, the fire. I've been here long enough that the hounded horns leave me be, Jangiby. Besides, the most of the beasts can't climb. Ceet's pastle is safe."

"Hrmph," Podo said, inspecting the tree house and trying very hard not to be impressed.

Nia elbowed him. "Peet, this is lovely. Can I help you with anything?"

Peet was glowing. He busied himself with pots and pans, rummaging through sacks of grain and dried meats and vegetables, tiny bottles of spices and herbs. While Peet prepared the meal, the others each found a nook and a quilt and made themselves comfortable. Podo refused a blanket and hunched against a wall, staring at his hands.

The rain beat on the windows and sides of the house, but Peet had sealed the structure well. Not a drop of water leaked in. The tree house swayed and creaked in its perch, and the smell of stew filled their noses. Janner, like the other Igibys, drifted off to sleep, thanking the Maker they were safe and dry in Peet's castle.

Even Podo.

49

The Jewels of Anniera

J anner woke long before his eyes opened. He lay beneath a warm blanket, feeling the rocking motion of the tree house, listening to the murmur of soft conversation and the rain on the windows. He didn't want to wake up just yet. The wail of the wind and the rumble of thunder intensified his gladness there in the shelter.

Nia noticed him stirring and kissed his cheek.

"Hello, dear Janner," she said.

He smiled, stretched, and forced himself to sit up. Tink and Leeli were awake and grinning at him. The trapdoor flipped open and Podo climbed into the room, his clothes soaked through.

"Ol' Nugget's got dry quarters now," he said cheerily.

"Thank you, Grandpa," Leeli said, hugging her grandfather's leg. She looked down the trapdoor at the makeshift shelter Podo had assembled from lumber and animal hides that Peet had lying about.

"Aye, lass. Yer dog's as dry as a bone and content just to be nearby," Podo said. "He sent a message for ye too."

Leeli looked confused, and Podo swept her up to sniffle around her chin and shoulders like a dog. She squealed with delight and everyone joined in the laughter.

Peet cleared his throat and declared the stew ready.

High in the boughs of a glipwood oak in the middle of the fiercest storm Skree had seen in a thousand years, the Igibys, Podo Helmer, and Peet the Sock Man shared a meal together. Though Peet was silent and at times somber, there was much laughter and thanksgiving for the Maker's provision and goodness while they ate and drank until their bellies were full.

Janner saw Podo's bundle lying in the corner and decided that it was time for answers. He wasn't the only one. Without a word, a feeling of gravity settled on them all, and they were silent while they chewed their food.

Finally, Janner set his empty bowl on the floor beside him. "The Jewels of Anniera," he said, folding his arms. "Where are they?"

Nia and Podo looked at one another, then at Peet.

Tink and Leeli barely breathed, as eager as Janner to know the truth.

Nia nodded at Podo and laid a hand on Peet's socked forearm as Podo retrieved his bundle from the door. The old pirate had a twinkle in his eye again, and crackling anticipation moved about like invisible sparks among the children. Podo paused, savoring the moment, then he said with bushy eyebrows raised, "To begin with, yer not asking the right question."

His statement hung in the air for a moment.

Tink squinted at his grandfather. "Uh…what's in the bundle?"

"Nope. The *real* question is…" Podo paused dramatically. "*What* are the Jewels of Anniera?"

Janner felt his arms tingle. There was something odd about the way the three adults watched them, smiling.

"The Jewels of Anniera," Nia said, "have been sought by Gnag the Nameless since the Great War fell on the shores of the Shining Isle and overcame it. Gnag destroyed all that was good and beautiful in that place…except for the jewels. And he has sought them ever since. He has obsessed over them and ruined nations in his search because he believes that the Jewels of Anniera hold a hidden power. His hunt for the jewels is what's led him to Skree. If he didn't believe they had come here, I don't think he would have bothered crossing the Dark Sea of Darkness at all."

"But he came," Podo said gravely.

"Did someone give them to you?" Tink blurted. "How did you end up with the jewels if they were from Anniera? Did you agree to hide them?"

Janner could feel his emotions rising again. "How could you do that when you knew it would put us—and all of Glipwood—in danger? Why would you give some of the jewels to Gnorm in the first place, if you knew they could lead Gnag here?"

"Janner, the jewels I gave Gnorm were worthless to me," Nia said gently. "Once, they might have meant something, but they were kept hidden for such a time as that. Gnag couldn't care less about those jewels. There must have been something I didn't notice in them that identified them as Annieran."

"Annieran?" Leeli said. "How did you get Annieran gold and jewelry?"

Nia paused. "Because I brought them here. From Anniera."

The children's confusion was so evident that Podo laughed. "Bitties, we came here from Anniera to escape Gnag and his army during the Great War."

"But Grandpa, you're from Glipwood! And so is Mama." Leeli grew more and more puzzled.

"No, dear," Nia said. "Your grandfather is from Glipwood. But I was born in the Green Hollows, far across the Dark Sea, where he met your grandmother. When I married your father, we all made our home in Anniera. But when the war came to us, we fled."

"We had to protect the jewels, see," Podo said.

"So where are they?" Tink demanded.

"I told you, lad. That's the wrong question."

"Fine. *What* are the Jewels of Anniera then?"

The question hung in the air like smoke or like motes of dust caught in a bright beam of light. The three adults sat and stared at the three children. The children stared back at the adults. Janner's stomach turned a flip and his head went dizzy. He didn't know what the answer was, but he felt in his bones that whatever it was would change everything.

Everything.

Peet the Sock Man cleared his throat and leaned forward. His big eyes bore less of their sorrow than Janner had ever seen, and he smiled into the

Igiby children's faces—first Janner's, then Tink's, then Leeli's, and then Janner's again.

"You," he said. "*You* are."

No one spoke. None of the children even breathed. Their hearts thrummed with the truth of what had been spoken. The air around Peet's words would have shimmered if it were possible to see such a thing, and the children knew it to be true.

Janner swallowed hard.

"What...what do you mean?"

"Your father—" Nia said slowly, tears choking her sentence and brimming in her eyes. "Your father was the High King of the Shining Isle."

50

The Throne Wardens

I was the queen," Nia said. "You three," she let out a long, tearful sigh, "are all that is left of the great kingdom across the sea."

"The Jewels of Anniera," Peet whispered, and he bowed so low his forehead touched the floor.

Podo, to their amazement, did the same.

Janner thought about the picture of his father at the prow of the boat, arms spread as wide as his smile. *A king? And not just any king, but the king of Anniera?*

Janner could scarcely believe what was happening. He didn't believe it, in fact. But he *knew* it. And now he realized that he had always known it, but the thought hit him with as much fear as wonder.

"So, if my father's dead, then that means…I'm…king?" Janner stammered.

Nia looked at him carefully. "No, son. No, you're not."

Janner's cheeks flushed.

"It's all right, dear," she said, placing a hand on his arm. "You see, in Anniera, the kingship is passed over the eldest son. For as long as there have been rulers in Anniera, the position of highest distinction is that of protector. Too many kingdoms have fallen because of envy, greed, and lust for power. So the second-born wears the crown." She looked at Tink. "Your brother is the rightful heir to the throne."

Tink blushed and averted his gaze from his mother's placid eyes.

Janner felt an unwelcome shiver of envy in his belly.

"But a great honor is bestowed on the eldest," Nia continued, taking Janner's hand. "The eldest son, upon the birth of the younger, becomes the protector of the king. It is his life's duty to serve and defend the younger from all harm. He is trained in battle, and his name is praised in every home in the kingdom."

Janner thought about all the pressure his mother and Podo had put on him to watch over Tink and Leeli. Not a day had gone by that they hadn't told him that it was his duty as the older brother to take care of them. It had always felt so stifling, and now he imagined his future as a groveling old man, chained to his brother forever, unable to do anything for himself—a lifetime of fretting over his reckless younger brother and crippled sister, while Tink reigned and Leeli did—well, whatever she wanted.

Nia sensed her son's thoughts. She took Janner's face in her hands and fixed her eyes on his. "It is no small thing to be a Throne Warden of Anniera. They have been sung about by bards for a thousand years and are accorded a place of honor like no other kingdom—like no other king—in the world—not because they're lords, but because they're servants. There were many days when your father wished he were a Throne Warden and not the High King."

But Janner had stopped listening. The burning envy in his chest cooled when he remembered something he had seen in one of Peet's journals.

"Throne Warden?" Janner said.

"Yes, it's the name for—"

"Artham P. Wingfeather, Throne Warden of Anniera," Janner said.

Peet lifted his head from the floor.

"Yes, my lord," he said to Janner.

Tink gasped. "But, that would make you—"

"Our uncle!" Leeli finished.

"Yes, Lady Leeli," said Peet, bowing to the floor again. Podo was watching Peet with a surly eye. His good humor was fading.

"That's enough, Artham," Podo said, trying for Nia's sake not to sound too gruff.

"But what happened to you? To your arms?" Janner asked.

"That's something I've been wanting to ask him myself," Nia said, turning to Peet.

But Peet shook his head violently. He scooted back against the wall of the tree house and fixed them all with such a look of terror that Janner leapt to his feet. Peet took in rapid, shallow gulps of air and was covered with sweat.

"Back up!" Podo said to the children. They scrambled to the wall of the tree house, and Podo put himself between them and Peet. Nia laid a hand on Podo's arm and stepped slowly over to the Sock Man.

"Shh," she whispered to him. "Artham. Artham, it's me, Nia. You're safe." Her voice seemed to have a calming effect even on the wind outside, and the rain fell slower. Peet gazed at her and his breathing eased a bit with each intake. She sat down beside him and pulled him tight. She held him like a mother holds a child who has woken from a nightmare, and like a child, Peet let his eyes finally droop shut. He was soon asleep. Nia's eyes shone with sadness as she held him.

"You should have seen him in Anniera, when he was Throne Warden," she said quietly. "His hair was as black as midnight, and he was in the eye of every maiden of the kingdom. He wrote the most beautiful poetry. He wrote high tales and silly poems and read them to you, Janner and Tink, when you lay in your cribs at night. Your father used to say that there wasn't a better man in the kingdom than his brother Artham."

Peet whimpered in his sleep.

"Shh," Nia said again.

The children eased back from the edges of the room.

Podo sat down with a huff, shaking his head. "He's dangerous, Nia."

"He would die before he would hurt these children, Papa."

"But what happened to him?" Janner asked.

"We don't know," Nia said. "When Gnag and his army attacked Anniera, they drove us into Castle Rysen, at Dorminey, in the center of the kingdom. That was where we made our home." Nia stared at the rain streaming down the tree house window glass. "The Fangs, trolls, and other foul beasts that we'd never before seen had breached the wall—Leeli, you had just been born. Janner, you were three; Tink, you were two. Your father told Peet to take us and go. There was an ancient escape route, a secret way out of the palace that led to the River Rysen and then to the Dark Sea. But your father wouldn't leave. He said that he would fight as long as he could, and then he would meet us at the river."

"Your father," Podo said, "insisted that we go. He said there was something in the palace that he had to get. Something he had to keep out of Gnag's hands."

"And you don't know what it was?" said Janner.

"No idea," Podo said.

"See, children," Nia explained, "it was in Peet's blood and bones to protect his brother. It's the very breath of a Throne Warden."

Janner and Tink glanced at one another awkwardly.

"But your father ordered him to see us safe to the river. Peet didn't know what to do. He loved us all and wanted to help us, but he couldn't bear the thought of leaving his brother behind. The monsters were in the palace, and they were looking for us. Artham—Peet—left your father—but only in order to help us." Nia stroked Peet's face. "It may have been the hardest thing he's ever done.

She was silent a moment, the only sound the pattering of rain against the windows.

"He swore to return once we were safe," she said, lost in memory. "Peet fought through the Fangs and led us to the secret exit where your grandfather was to meet us with a boat. I held you, Leeli. Janner, you were old enough to hold my hand and keep up. Tink, my mother carried you."

Podo looked away.

"Our grandmother?" Leeli was suddenly wide-eyed. "She knew us?"

"Aye," said Podo, his voice thick with sorrow. "And she'd know you now if it wasn't fer that uncle of yours." Podo spat.

"Papa, enough!"

Podo wiped a tear from his face.

Janner had never seen him cry.

"We got to the riverbank before your grandfather," Nia continued. "Fangs and trolls came out of nowhere and attacked us. Peet was the finest swordsman in the kingdom, but even he couldn't fight back that many." She paused to push down the lump in her throat. "Mama—your grandmother—was killed."

"But how could you blame Peet for that?" Janner said. "You just said that there were too many Fangs."

Podo glowered at Peet, his eyebrows quivering, and an uncomfortable silence followed.

"What happened to her was no one's fault," Nia said firmly. "That's all that needs to be said." Podo sputtered a protest, but the look in Nia's eye silenced him. She turned to Leeli and placed a hand on her cheek. "Peet held them off as best he could while we boarded, but—one of the Fangs grabbed you, dear." She took Leeli's hand. "He tried to tear you from my arms, and…"

"My leg," Leeli breathed.

"I'm sorry," Nia whispered. She covered her eyes and struggled to keep her composure. Leeli scooted over to her.

"It's okay, Mama," Leeli said. "I have Nugget now."

Nia took a deep breath and hugged Leeli tight.

"We made our way down the river," Nia said after a moment. "Peet ran back through the Fangs and into the palace to find your father, even as it burned. The last I saw of Anniera was fire and death. We sailed the river for hours to the estuary at the Dark Sea and saw nothing but towering flames on either side of the river."

"I couldn't see anything," Podo said, staring out at the storm. "I was sailing on a black river between walls of fire. We rode the River Rysen all the way to the Dark Sea. Gnag had sacked every village we passed, and I saw things I'll never forget, though the Maker knows I've tried to." He was silent a moment. "When we got to the sea, we asked the Maker to guide us, to protect the Jewels of Anniera, and I tell you, he did. He sent up a mighty storm that nearly tore that little ship to pieces. The waves were high mountains, and sea critters like I'd never seen churned up from the deep and watched us pass with eyes as big as a house. I've never been so afraid, and I tell ye I felt like the Maker had cursed us sure. But when the storm cleared, I saw we were better off than before—we were in the Phoob Islands, just north and east of here, on the other side of Fingap Falls. We had crossed the Dark Sea in *five days*. That's something I've never told anybody for worry that they'd think I was crazy. And besides, we were in a little skiff with naught but one sail. It's impossible, I tell ye." Podo spread his hands. "But here we are."

He looked at his grandchildren intently. "Your grandmother's name was Wendolyn Igiby," he said. "You took on the Igiby name when we came here and left the name of Wingfeather behind."

"So how did Peet find us?" Janner asked.

Nia looked puzzled. "We still don't know. About five years after we settled here, we saw him in town. We barely recognized him, and when we did we were frightened. We were sure that somehow he would lead Gnag to us. For all we knew, Gnag had turned him into one of his own. Podo told him to keep away from you, from us. And he would, for a while. Then he'd be back in town, carrying on and making a spectacle of himself for some reason. I can't explain it."

Nia continued, shaking her head.

"Before last night I didn't understand why he wore the socks. I thought the old Artham was lost forever. But he's in there." She stroked his wild hair. "Whatever happened to you," she whispered to Peet, "I'm glad you've got it in your head to protect my children the same way you would have protected Esben." Nia looked up at Janner. "And I tell you, you should rest easy knowing that a Throne Warden of Anniera is keeping watch."

Janner felt a surge of pride.

Nia smiled at him.

"Grandpa, what's in the bundle?" Tink asked.

"Ah, yes," Podo said as he laid the blanket on the floor between them and folded back its edges.

51

A Letter from Home

For you, lad," Podo said to Janner, handing over an ancient leather-bound book. "It's one of the oldest books in the world, one of the First Books, according to some."

Janner looked at it with wonder.

"Among the treasures of Anniera were several ancient books that were passed down to the Throne Wardens over the ages," Podo explained. "This one's said to give 'wisdom to the wise,' whatever the deep that means. I never took to readin'. Artham here, if he's not too crazy, will be able to tell ye more about it. Yer father gave it to me before we were run out of the palace. Told me no matter what, to make sure it got to you."

Janner held the big book gingerly but didn't open it.

"And for you, young Tink. High King Kalmar, I should say. That *is* yer real name, after all."

"Can you just call me Tink?" he asked, blushing.

"As you wish. Tink, then. This is for you." Podo handed Tink an old, tattered notebook.

"Your father's sketchbook," Nia said. "He was an artist, just like you. He filled this book with pictures of Anniera, along with his own writings. I wanted you to have something to remind you of your homeland. It's a prettier place than any picture could tell, but your father loved his land, and you can see that love in these pictures. I fetched it for him on my way out of the palace because he never let it leave his side. I thought he'd want it once we were all safe and away. But it's yours now."

Tink's eyes shone as he accepted the gift.

"And for you, my lass." Podo lifted the last fold of the blanket and handed Leeli a silver whistleharp. This belonged to your great-great-great-aunt Madia, Queen Sister of Anniera, and it's been in the kingdom longer than that. See, whenever a third child is born, that child, according to Annieran tradition, is to learn to sing and make music. That's why we've taught you all these old tunes over the years. Legend says there's a power to protect Anniera in the music of a Queen Sister who knows the right songs. Nobody believes that anymore, mind you, but this very whistleharp has been in Anniera since the beginning of the Second Epoch."

"That's three thousand years ago," Janner said with astonishment.

"Aye," he said.

Leeli held the gleaming whistleharp to her lips and hesitated.

"Go on," Podo said, smiling.

Leeli played "The Fisherman's Elbow," one of Podo's favorite tunes, and the happy music filled their hearts.

Peet woke to the familiar song of his homeland. He seemed more like a man and less like an animal there in the brightness of the melody. He stretched, then rose to stoke the fire, pushing back the wet chill even further.

Night had come and the storm yet raged outside their haven.

The Igiby children laughed with one another and felt the bond of their blood grow stronger than ever before. Nia and Podo, relieved of secrets carried too many years, leaned back in reverie of memory and song.

Janner thought Tink didn't look much like a king, but maybe in a few years. He was only eleven, after all.

Tink opened the first page of his father's notebook and saw a sketch of an island rising out of a fitful sea. In the center of the picture, lifting out of the trees, were the lofty spires of a castle. Next to it, beneath a drawing of a puffy cloud, was written one word by the hand of his father: *Home.*

While Tink marveled at his father's sketches, Janner opened the ancient book in his lap. The pages were yellowed and tattered. The handwritten words were in another language, but it was beautiful to look at nonetheless. Janner felt a familiar tickle in his stomach as he turned the pages of a book he hadn't yet read. To his surprise, a folded piece of paper fell from the book and into his lap. The paper was white and crisp compared to the book's old leaves, still Janner was careful in unfolding it.

Janner,

You're only two years old now. Everyone says you look just like your father, and I take it as a high compliment. A handsome boy you are! I'm no poet like your Uncle Artham, but seeing you sleep here tonight bid me sit and put down some words for you to read one day. Your mother loves you and your brother well. And she has another little one bursting to come out! Foes to this kingdom beware! These three little Wingfeathers will keep this island safe and good. I know it. You've royal blood in your veins, no matter what your name or place in this world. The Maker made you the Throne Warden to your little brother, and I wouldn't wish anyone but you to keep him safe. There are rumors of war, and though I scarcely believe the half of it, should Anniera fall (and I'm sure it won't!), remember your homeland. Ancient secrets lie beneath these stones and cities. They have been lost to us, but still, we mustn't let them fall to evil.

It occurs to me how silly it is to be writing this to a two-year-old boy. But maybe one day when you're alone, unsure, doubting yourself, you'll need these words. Remember this: You are an Annieran. Your father is a king. You are his son. This is your land, and nothing can change that. Nothing.

Ah, and no one can change your underclothes but me. I can smell that you've soiled them again. Should I fall over dead from the stench in your britches, know when you read this that your father loves you like no other.

Your Papa

At the end of the letter was a sketch of a little boy sleeping peacefully in a crib surrounded by flowers that had withered from the smell of the child's soiled underclothes.

Janner's heart felt large and full. He lay down in the tree house and stared up at a dark, rain-battered window, thinking of his father. *Esben.*

He heard Nia and Podo in the other room talking softly, but he made out enough to understand they had agreed it would be best to stay in the tree house with Peet for several weeks, maybe longer. Peet assured them that he had learned how to live safely among the creatures of Glipwood Forest, and the Fangs wouldn't be coming near the forest for a long time once they saw the remains of the battle at Anklejelly Manor.

Skree, meanwhile, was shrouded in darkness. The black storm roiled in the sky, and the bright moon could not penetrate it.

The Dark Sea of Darkness moaned and heaved beneath the thundering expanse.

Among the glipwood trees, chorkneys and thwaps and toothy cows alike sought shelter from the mighty wind and rain, and the town of Glipwood sat as barren and windblown as a ghost town. The hearts of the people and trolls and Fangs all across Skree were black on this night while they tossed and turned in gloomy beds.

Darkness was everywhere.

Except, of course, in a tree house, deep in the murky heart of Glipwood Forest, where the Jewels of Anniera shone like the sun.

APPENDICES

The Legend of the Sunken Mountains

Traditional
(from Fencher's *Comprehensive History of Sad, Sad Songs*)

Come forth from sunken mountain calls the sundered summer
      moon
The eyrie's fallen dragon king hath groaned his grievous tune
The halls that rose in cloudy steeps now lie beneath the waves
And Yurgen's fallen kingdom sleeps in bouldered ocean graves

Yurgen's son, the dragon fair, met Omer son of Dwayne
And so the knight and Yurgen's heir did battle in the rain
And lo, the dragon wounded lay from Omer's mortal blow
The knight, in grief, did haste away to save his mortal foe

And Omer, bent with sorrow, bowed in Yurgen's mountain hall
And told the ancient dragon how his only heir did fall
So Yurgen, mighty dragon king, atop his mountain keep
Asunder tore the glistening and rocky mountain steep

He summoned every dragon for to burrow through the ground
And find at last the fabled ore that makes the maiméd sound
But Yurgen's heir was cold and killed, and buried in the mount
As dragons tunneled deeper still below the ocean fount

And then at last with thund'rous din the misty mountain climbs
Collapsed upon the beasts within the darkness of the mines
From ocean then did Yurgen rise to seek his dying son
But where his mountain once arrayed a half-moon golden hung

His dragon kingdom moldered, his dragon scion slain
King Yurgen's sorrow smoldered and he sank away again
The halls that towered in cloudy steeps now lie beneath the waves
And Yurgen's fallen kingdom sleeps in murky ocean graves

The summer dusk hath split in twain the gilded summer moon
And all who come shall hear again the dragons' lonesome tune

PERMISSION TO HOE
GARDEN FORM

I, _Podo Helmer_ , request permission to hoe a garden. By signing this form, I also acknowledge the superiority of the Fangs of Dang, both general and specific, generally over all mankind, specifically over me, _Podo Helmer_ , and when I say superiority, I mean drastic superiority, like in the way a bomnubble is superior to a meep, which is to say that I, _Podo Helmer_ , would represent the meep, and the distinguished Fangs of Dang would represent the mighty bomnubble, which is drastically superior to the meep.

Day of Use: _Seven Day_

Hour of Request for Permission: _Dawn_

Signed by _Podo Helmer_ , this _Thirtieth_ day of _Five Moon_ , Year _451_ of the Third Epoch.

Fang on Duty: **Brak**

ADDENDUM TO THE PERMISSION
TO HOE GARDEN FORM:

PERMISSION TO USE HOE

Please Check All That Apply:

☒ I Would Like to Use a Hoe

Initialed: _____*PH*_____

PERMISSION TO SHOVEL HOGPIG DROPPINGS FORM

I, _Podo Helmer_, request permission from the dominant, clever, witty, superior authority of Glipwood, Commander Gnorm, most distinguished Fang of Dang, or one of his Fang associates, whoever may be on hand at the time of said request, to use one (1) shovel for the purpose of shoveling hogpig droppings from the hogpig pen and into the wagon, wheelbarrow, basket, or bowl to be used for fertilizing various plant life only, and not to throw, smear, or otherwise misuse said droppings in any way, whether with malicious intent or mischief, unless that malice or mischief in some way belittles, humiliates, or causes discomfort to a non-Fang entity, in which case, misuse is strongly encouraged.

If said shovel is not returned to the Fang facility by sundown on the day of use, I, _Podo Helmer_, admit that the woeful punishment I receive is a result of my foolishness and disregard for Gnag the Nameless and his most distinguished Fangs, such as Commander Gnorm, and will not squirm either while being tortured or forced into the Black Carriage, because while the Fangs enjoy hurting people, they would also rather be sleeping than tying up a victim for whipping or carriaging.

Day of Use: _Second Day_
Hour of Request for Permission: _Forenoon_
Signed by _Podo Helmer_, this _Fifth_ day of _Six Moon_, Year _451_ of the Third Epoch.

Fang on Duty: _VOP_

Toothy Cow (Skrean)

fig.1

eyes
malicious gleam therein

toothiness
hideous

cloven hoofs
more evil than the regular sort

udder
feeding violent, given toothiness of calves

long tail
serves to whip flies away as well as to distract prey before pouncing

From Pembrick's *Creaturepedia*.

Author Andrew Peterson is a natural-born storyteller, being a preacher's kid from the South (mostly).

He wrote and produced the acclaimed epic song cycle *Behold the Lamb of God: The True Tall Tale of the Coming of Christ* (awarded the 2004 Best Album of the Year, World Christian Music Editors Choice), part of which inspired his children's book *The Ballad of Matthew's Begats: An Unlikely Royal Family Tree.*

A singer-songwriter and recording artist, he has just released a new album, *Resurrection Letters, Vol. II,* having written and recorded seven others over the last ten years, including:

Slugs & Bugs & Lullabies (with Randall Goodgame)
Behold the Lamb of God: The True Tall Tale of the Coming of Christ
The Far Country
Love and Thunder
Clear to Venus
Carried Along

Andrew and his wife, Jamie, have two sons, Aedan and Jesse, and one daughter, Skye. They live in the Nashville, Tennessee, area on a wooded hill in a little house they call the Warren—where they're generally safe from bumpy digtoads and toothy cows.

You can find Andrew online at his Web site www.andrew-peterson.com or visit The Rabbit Room (www.rabbitroom.com), an online writer's collective inspired by the Inklings (C. S. Lewis, J. R. R. Tolkien, Charles Williams, and other friends), for more fun facts and delicious details.

Illustrator Justin Gerard spent most of his childhood in Pittsburgh, Pennsylvania, drawing imaginative characters informed by comic books, science fiction, and Disney films. As his art developed, Justin found inspiration in N. C. Wyeth, Caravaggio, Peter de Sève, and Carter Goodrich. He's illustrated several children's books, including *The Lightlings* storybooks for young readers by R. C. Sproul (Reformation Trust/Ligonier Publishing), as well as numerous short stories published in elementary reading texts. He lives in Greenville, South Carolina, and works as the chief creative officer for Portland Studios. He holds a bachelor of fine arts degree in studio art.